SIU7 Series

Book One

Wild Obsession

Angela
I had a great time hang out with y'all ♥
[illegible]

SIU7 Series

Book One

Wild Obsession

By

Genevieve Williams

SIU7 Series

Book One: Wild Obsession
Book Two: Cold Obsession
Book Three: Past Obsession
Book Four: Undeniable Obsession
Book Five: Ian's Obsession

Desert Breeze Publishing, Inc.
27305 W. Live Oak Rd #424
Castaic, CA 91384

http://www.DesertBreezePublishing.com

ISBN 13: 978-1-68294-946-7

Published in the United States of America
Publication Date: August 1, 2016

Editor-In-Chief: Gail R. Delaney
Editor: Christy Dyer
Marketing Director: Jenifer Ranieri
Cover Artist: Carol Fiorillo

Dedication

To Genny Falgout -- cohorts in crime forever! It has taken hard work and dedication, but here it is! Let us revel together in its success.

Acknowledgments

First and foremost, to the many friends and fans who believed in this book from its inception, you deserve undying gratitude for your input and loyalty which you will receive forever.

Travis Gaspard, thank you for years of friendship, guidance, suggestions, and allowing your name to go down in infamy (and yes, as requested, your namesake has a hot body).

Mary Stein, you are by far the best beta reader in the world, not to mention a fantastic friend. Thanks for sticking around.

Timmy, you are sorely missed. It was fun immortalizing you.

To our service men and women both here and abroad, thank you for your service. Because of you, we are alive and free.

Last, but definitely not least, to family members (and you know who you are, both immediate family and extended), thanks for never doubting where this writing "thing" was headed. Your constant belief it would happen someday is what has made it so. You have undying love forever and ever.

Chapter One

Tara clutched the tee shirt over her fast beating heart. Beads of sweat trickled between her breasts as she tried to slow her heart rate down to a level less likely to cause a heart attack.

Every night it was the same old thing: go to bed, dream, and wake up in a sweat from the nightmare. Not just any old nightmare... oh no. *The* nightmare. The one she re-lived over and over every night for the past six years. The one where she watched one or all of her family members die right before her very eyes. The one which was a constant repeat of the reality suffered at the hands of a madman.

The night of the murders still haunts her. She'd been asleep a short time before she awoke to a cold hand clinched over her mouth. She remembered staring into the face of the guy who'd been stalking her for six months -- Alvin Cruz. The long strands of his disheveled hair hung haphazardly around his face. His electrifying ice blue eyes glinted with pure evil.

Tara tried shaking the memory from her brain. Her sleepy eyes roamed over every corner of the room adjusting to the beams of the harsh Las Vegas daylight filtering in through slits in the blinds. Her heart rate, still tapping out a staccato rhythm, began a slow, lazy descent back to normal as realization dawned. She was safe and sound in the confines of her own bedroom.

She spotted Timmy perched on the top of her feet, his furry paws sticking up in the air. A rumbling snore emanated from the feline's throat. *The damn cat is snoring and I'm wide awake. What's wrong with that picture?*

Rubbing sore neck muscles, she again tried vanquishing the vivid images of her family's torment, the ones conjured up by her dream. She knew Alvin was captured three years after he'd murdered her family. She also knew he was still confined to a psychiatric facility in Los Angeles, California. There was no way for him to get to her now, and despite knowing it, fear still managed to keep a stranglehold on her.

Unable to go back to sleep, she rolled out of bed and headed for the kitchen. Retrieving a tempered mug from the cabinet, she poured milk into it and popped it in the microwave.

While the milk was warming, she envisioned her parents and siblings. Her younger sisters, Tracy and Meagan, were happy children. Her dad was a good, loving father and her mom was a kind and gentle woman. None of them deserved the horrific deaths they'd suffered.

In one twisted turn of fate, Alvin took from her the one thing she ever wanted or needed -- a family to love with her heart and soul. His actions left her alone and lonely. She blinked, her eyes stinging from threatening tears.

The microwave pinged bursting the bubble of regret enveloping her. Taking the mug with her, she moved into the living room and plopped down on the soft overstuffed couch. She sipped the warm liquid and hummed with pleasure as its smooth texture slid down her throat.

Work popped into her mind. *Ugh.* As sleep deprived as she was thanks to the nightmare, she would have a difficult time staying alert. Maybe there would be a big crowd for the afternoon's live broadcast of *Party Hard -- Las Vegas* where she worked as a server. Maybe the party atmosphere, loud music, and boisterous patrons would help keep her alert. She yawned... and maybe not.

Timmy meowed at her feet. "Well, if it isn't Rip Van Winkle. Did *you* get enough sleep today?" The fluffy grey feline meowed again and rubbed his chubby body against her leg, his way of letting her know he wanted to be picked up.

Weighing in at nearly twenty pounds, Timmy seldom managed to hop up on his own. Tara bent and pulled the hefty tabby into her lap with a grunt. He made himself comfortable. Then, like an afterthought, his head popped up and his rough wet tongue licked the side of her face like he was enjoying a tasty lollipop.

"Sheesh, Timmy. You're slobbering like a bulldog, for heaven's sake," she chided as she grimaced and rubbed the back of her hand across her wet cheek. Feigning apathy, the cat plunked back down on her lap with a thud and fell asleep.

"Great. I have to get dressed for work without benefit of a decent night's sleep and you're the one out like a light again." A soft, raspy snore came from the feline's throat in response to her gripe. She couldn't help but laugh.

Chapter Two

FBI Headquarters
Quantico, Virginia

"I don't give a rat's *ass* what the evidence shows!"

The angry words shattering the silence in the glass-encased room came from a man with an imposing six foot plus frame. He towered over his opponent who appeared to be of a more common five nine, five ten height. Neither man was giving up so much as an inch of ground in their heated debate.

"I'm telling you, Joe." The man's deep voice reverberated with passion for the subject at hand. "The boy is not now nor has he ever been involved with a damn biker gang. There's no way he went rogue for them; he's just not that stupid!"

Standing in the doorway of the FBI office known as "the bullpen," Chance Anselmi scrutinized the drama unfolding as he listened to the scorching exchange. So these were his new team members. When orders for his transfer to the elite task force known as Strategic Investigative Unit Number Seven, or SIU7, came down from the higher ups, he'd been shocked because of the team's exemplary record and also their rather questionable reputation.

The FBI rumor mill had it the team liked to work "outside the box" rarely abiding by the rules. Even so, they had a solid ninety-nine percent success rate, their last case being the one marring their once perfect record. When Chance was told of his transfer, he tried to find out what caused the team's one failure, but the ones talking were the not-to-be-trusted gossipers who recounted vague details. According to those who thought they knew all, when the jeopardized case was over, everyone was left wondering what the hell had gone wrong. In the end, one of their top intelligence agents, Ian Maguire, was escorted out of FBI Headquarters never to return.

Because of his inherent nature to question things thanks to Ranger training, Chance dug up as much as he could about the exclusive team. Their unconventional methods always got first-class results which he could tolerate. Being a Ranger meant doing what needed to be done in whatever manner the situation warranted, so not-by-the-book was something he could handle.

What he wasn't comfortable with was the discord happening because of Maguire's departure. They were on different sides of the fence when it came to Maguire's guilt or innocence, and it just didn't translate to a level of trust which meant everyone watched out for everyone else just like with his Ranger brothers. It was something he didn't like and would not tolerate. Having each other's backs must be a given.

Chance sighed as he wondered just what kind of mess he'd gotten himself into. He watched as Joe poked the other guy in the chest to emphasize his point.

"And I'm telling *you*, Travis. Evidence never lies. Maguire is not in jail because the wimp of a DA refused to indict based on what he claims is a strictly circumstantial case." Joe's eyes narrowed as he stared at his opponent. "For once, take your head out your ass and look at this objectively. The boy isn't just involved in it. Evidence proves he's the mastermind of the whole gang!"

Another man jumped up and interjected himself in the argument. "Well, in my opinion, Joe's right. Evidence never lies. Ian Maguire is as dirty as dirty gets and therefore I believe he is guilty as sin."

Travis shoved the guy on the shoulder so hard, the man's stance faltered.

"Shut the hell up, Jason. You know nothing." Travis huffed. "Nobody asked for your opinion anyway. Besides, you've been with this unit less than a year which is not long enough for you to even have an opinion worth more than a plug nickel."

Chance observed as the lone female in the room stood and pushed her way between all three men. As she extended her arms placing her palms against the chests of Travis and Joe, her voice boomed bouncing off the glass walls.

"*Hey!* Cool it, all of you. Bank the testosterone for a minute. We are a team here and we're all worried about Ian. Arguing is not going to help us or him."

Her chin jutted toward Jason. "And you. Quit trying to act like you know what the hell happened. You can't know Ian Maguire as well as the rest of us who've worked with him for years. You've been with this team for what? Six months? Which means Travis is right. Your opinion doesn't count."

Chance shook his head. With orientation and two months of FBI service under his belt, he had yet to work a full case which made *him* even more of a rookie than Jason. He now knew without a doubt the task force rumors were true. This group *was* unorthodox. Just what he needed -- a bunch of hot headed, opinionated cohorts.

Breathing deep, he straightened the books in his hands and heaved his backpack higher on his shoulder as he let the door slam behind him. All heads turned his way as silence ensued.

Chance cleared his throat. "Now don't let me interrupt your discussion, folks. I'm here because I was told to report to SSA Ross and they said I could find him here."

The woman shoved passed the agents surrounding her. Chance

watched as she crossed the expanse of the bullpen with an air of confidence, her long brown tresses bobbing, until she stood directly in front of him. Her head tilted back until her pale blue eyes met his. Her brows rose as she whistled, bewildered by his enormous build.

Amused, Chance looked down his nose from his six-four height meeting her gaze. She extended her tiny hand toward him. He reciprocated but couldn't hold back a grin.

"Agent Ross will be here shortly. I'm Katrina Wright. Just who the hell are *you*?"

Before Chance could open his mouth, Travis spoke, "He's Chance Anselmi, the fresh meat they've sent to replace Ian."

Katrina turned to glare at Travis. "And how the hell do *you* know this when the rest of us are in the dark about it?"

Chance wondered the same thing.

Offering no answer to Katrina's question, Travis shrugged and returned to his seat.

Spotting an empty chair, Chance followed suit and deposited his books on the table, his backpack sliding down his arm and landing with a clunk on the floor next to his chair. The three agents standing also returned to their own seats. All chatter ceased.

Silence.

Antsy and feeling uncomfortable, Chance glanced toward the door hoping Agent Ross would make a sudden appearance. He drummed his fingers against the glass topped conference table and then glanced at his watch. A full three minutes passed.

The only sound was the clicking of his fingernails against the glass which now matched the tapping sound of his soled heel, the thick-piled brown carpet doing nothing to muffle the new distraction. Everyone was staring at him. Another glance toward the door and another check of his watch.

He felt like a new animal at the zoo.

Another minute passed. His instructions were to stay put in the bullpen until Derek Ross arrived. By reputation, Ross had a by-the-book attitude. From the looks of his team, Chance doubted the man's reputation was accurate.

Glancing around the table at the other agents, Chance realized he didn't know anything about any of them. As a distraction, he thought of the rumors he'd heard around Quantico about the team. They stayed in trouble with the brass because of their refusal to follow protocol. In fact, he'd heard Ian Maguire, the one he was replacing, was drummed out of the bureau because of a suspected connection with a volatile crime syndicate operating under the guise of a biker gang. From the conversation he'd just interrupted, not all of Maguire's team members believed in his innocence.

A touch of claustrophobia niggled at Chance's nerves as time marched on with no team leader in sight. He ran a finger under his restricting collar. All this waiting was beginning to make his skin itch... or maybe it was just his suit.

Man, he wished he didn't have to wear a suit. He hated suits; they were so not him. Now a well-worn pair of cut-off jeans and a muscle shirt would be just fine like the ones he wore on lazy summer afternoons at his family's camp in the swamplands of south Louisiana. He could almost feel the warm southern breeze as it dried off his wet skin after a dunk in the canal running in front of the camp.

A distinctive click floated through the still air breaking into his daydream as the door to the bullpen swished causing everyone's head to swivel toward the door.

Two gentlemen entered. One, in his early fifties, Chance knew. He was Reginald Lyons, the director who rode roughshod over SIU7 and the person who requested his transfer to this team. The second man he figured must be Derek Ross.

All eyes were now focused on Lyons as both men settled in chairs. "Before we get on with this debriefing, I'd like to introduce you all to our newest team member, Chance Anselmi."

Chance felt heat rise to his face as he once again became the object of everyone's attention. He pulled his gaze toward the director.

"I've reviewed your file, Anselmi. Quite an impressive background. You started training in high school with Junior R.O.T.C. and upon graduation enlisted in the Army?"

"Yes, sir."

"You spent eight years in the Army, Special Forces, as a Ranger. Your service record is exemplary and is chock full of awards and commendations. You served in Afghanistan until you were wounded in combat, then you turned to the FBI, correct?"

Dismayed at the director reciting the facts of his life without looking at notes, Chance wondered why he was being put on display in the first place, and he didn't like it one bit. "Yes, sir, correct, but why the oration on my background? Is this necessary?"

Lyons glanced at Ross and smirked like he found something amusing.

"Well, if you haven't heard about this task force before, one thing we always do is finalize our cases. Special Agent Ross is senior agent on this team and has full control of this unit. He issues the orders and you all fulfill them. His word is final. He has been given the objective to complete the case no matter what has to happen to achieve the end results of case completion.

"Your background reveals you are used to following orders and are structured and disciplined." Lyons leaned on the table and pinpointed his gaze on Chance.

"Understand this, Anselmi. This unit is not like most. We don't always play by the rules. Even though your history suggests *you* do with your commendations and awards, you also have a history of accumulating write-ups which leads me to believe you're not so straight-laced.

"You're from deep down south Louisiana. I've trained others from your neck of the woods and all you boys are rough, ready, and cunning. Hell. A bunch of you hid from us on an escape-and-evasion exercise for six hours before we found out those swamp rats were within a hairsbreadth of the observation site all along watching us being fools. I've never met anyone from the south who didn't have a temper. Cajun men are known hot heads, which also leads me to believe you'll fit in just fine with this bunch of misfits."

Chance felt the blood rising to his face, his famous Cajun temper barely in check at the way the director was dissecting his persona, but he knew better than to argue with the man. Acting like a hot head would only reinforce the man's point.

Lyons sat back in his chair, the corner of his mouth rising in a smirk. "With all the pleasantries said and done, I now relinquish this session to Agent Ross."

"Thanks, Reggie. We've lost a member of SIU7 -- Special Agent Ian Maguire."

"You mean *former* Special Agent," Joe interjected.

Ross's glare directed toward Joe did its job and squelched further comment. "I know some of you aren't happy about losing Maguire, but I expect each and every one of you to forge past this bump in the road and welcome Agent Anselmi to our team. Now let me introduce you to the rest of the team," Derek continued as he turned to his right. The man who'd been arguing with the guy named Travis was sitting next to him. "This is Special Agent Joe Scott, my second in command. If I'm not around and you need something, he is your go-to man unless you are informed otherwise. Next to Joe is Special Agent Jason Navarro who is also new to the team. Special Agents Katrina Wright and Travis Dean are sitting to your left. Those two have been with us for several years now."

Glancing around the table, Chance felt the frisson of tension emanating from some of his new team members and wondered if, as the new guy, he'd be branded as the one who'd replaced their buddy and friend. He got the feeling it might take some time before this group as a whole accepted him, especially in light of their recent loss of Maguire.

He took in a deep breath and steeled his conviction. If they wanted to play, then he would just play right along with them.

*****

Damn. I've finally found her.

Alvin jumped up from his seat in the recreation room, a magazine in his hand he'd found on the chair next to his own. He surveyed the ad which had grabbed his attention, an advertisement for a new reality show. There were lots of guys partying poolside being served cocktails by an auburn haired beauty, her radiant smile on display.

He couldn't believe his eyes. Both his waking and sleeping hours were filled with thoughts and dreams of the one who'd gotten away, his woman. His eyes transfixed to the server in the ad, he imagined how her shiny hair would tumble across his chest as she wiggled down his torso. He could almost taste the slight saltiness of her skin against his tongue, feel the softness of her silky skin against his fingertips and smell her sweet nectar.

Taking in a deep breath of air, her scent locked into memory filled his nostrils, a whiff carrying a hint of vanilla and sugar. He throbbed with the need to be inside her and claim her as his alone. Hell. Just imagining those fiery waves bouncing around her face was enough to make him go hard. Someday soon he'd show her how much he wanted her, and he'd damn well make her know she was his.

"I'm coming for you, Tara."

Perfect timing. Not only would he own her body, he would also possess her soul.

Chapter Three

The door to the bullpen swung open as a young woman entered waving a piece of paper over her head.

"Case! We've got a new case!" She came to an abrupt halt just before running into the conference table. "Well, it's not new. It's about a guy the team captured some years back, the one who killed a family in California. Well, the case is new now because it is about his escape but it's still old because of the subject."

Chance watched fascinated as Derek stood drawing the woman's attention.

"Izzy? What the hell are you talking about? We can't go on a new case. We haven't debriefed from the last one."

"Remember the Cruz case?" She cocked her head in thought.

"Yeah, I remember. What about it?"

"Well get a load of this." She handed him the paper she'd been flailing in the air.

Derek did a quick perusal of the paper and turned giving it to Reggie. "She's right. We have a new case."

Above the moans and groans of the others, Katrina's voice boomed. "Wait a minute. We need time to regroup considering we have a new team member." Chance felt all eyes shift his way. "You said so yourself, Reggie."

The director finished reviewing the paper and stood, his voice strong and steady. "There's no choice. This assignment has come from higher up. You should remember Mr. Alvin Cruz from Los Angeles. This says he escaped this morning and is on the loose." He handed the paper back to Derek. "Izzy, you're with me." He and Izzy left the bullpen.

Chance pointed at the door where they'd just disappeared. "Who is the woman, and who is Alvin Cruz?"

Derek answered. "Her name is Izabelle Roth and she is the best technical analyst the FBI has ever seen. I'll get you up to speed on this case later. Okay. We play it this way. Lucien and Kat will cover airports. Eric and Stephen will cover bus and train terminals. Travis and Jason will set up a safe house. Joe? Gather up a team and find his trail."

"On it, boss." Joe stood and headed for the door. Everyone except Chance got up and left. Derek sat back down and took in a deep breath.

"Here's the deal, Anselmi. You'll be partnering with me since this is your first case. As Reggie said, I'm the lead agent for this team. Not trying to cut you down or anything, but I've been with the bureau for twelve years which makes me a bit more experienced than you. If you're wise, you'll follow my lead for your first few assignments and learn the ropes out in the field. We need a constant flow of communication between us for our partnership to work. From the looks of you, I'm confident you'll be able to watch my back and I've *never* let a partner's back go uncovered, so I fully intend to cover yours. Do we understand each other?"

Chance stared at him for a few seconds taking in the agent's tall and muscular stature. He was pretty sure Derek could cover even his big back. "Yes. We understand each other."

"Great. Do you have any residual effects from your stint in Afghanistan?"

The corner of Chance's mouth lifted. "Just one."

"And what would it be?"

"An insatiable desire to find a few terrorists and blow their asses to kingdom come."

Derek smiled. "We do those things too, but you do realize you have to go wherever needed?"

"Sure. I'm up for whatever the FBI can dish out. Actually, the dirtier the better."

Derek stood and Chance followed. "Well here's your chance. Meet us on the tarmac behind the building in thirty minutes. Pack a go-bag and be prepared for anything. I'll brief you on the case once we're in the air."

Strolling toward the door, Derek paused just before opening it, turned around and faced Chance. "Any questions?"

"Where are we going?"

"On a road trip. School starts now, rookie. Oh. And one more thing."

"What?"

Derek grinned. "Lose the suit. You look like an overgrown ape in it."

*****

Thirty minutes later, Derek gave a shout out. "Anselmi!"

Now in a pair of black jeans and a black polo shirt, Chance grabbed his go-bag from where he'd dropped it at his feet and took off toward Derek meeting him half-way.

"Where are we headed?" he yelled over the roar of the nearby plane.

"LA," Derek shouted.

"What's in LA?"

Approaching the steps of the Cessna CJ4 parked on the private FBI airstrip, Derek took two steps up and stopped, turning around to face Chance who was still rooted in the same spot. "A psychiatric hospital where a psychotic killer escaped and left a trail of dead bodies in his wake. *Get a move on, rookie!*"

Chance's eyebrows shot up as he picked up the pace and boarded the plane. He spotted Joe Scott and a few other agents he didn't know sitting in the back talking amongst themselves. He assumed they were Scott's scouting team. He grabbed a seat across from his leader and decided to just keep his mouth shut for now and start learning from the veteran.

As the plane taxied down the runway, he contemplated if this, his first official assignment as an FBI agent, would be typical of future assignments. His extensive experience as an Army Ranger would be a big plus in how well he could handle this job along with his recent FBI training but he just wasn't sure he was prepared enough. Right now, he *felt* like a damn rookie.

At thirty, this new career was his opportunity to remain in an adrenaline charged work environment without suffering the rigors being a Ranger inflicted on his mind and his body. He had to face the fact he just wasn't physically or mentally adept as a twenty year old. Derek spoke interrupting his musings.

"Meet twenty-six year old Alvin Cruz." He slid a file folder across the desk toward Chance. "Eight years ago at the ripe old age of eighteen, he broke into the Roberts home and murdered them by slitting their throats. He killed dad, mom, and two daughters."

Chance opened the file now in his hands. The mug shot of Cruz revealed a tan young man with shoulder length blonde hair and typical California surfer dude looks. What set him apart from the stereotype were his eyes. Something evil lurked behind the crystal blue orbs which made warning bells go off in Chance's head.

He flipped the picture over to reveal another picture, one of a teenage girl. Rich auburn hair framed a face kissed by the sun. Her emerald eyes were haunting as they gleamed with flecks of gold and appeared to be staring straight through him.

"Is she one of the daughters killed?"

"No. The two murdered were ages ten and eight."

Chance felt a knot form in his gut. *Such young children.* "So who is she?"

Derek's lack of urgency to answer told him things were getting ready to get complicated. Derek inhaled and gave him the gory details.

"*She* is Tara Roberts, the oldest daughter. The picture was taken at Cruz's trial. She testified he broke into the family home in the dark of night. He slit the father's throat, took the mom into the kitchen where he gagged her and tied her to a chair and then found this daughter, Tara. He pulled her into the parents' bedroom to flaunt his handiwork with the father.

"He dragged her into the kitchen and tied her up like the mother. She was forced to watch as he did the same to her two sisters. Then, one by one, he slit each of their throats while Tara was forced to watch. Neighbors heard her screams and called nine-one-one. When sirens alerted him, he escaped through the back door hiding out in the woods behind the property."

"*Merde,*" Chance cursed in his Cajun French. "So she escaped his wrath because he got interrupted by the cops."

"No."

Chance lifted his gaze, puzzled. "Then why'd he leave her alive?"

"He stalked and harassed her for at least six months leading up to the murders trying to force her to go out with him. She repeatedly rejected his advances. While in the act of killing her family, he told her she was the only woman who ever rejected him and she belonged to him. He confessed he killed her family because they vied for her affection and they were trying to keep them apart. *She* is the reason he murdered her family; he is obsessed with her."

Derek blew out an anxious breath before continuing. "His last words to her were, quote: 'I will hunt you down wherever you go, my baby. You're mine and mine alone.'"

"Dammit!" Chance couldn't hold back his anger. A shiver ran down his spine. This Cruz was a loose cannon and wouldn't be easy to take down. "Where is she?"

"She is twenty-four now and lives in Nevada." Derek handed him a picture of her current driver's license.

Chance studied the picture running his finger over her face. He contemplated why the FBI was part of this case at all. "So why are we involved with this? It doesn't fall into the scope of FBI jurisdiction."

"Good observation, rookie. It normally wouldn't fall to us, but SIU7 was on assignment in California when we stumbled upon Cruz. We were the ones to capture and arrest him, which made this case part of our jurisdiction. Besides, these new murders took place on the grounds of a federal mental institution so we automatically take lead on the case."

"What's the last known whereabouts of this asshole?"

"M.I.A."

"So why are we headed to LA if he's not there anymore?"

"The psychiatric hospital where Cruz was being held under high security is where our hunt begins. We'll go in and talk to the staff while Joe and his team scour the area for Cruz."

"And just how did he escape if he was under such high security?"

Derek eyed him for a couple of seconds before responding. "Simple. He just killed everybody who got in his way."

Chapter Four

Sitting on a bed with a wafer thin mattress and squeaky springs in a cheap motel, Alvin picked up his pre-paid cell. He was going to need more money. The paltry bit he got off the people he carjacked to get a set of wheels was almost gone.

He dialed and listened as the phone rang... and rang.

"Come on, come on. Pick up." He chewed on his thumbnail.

"Yeah," a familiar voice answered.

"Hell, Junior. It's Cruz."

"Alvin? Where the hell are you?"

"Oh, no, not yet. I need your help."

"And just what makes you think I can help you?"

"Look. You owe my family big time."

"I don't owe you or your family a damn thing. And don't call me Junior."

"I don't think so. Daddy did you one huge favor protecting your ass all these years. The least you can do is pay back some of the debt you owe him. And I'll call you whatever the hell I want to call you."

There was a long pause. "You know about that?"

"Hell yeah. I know all of it. If it hadn't been for my daddy covering up the mess you made in college, your sorry ass would be in jail."

"What is it you want from me?"

"I figured you'd come around, *Junior*."

"What do you want, you piece of crap!" Junior yelled, evidence his temper was rising.

"First off, do my parents know I'm out?"

"No, but I'm sure FBI agents are probably knocking on their door this very minute."

"I don't want them finding out just yet. I need time to get things done. You need to get me clothes, fake IDs, and some spending cash."

"And how am I supposed to get all this to you if you won't tell me where you are?"

"Just meet me at the Starlight Café on the edge of town in two hours," Alvin demanded.

"Two hours? What makes you think I'm close enough to you to get there in two hours? Can't you give me a little more time? The damn IDs alone will take..."

"Shut up and listen to me. I knew you would run here the minute you heard I broke out of the hellhole institution. You're nothing if not predictable, Junior. Two hours, Starlight Café, clothes, IDs, and cash. Got it?"

"All right, all right. Stop crying like a baby. Two hours."

"Better."

"One more thing, Cruz."

"What, *Junior*?"

"You'd best not screw around with me on this or I'll serve your head on a platter to the first FBI agent I run across."

Two hours and twenty minutes later, Alvin sat in a dark corner of the dimly lit Starlight Café. The smell of strong coffee and stale grease wafted through the air. He had a clear view of the front door and the street. *Where the hell is he*? His anxiety level ramped up a notch.

Just then, he spotted an SUV rolling up across the street. A man in his mid-to-late forties with semi-balding hair approached the front door carrying a black leather bag. As he entered the café, the man slid his sunglasses off and dropped them in the inside pocket of his jacket as he headed in Alvin's direction.

"Well, well, Cruz. You finally managed to break out of the nut house." The man pulled out a chair across from him as he dropped the bag at his feet.

"And it's about damn time you showed your ass up, Junior. You're late." Alvin was sarcastic as a waitress approached their table.

"What can I get for you guys?"

"Just bring us coffee," Junior responded. She nodded and left the table disappearing behind the swinging doors leading to the kitchen. "Tsk, tsk. Come now, Cruz. Is that any way to treat your best friend? Come to think of it, probably your *only* friend?"

Alvin fought his rising temper. "You're not my damn friend and you know it. If it weren't for my daddy, your ass..."

"We've been over this already. Drop it.

Alvin glanced around the mostly empty café making sure no one was listening in. "Did you bring everything I asked for?" His voice was barely above a whisper.

Junior nodded. "Clothes, IDs, spending money. What's your plan for a ride?"

"Don't worry about my ride. I can find my own."

"You do realize the FBI is going to be on your ass like white on rice?"

"Yes, I do. But guess what? Here is where you make yourself useful. *You* need to keep them off my ass."

"Where are you headed, Cruz?"

"Un, un. Info for you is on a need-to-know basis and right now, *you* don't need to know."

Junior sighed in obvious disgust. "You are such a dumb ass, Alvin. How the hell do you expect me to keep your ass clear if I don't know where you are?"

"Listen up. When I need you to know, you'll know. Until then, I'm better off alone. So keep your damn phone handy in case I need you."

"Yeah, yeah, and remember. No more crap. You're skating on thin ice as it is."

Alvin gave him a wicked grin. "Don't worry, Junior. I won't do anything more than *you've* already done."

"Humph. That's exactly what worries me." Junior stood and left without a backwards glance.

*****

The oversized gaudy billboard at the far end of the car lot boasted the cheesy slogan "*Cruise the highway in a new Cruz Porsche.*" John and Deborah Cruz, owners of Cruz Porsche Car Dealership, were proud of their flourishing business. Lots of California's celebrities bought their expensive toys from them, especially those who wanted to buy cars from the parents of a mad man. The phone rang breaking into John's thoughts.

"Cruz Porsche."

"We've got a big problem."

John's throat constricted at the sound of the familiar voice. "Junior. What's wrong?"

"He's escaped." Junior's voice held a note of discontent.

A single drop of liquid formed at John's temple. "When?"

"About six hours ago."

"Where is he now?"

"Who the hell knows? He went on a damn killing spree again and left bodies everywhere. He's over the edge, John. He can't be trusted."

John expelled a shaky breath. "What do you expect me to do? He hasn't contacted me."

"Don't get all huffy, okay? I think I know where he's headed. Let me know if he contacts you. You know he'll need you for money."

"Yes, no doubt. Find him, Junior. Get him back to me in one piece, you hear? I'll see to it he's out of the country and untouchable within twenty-four hours of his return."

A long pause ensued. "This one's going to cost you, John."

"Haven't I done enough already protecting your sorry ass all these years?"

"Well it's just not enough anymore. It'll take money to keep him out of FBI hands."

A drop of sweat trickled down between John's eyes. "How much?"

"At least a hundred grand to start."

Beads of sweat blossoming, John felt his face go flush. "You're a sorry SOB, Junior."

Junior snickered. "Take it or leave it, Cruz."

John swiped a hand through his thinning blonde hair. The boy was going to be the death of him yet. "All right. I'll transfer the cash. I want the boy standing in front of me and soon."

"Deal."

"And he'd better still be breathing or the deal is off. Do you understand?"

"No problem." The phone line went dead.

*****

High atop a telephone pole across the street from Cruz Porsche Car Dealership looking like a typical telephone repairman, he disconnected the line. The corners of his mouth lifted. Raising his mirrored sunglasses to the top of his head, he glanced down at the recorder in his hand. Rewinding the tape back a few seconds, he hit the play button and listened as John Cruz was informed by someone referred to as "Junior" of his son's escape. A mile wide smile broke out on his face when he realized he recognized Junior's voice.

When he thought about the images he'd taken earlier of the man and his black SUV leaving the Starlight Café, he realized he was so much closer to attaining his goal of revenge.

With the reflexes of a cat he shimmied down the pole, jumped in the telephone truck, and left.

Chapter Five

Thirty minutes after landing in Los Angeles, Derek, Chance, and Joe along with Joe's team were all escorted by LA detectives into the recreation room at the psychiatric hospital where they headed in different directions. Derek and Chance were escorted to the recreation room. The cordoned off crime scene could have come straight off the pages of a gruesome murder mystery book. Two bodies lay next to each other in the middle of the room while several of LA's finest law enforcers took pictures and dusted for fingerprints. Donning protective gloves, Derek leaned over the woman's body while Chance examined the man.

"She took one blow from behind straight through the heart. The wound is jagged suggesting the weapon was a crudely made sharp blade. There are no other visible signs of trauma. She probably died before she hit the floor. What about the guard?"

Chance stood looking over both bodies. "His throat was slit. The edges of the wound are also consistent with a jagged edged or crudely made blade. Two hypodermic needles are still impaled in his chest right over the heart. No other visible signs of trauma noted. From placement of the bodies, I'd say the nurse approached Cruz with a tray of meds in her hands. Pills and hypodermics are scattered around both bodies. The nurse, distracted by the guard, gave Cruz the opportunity to react. My guess is he pilfered the hypodermics from the tray while she wasn't looking, stabbed her from behind with a makeshift blade, and then drove the needles into the chest of the guard to stun him before he slit the man's throat. Keys and walkie-talkie are missing. Oh, and Cruz is left handed."

Derek quirked a brow. "Good work, rookie. Let's take a look at his living quarters."

They walked down the hall to a room barricaded by crime scene tape and flashed their badges to a guard. He lifted the tape letting them enter.

The fine hairs on the back of Chance's neck stood on end from the evil permeating the room. The air was thick with the stench of it. An unmade hospital bed stood against the left wall with a night stand to the right of it. Solid steel bars glimmered through the glass of the lone window facing the western courtyard. Two opened doors on the right wall led to a closet and a bathroom. When Chance peeked into the bathroom, he made mental notes. There were no visible signs of sharp objects such as razors or scissors. Derek checked out the closet. While they were examining the rooms, an elderly gentleman in a long white coat entered clearing his throat. They both moved back into the main room.

"I'm Dr. Aveda, Mr. Cruz's psychiatrist. What can I do for you gentlemen?"

Both agents flashed their badges to the doctor as Derek made the introductions. "Derek Ross and Chance Anselmi, FBI. You can start by giving us a rundown on Cruz's mental state at his last exam, and please, excuse us if we continue our work while you talk."

"No problem. I was reviewing my notes on Mr. Cruz's case when I heard about this tragedy. Such a shame. The poor nurse who was killed worked here for ten years. She was very good with our patients. I didn't know the guard personally, but he looked like a nice young man. And those poor laundry workers. They were all so very young to lose their lives so violently."

"Uh, Doc?" Chance rolled his hand over and over to speed up the doctor's rambling.

He grinned sheepishly. "Oh. Yes. Sorry." He recounted Cruz's tempestuous mental history while they continued searching for more clues. "I don't understand why this happened. Mr. Cruz was making remarkable progress toward calming his aggression."

Derek walked out of the closet carrying a worn shoe box. He flipped the box upside down onto the rumpled unmade bed.

"Here's his good progress, Doc." A myriad of pills lay across the bed, all different shapes, sizes and colors.

The doctor's face paled. "You mean he hasn't taken his medicine recently?"

"I'd say he hasn't taken his meds in a long time."

"Oh my." The good doctor was horrified by the evidence.

Derek walked to the desk at the far end of the room. He fumbled through the drawers but found nothing of interest. Withdrawing a slim pocket tool from his jacket, he broke the seal on one of the drawers revealing a false bottom. "Chance. Take a look at this."

Chance walked over and peered inside the open drawer. Sitting on top a stack of papers was a picture of Tara Roberts identical to the one he'd seen in her file.

Derek pulled out the contents of the drawer. There were several old newspaper clippings from the trial. Underneath those were hand sketched diagrams and schematics resembling the hospital. Clear plastic overlays, each one showing a different detailed route, were draped over the diagrams. "He's been planning his escape for quite some time," Derek confirmed.

Chance nodded and pulled out the next set of papers. His gut clenched. The psycho had a hidden talent. There were well drawn pictures depicting a man resembling Cruz in various sexually explicit positions with a woman.

"The Roberts girl," Derek murmured. The last drawing in the stack was of the woman alone, bound and gagged, hooked in handcuffs against a wall with her head dangling and bright red -- blood red -- smeared across her chest.

Overcome with a foreign amount of anger, Chance closed his eyes and took in a deep breath. What kind of deranged maniac were they dealing with here?

Derek nudged Chance's arm forcing him to reopen his eyes. "Look here." Derek shoved another box into Chance's hands which contained several different crudely made sharp blades.

"We've got to find this asshole before he finds the girl." Chance's voice was shaky.

"Agreed. So, Dr. Aveda. Can we have copies of your notes on Cruz?"

The doctor's pale face flushed. "Sorry, gentlemen. Doctor-patient privilege, but, I'll be more than happy to discuss this again with you at a later time if you come back with a warrant."

"All right." Derek gave in since legally he couldn't force the issue.

"Oh, and don't forget the three bodies in the laundry room," the good doctor added.

"We'll get to them in a minute, but first, I'd like to see the surveillance tapes from the recreation room this morning," Derek requested.

"Of course. I'll have the guard take you both to the control room."

*****

A bank of computer monitors displayed several live shots of every nook and cranny of the facility. "It will take just a minute to pull up the feed from this morning. Keep your eyes on the monitor in the middle." The tech manipulated buttons on the keyboard.

As the tape began rolling, Chance realized they were viewing a shot from a camera mounted behind Cruz's chair. The angle helped him visualize things from Alvin's perspective. After a few minutes, he noticed Cruz pick up a magazine on the chair next to his own. Chance peered at the front page holding Cruz's attention but the grainy texture of the video made it difficult. After a minute or so awareness dawned.

"Stop the tape!" He turned to the technician. "Can you rewind about one minute?"

"Sure thing." The tech set the tape in reverse. Once it started playing again, Chance squinted and leaned in closer for a better look.

"Stop it right there."

"What do you see?" Derek asked.

"Can you enhance the magazine?"

The tech nodded and fiddled with a few more buttons. The image of the magazine grew in size. Bit by bit, the picture sharpened and cleared. As it came into full focus, Chance's heart skipped a beat. "Freeze it." He turned and faced Derek.

"Did it make you wonder why Cruz picked that particular moment to escape? I'm sure he's had plenty of chances before this. We saw the plans in his room. He's been making them for at least a year. This scenario which occurred? It wasn't one of them."

Derek looked a little puzzled.

Chance pointed to the blown up magazine on the monitor. A full frontal crystal clear view of a woman was on the screen.

"He's found her, Derek."

Chance's heart was pumping hard. His worry for this girl whom he'd never laid eyes on was beginning to escalate. They both eyed the monitor showing a picture of none other than Tara Roberts. The caption on the magazine ad read "*Join us at Party Hard -- Las Vegas.*"

"Cruz now knows exactly where to find her."

Derek frowned and uttered one word. "Dammit*!*"

Chapter Six

Holding two jobs was beginning to wear on Tara's nerves, but it was the only way she could afford living in Vegas on her own. She bartended at a popular bar on the Strip five nights a week. The job wasn't so bad except she spent three of the four nights putting up with over-the-top drunks who had no respect for themselves much less anyone else. The tips, however, were good and helped her keep cash on hand.

Her second job was much better. On weekends she worked as a poolside cocktail waitress for the show, *Party Hard -- Las Vegas,* which was also taped at the same facility where she bartended. The setting was much more pleasant plus management provided a ton of security poolside. It made her feel safer than at the bar where she had to fend for herself.

Ever since Alvin's possessiveness had begun she struggled with many things she never worried about before. The first few years after the murders gripped her with fear. There were days when she wondered if she could make it out of bed each morning much less function like a normal person. Then depression settled into her heart like a huge boulder. When she managed to get it under control, loneliness engulfed her causing the opposite effect. Her heart felt hollow and empty now. There were times when all she could do was put one foot in front of the other. Her family members were a happy bunch. Love was the primary thing in their household. She missed them all so much.

She sighed resigning to continue on with her life. She donned her *Party Hard* uniform, a rust colored bikini which heightened her summer tan. She pulled on a pair of snug black jeans and skimmed a white *Party* tee shirt over her head. Slipping into her favorite shoes, she grabbed her purse and keys and walked out.

Man, she wished money wasn't so tight. Trying to keep her little dark blue Mazda in good working order was becoming difficult. The door handles stuck sometimes, the radio played only when hitting a bump in the road and the faux leather seats were worn and tattered, but it ran great. Well, most of the time it ran great. Truthfully, sometimes it coughed and wheezed like it needed intensive care, but at least it was paid for and was all hers.

Two hours later, she was poolside at *Party Hard.* They were filming a special live shot. A heavy crowd covered every inch of the facility. She wormed her way through a throng of people. *Sheesh! Where did all these people come from?* When there was a big crowd, servers were terrorized by guys hitting on them, which was when she displayed her best be-a-bitch attitude.

"Hey, Tara! Over here!"

Scanning the crowd, she spied her best friend, Tiffany Summers, waving frantically. They both started walking eventually meeting in the middle.

"How's it going, girl? Is this wild or what?" Tiffany's eyes glistened with excitement. This type of scene was so Tiff. A bit of a wild child originally from Texas, Tiff loved drama, but all in all, she had a good nature.

"Tiff. Where did all these people come from? Something special happening today?"

"Didn't anybody tell you?" Tiffany's Texas drawl thickened with her excitement.

"Tell me what?"

"We have a celebrity guest today."

Tara's brows furrowed. She wasn't into the see-a-movie-star-and-ogle-them scene, but she did have the curiosity of a cat. "So who's the latest glamour gal?"

"Not a gal, a guy. Or should I say, man." With her love for the dramatics, Tiffany drew out the moment.

"Well, who is it?"

"None other than a magnificent MMA stud. Over there."

Tara's gaze slid to where Tiffany was pointing. Standing in front of one of the celebrity cabanas only the rich and famous could afford was one of the legendary mixed martial arts champions. She didn't get to watch much TV, but she was fascinated by the ultimate fighters. She never missed an episode and knew them all by name.

"Wow!" She was star struck.

Tiffany beamed at her. "I'm working his cabana." Tiffany shoved her elbow in Tara's midriff. "Lucky me, huh? Hey. You want to meet him?"

Tara's eyebrows shot up. It would be cool to meet one of her favorite MMA legends.

"Sure, why not?"

"Okay! Let's go!"

*****

Feeling a sense of urgency, Chance voiced his concern to Derek. "If we don't get a move on, Cruz will get to her first and we might not be able to save her."

"I know. That's why I called in a heads up to her boss, Bob Gorman, and apprised him of the situation. His security's dogging her every footstep. He'll pull her out as soon as we arrive."

"Is the safe house ready?"

"Yes. Travis and Jason are setting up surveillance as we speak."

"Good." Chance was getting antsy, his gut reacting to the urgency of the situation. He was ready to get this over with. Things could escalate at any second and he'd prefer to have the Roberts girl under their watchful eyes. She would be safe from harm with them.

Chance sat in the back of the SUV watching the special live broadcast of *Party Hard -- Las Vegas* on the mini TV. They were headed to the set of the show where they would take the girl into protective custody.

Every few minutes as the camera panned out over the crowd he caught a glimpse of her. The rust colored bikini she wore showed off her tan and barely covered her assets, and what assets they were. The tiny swim suit was hugging her body like a second skin. Just imagining what lay beneath those scraps of cloth had him squirming in his seat.

Since the split with his ex-girlfriend, he'd lost his appetite for a steady relationship. In fact, these days a steady relationship was the last thing on his mind. Oh, he indulged in an occasional one night stand every once in a while just to relieve sexual frustration.

The ex made him believe there wasn't a woman available who was trustworthy and loyal. They all had hidden agendas, and his grandfather and grandmother instilled in him a belief in commitment where relationships were concerned, which was why he wasn't in one. Besides, his new career occupied most of his time leaving none to develop any kind of relationship. He wasn't even sure he wanted one anyway. FBI work could be dangerous and required trust between partners. *Lots* of trust.

So he wasn't ready to involve himself with a woman any time soon, in particular, not a woman who looked like the one he was watching on the screen. Besides, FBI regulations mandated no personal involvement with subjects on a case. It could turn out to be bad.

Refocusing his mind, he gazed at the screen. Tara was talking with a woman who looked like a co-worker in the middle of a mind boggling crowd.

"See anything significant yet?"

"Nope. She's just talking with one of the other servers right now." He watched as the other girl pointed toward one of the cabanas. Trying to see where she was pointing, he focused on a gentleman. Was that... nah, couldn't be. Both girls turned at the same time and headed toward the guy. As the shot zoomed in on the man, Chance freaked. "Whoa!"

"What?"

"You're not going to believe this."

"What? What's going on?"

"Guess who she's talking to right now?"

"She's talking to someone we know?"

"Yep."

"Dammit, Chance! Who is it?"

"Ray Rains."

A moment of silence ensued before Derek spoke. "Who the *hell* is Ray Rains?"

"Come on, man, you don't know Ray Rains?"

Derek glanced back at Chance through the rear view mirror and gave him a dubious look.

Chance let out an exasperated breath. "He's a legendary mixed martial arts champion." When Derek glanced back at him, his dumbstruck look told Chance he didn't get it.

"Ultimate fighting?" Still no look of recollection on Derek's face.

"The fighter on the dancing reality show a few seasons back?"

Recognition dawned in Derek's eyes making Chance roll his own.

"You mean the guy with the Mohawk and two left feet?"

"Yeah! He's the one."

Chance watched the screen as Tara moved away from Rains and walked poolside stopping to hand out drinks. One guy put his hand on her back and started rubbing it. Some strange unfamiliar emotion simmered just under his skin. Anger, perhaps? Huh.

What made her like being pushed, shoved, and groped around in a place like that, he pondered. He thought she could find better, safer work. She jerked her shoulder away from the guy's hand and, from the look in her eyes and the set of her jaw, she took care of telling off the jerk in question. *Good for her!* His sudden emotion of anger ebbed.

Another guy tried to grab her arm. A hint of a new emotion surfaced in him. A need to protect? *Whoa. Note to self: no involvement with subjects while on a case.*

He wondered how the woman would handle this latest show of aggression from the patron. It didn't take long for him to find out. Loads of security personnel were converging on her and the idiot but they got there too late.

Ceremoniously, she dumped the contents of her tray over the guy's head, cups flying and liquor running in rivulets down the man's face and torso, his face turning as red as the board shorts he was wearing. People around him were laughing and pointing at him but the moron didn't know when to stop while he was ahead. He attempted to grab her again yelling God only knew what at her. Tara moved out of his grasp. She then bashed him on the head with the tray then threw it to the ground. The loser folded up his body like a wounded five year old and started wailing like one too.

A small chuckle passed Chance's lips. *Damn, but she's spunky.* He liked the personality trait in a woman. Maybe she was the kind who could take care of herself after all.

"What are you finding so funny?" Derek asked.

"Nothing."

"Well we're here."

Chance peeked back down one last time at the screen but she was no longer in sight. He was actually getting anxious to meet the little wildcat.

Chapter Seven

There was a chill inside Bob Gorman's office and it was coming from Bob himself. Some days his job got the best of him. He liked most of the servers who worked for him at *Party Hard*. The money he paid them was nothing to sneeze at and he respected them one and all, but sometimes they did things which made him feel like an old man.

Tara Roberts was one of those gals. She always managed to do something once or twice a week to make him feel aged. After going through a rough youth, she was trying to make her way back into a normal life. Some days she made him feel light hearted and young. Some days she was such a hellion she simply pissed him off. Today was turning out to be the latter.

"But he deserved it, the jerk!" Tara gave him her best pouty lip service.

Pinching the bridge of his nose, he blew out a breath in frustration. "I know he did and it will probably boost our ratings big time, but you can't go around hitting people on the head with your tray, Tara. We have liability issues to contend with here."

He watched her eyes as she looked at everything in the room except him. Inwardly he grinned. When she'd first started working for him, he wondered if she was going to make it having lost her entire family and being all alone. He could see she carried the weight of the world on her tiny shoulders.

It was why he took on the role of substitute father. He couldn't help it. He liked her determined attitude. After another steadying breath, he took his good old time speaking in hopes his silence would make her think. "Take this tray and get your ass back out there."

He could tell Tara was trying not to grin which frustrated him even more. He felt like an exasperated father of a wild teenager.

Grabbing the new tray he'd placed on the corner of his desk, she let her grin loose and walked out the room without speaking another word. He couldn't help but smile.

*****

Out on pool deck once more, Tara stepped right back into her rhythm. At least the crowd wasn't quite as intimidating now as it was before. In fact, they all appeared to be giving her a wide berth. Not the damn camera, though. It was dogging her every move. Great. Just what she needed -- more media attention. She'd had her fill during Cruz's trial.

In truth, public attention never died down, she just learned to live with it.

*****

The squeaky sound of Tara's tennis shoes squishing against the tiled hallway had her nerves jingling. Having been delivered a message to get dressed and report to Bob's office once again, she began worrying. Something was seriously up for him to summon her twice in one day much less twice in the same hour *and* specifically telling her to get dressed. The filming of the show wasn't over yet. Hopefully her ass wasn't in a sling from the tray incident.

She gathered her courage and swung Bob's office door open. Then, she did what she did best -- met the problem head on by shooting off her mouth. "Look. I know I shouldn't have slammed the tray over the loser's head, but let's be real here, all right? The jerk was asking for..."

Her tirade ceased as she took in the scene. Bob was perched on the corner of his desk as usual. *Uh oh.* Two men stood next to him staring intently at her. Without so much as a cursory glance toward them, she refocused on her boss.

"What? The jerk sent his lawyers already because I clobbered him with a tray?"

She eyed both men. Guy number one wore a black suit and tie. He looked in his mid to late thirties, quite handsome, but definitely not her type. Too straight laced, too clean cut and too professional looking. She knew without a doubt this guy was no lawyer. He dripped authority, the kind involving guns. She was pretty sure he was a badge of some sort, some level of law enforcement. Maybe plain clothes cop? Something about him made him look familiar even though she couldn't pinpoint why. She shifted her gaze to guy number two.

Whuh!

There stood a mountain of hot, rippling, bulging muscles wrapped up like a Christmas present in warm bronzed skin. The polar opposite of the suit, Mountain Man was wearing tight fitting black jeans worn in all the right places and a snug black Polo shirt which was having trouble containing his massive biceps. Aviator glasses were hooked onto his shirt. His biceps were flexing away and... *oh look*! The right one sported a tattoo -- her weakness.

Wow was her only intelligent thought. It had been a very long time since she'd seen such a fine specimen of man like him, and it was extremely difficult to peel her eyes away from him and plant them back on her boss, but eventually she managed to do just that.

"Okay. They're not lawyers. What's up, Bob?"

"Tara. These men are here to talk to you." Bob spoke in his fatherly voice.

She placed a hand on her hip and cocked her head sideways. "So. Which Mafia king pin are you?" She addressed the suit and watched as the corner of his mouth lifted. "And him." Her chin jutted in Mountain Man's direction. "He's what? Your muscle?"

The suit's grin grew lopsided as Mountain Man's eyebrows drew together in a frown.

"Afraid not, Miss Roberts." Mr. Suit flipped out his ID and shoved his coat tail aside so she could see the badge attached to his belt. "Supervisory Special Agent Derek Ross, FBI. And this is my partner, Special Agent Chance Anselmi."

Tara could feel the blood draining from her face. This couldn't be good. What on earth would the FBI want with her? Then it hit her. "I remember you. The trial. You're one of the agents who captured Alvin, right?" She didn't wait for him to answer. "What the hell does the FBI want with me?" Her voice sounded weak even to her own ears, the confident vibrato she carried in her voice vanishing.

Bob jumped off the desk and approached her. "Now stay calm, Tara. These men need to talk to you for a minute."

"Bob? What the hell does the FBI need with me?" She couldn't keep worry from infiltrating her voice. The air in the room frosted.

"Miss Roberts. Why don't you sit down for a minute?" It was the suit who broke the ice.

"Oh, no. I prefer to do my freaking out standing up, thank you very much. If you have something to say to me, Agent Ross, just spit it out."

"Derek, ma'am. And all right, if you insist."

"I do, Derek. So get on with it." She rolled her hand over and over nervously as she watched him take a deep breath.

"Early this morning, Alvin Cruz escaped from the psychiatric hospital in California and the FBI has reason to believe he's coming after *you*."

Already lightheaded, Tara felt a strong wave of nausea hit her gut like a wrecking ball. Her knees wobbled and buckled. A multitude of little black dots wavered in front of her eyes mere seconds before darkness enveloped her now topsy-turvy world.

Chapter Eight

Miss Roberts? Wake up, Miss Roberts."

Was her mind playing tricks on her? Did she just dream someone from the FBI just told her Alvin was on the loose and was coming for her? No! It couldn't be. Her life just started to settle. Then she heard it again, a voice sounding like it was coming from the deep depths of a tunnel.

"Come on, sugar. Wake up, Tara. It's me, Bob."

Tara's eyes fluttered open. She looked around and saw three sets of eyes peering down at her. She recognized Bob's baby blues but not the other two. One pair was blue like ocean waves crashing off some breezy tropical island. They were pretty but nothing unusual as far as she was concerned. As for the other pair? Wow! They were a shade of semi-sweet to dark chocolate, big, warm, and gorgeous.

Maybe she was asleep and just dreaming, and maybe Alvin was still locked up which meant she was safe. Maybe her subconscious was trying to tell her something. A strong smell of ammonia fully awoke her senses. She bolted upright and started hacking.

"Damn! What are you guys trying to do, kill me by lethal inhalation?" She became more aware of her surroundings. She was in Bob's office and those two new pairs of eyes belonged to FBI Suit and FBI Mountain Man. Reality smacked her in the face.

"Crap!" She scrambled off the couch. "Okay, I remember now. Alvin's on the loose and headed my way. Dammit, dammit, *dammit!*"

"Nice vocabulary." Mountain Man's voice was rich and deep.

Bob stepped in front of her placing his hands on her shoulders, his substitute father persona in evidence once more. "Calm down, Tara. You need to get a hold of yourself if you're going to make it out of this mess."

"All right, all right. I get the picture." She chewed nervously on her lower lip. "So where do we go from here?"

*****

Chance was one hundred percent intrigued with the wiry little female especially as he watched her chewing on her very nice lip. She'd grown into a voluptuous, curvy little woman. Even though fear was radiating from every pore on her body, he could tell she was a strong, independent woman. *Yeah, maybe a little too strong and a little too independent.* She would be a handful for sure.

"Miss Roberts." He tried snagging her attention.

"Tara. Call me Tara."

Chance gave her a little lopsided grin hoping to gain her confidence. "Okay. Tara. We need to be expeditious here. The sooner we place you under protective custody and tuck you away in a safe house where Cruz can't get to you, the better." Chance saw Tara stiffen her spine.

"Whoa, wait a minute, buster. I am not going to some safe house."

"Tara. Hear them out." Bob warned.

"No. No safe house," she repeated.

Chance knew from her file that she'd spent a lot of time in safe houses after her family's murders and she must be reluctant to go through that again.

Bob attempted to gain her cooperation. "Come on, Tara. Please let them protect you."

Derek stepped forward. "Rookie's right, Tara. We know Cruz is headed your way. We uncovered evidence proving he's located your whereabouts -- where you live and where you work. He's not going to stop until he finds you."

Tara frowned. "Why do I have to hole up in some safe house somewhere? Why can't the FBI plaster guards around my ass and keep him away from me?" She flung her arm in Chance's direction. "And I am *not* going anywhere with some rookie suit or rather some rookie muscle man or whatever the hell rookie here is supposed to be!"

Her statement amused Chance. It was his turn to try and be persuasive. "Cruz is psychotic, Tara. He's one hundred and fifty percent obsessed with you. Don't you get it? He is not ever going to give up. He'll hunt you down until he catches you."

She looked him straight in the eyes. He could tell she was trying to hide the fear pinging through her body. "And if he does catch me?"

He moved to stand in front of her and shoved his body as close to her as he could get without skin-to-skin contact. He overshadowed her tiny frame and forced her gaze upwards. A split second passed before he answered keeping his voice low and menacing. "We found pictures Cruz drew with his own hands, Tara. Pictures of him and you... sexually explicit pictures, if you catch my drift."

She sucked in a deep breath and gasped.

"Anselmi!" Derek warned.

Chance turned and faced his leader. "She needs to know the truth, Derek. She needs to be aware of what she's up against.

"He still wants me, doesn't he?" Tara's voice was noticeably weaker and more resigned as she faced the truth of the situation.

Chance swung back toward her and lowered his voice too, looking her straight in the eyes. "Yes. He still wants you, but we're here to protect you and stop him." He paused a moment before speaking in a whisper. "Tara. Please let us do our jobs and protect you."

She took in another deep, shaky breath and glanced at Bob. She was seeking his reassurance and fatherly approval. Bob nodded his head and gave her a wink.

"Okay. Fine. I'll go. Just let me finish my shift and go back to my apartment to pick up a few things. We can go then."

Derek stepped forward. "Uh, no. You're leaving with us right now."

Tara shook her head in denial. "Not going to happen. I am not leaving here to go anywhere with you two bozos without my own clothes and my cat."

"Nope. No cat. You and you alone."

"No cat? Then no Tara, bud." She gave Chance a stern look.

Chance stood a little taller and inched even closer to her. "I said *no cat.*" His tone reflected his growing unstable Cajun temper.

Tara inched closer as well, her head back in an effort to stare him down, or up as the case might be. Punctuating each word with a stiff finger to his chest, she replied, "And I said *no cat? No me!*"

Derek stepped between the two of them. "Enough you two. Rookie? Back off. And, Tara? Won't you *please* consider leaving the cat in the care of a neighbor?"

She replied by pursing her lips and crossing her arms over her chest, holding her ground and drawing Chance's gaze to the swollen mounds of her breasts.

"Humph." His gaze remained fixated on her cleavage. "Stubborn woman."

"Humph." Her gaze was glued to his chest. "Stubborn Neanderthal."

Derek waved his arms about. "Enough already. Here's what's going to happen. Anselmi, you take the SUV to her apartment, pack up a few things for her, and pick up the cat." Tara tried to stifle a little giggle at her momentary victory but failed irritating Chance.

"Oh, no. Cats and I don't see eye-to-eye. I'm not layin' my hands on some skinny assed, mangy cat which probably hasn't been declawed." His Cajun accent was spilling thick.

Derek gave him a look of authority saying you'd better follow orders or else. He inhaled and let his breath out on a sigh caving in. He turned toward Tara and held out his hand, palm up. "Keys."

She looked down at his palm like it was moldy and covered with moss.

Bob yelled at her from across the room. "Tara! Give him the damn keys."

Chance watched her shoulders slump in resignation like she were a five year old being reprimanded by a parent. She fished the keys from her pocket and slammed them down in his hand. An unexpected jolt of electricity shot up his arm at the intimate contact of skin-on-skin.

Well just what the hell was that? He pulled his hand away. It took a couple of seconds to regain his composure. Turning to his partner, he put out his other hand palm up.

Derek took the SUV keys from his pants pocket and plopped them in his hand. "I'll call for another unit and we'll rendezvous with you at Tara's apartment in thirty."

Chance nodded and started heading for the door.

"Anselmi!" Tara called out to him.

He halted his steps, pivoted and glared at her.

"Good luck with the cat." Her sickly sweet comment was accompanied by a wicked grin.

"Yeah, yeah," he muttered, turning back around.

"And water my damn plants!" she yelled at his back as he slammed the door shut.

Chapter Nine

Twenty minutes later, Chance was parked in front of Tara's apartment building. It wasn't in the best shape but it wasn't a rundown shack either. The first thing he noticed was an obvious lack of security. Sure, the front door had an automatic lock system, but all a yahoo needed to do was ring any doorbell on one of the mail boxes to gain entrance. In fact, while he sat in his car watching, he saw two people enter the building by doing the exact same thing.

As he walked through the main floor of the building, he once again noted a lack of security. There was a stairwell trailing down to the left appearing to lead to a storage area. On the right was the main stairwell leading up to the apartments. He looked around once more and spotted an elevator tucked unobtrusively in a corner.

When the elevator arrived on the third floor and he started walking toward Tara's apartment, he remembered she owned a cat. Damn. He wasn't fond of felines. Back home in Louisiana, he'd grown up around dogs except for stray cats that made their family camp grounds home but they pretty much kept to themselves. Dogs were more his style.

He inserted the key in the lock and twisted the doorknob nudging it open. Last thing he needed was the damn cat shooting down the stairs and wandering off. She would be some pissed at him then. He stuck his nose through the crack in the door and glanced around looking for the cat but it was nowhere in sight.

"Here, kitty, kitty, kitty." He chuckled at the way the call sounded. "Come out, come out, wherever you are."

When the cat didn't materialize, he checked out the living room. It was small but efficient. The furnishings were sparse but were well kept. A soft looking overstuffed brown couch faced a small entertainment center. An end table stood sentry between the couch and a matching armchair. The walls were neutral beige and held pictures of what looked like a happy family. The only splash of color was a vibrant rainbow hued throw rug in front of the couch.

Spotting a hallway, he headed there seeking the cat. Opening the first door on the left, he discovered the bathroom which was neat and clean, not a towel out of place. No cat.

He closed the door and headed to the one on the right. Before he could open it, he heard a soft meow but the sound wasn't coming from behind the door. It came from the front of the apartment or maybe from the kitchen. He headed in that direction.

Swinging doors served as an entrance to the kitchen. He entered glancing around and took note of food and water dishes near the door but still no cat.

He saw a set of glass sliding doors at the other end of the kitchen leading outside. When he crossed the floor to the doors and opened them, he couldn't help but smile. There was a tiny balcony strewn with ivys, bamboos, and cacti. All of them were shiny and healthy looking which reflected how much love she gave them.

Tara obviously learned how to adjust to life on her own. She not only managed to keep herself afloat, she also found enough love within her heart for a balcony full of plants and a cat which he found amazing.

He heard the meow again and this time it sounded closer. After locking the sliding door behind him, he headed for the swinging doors. He pushed them open and halted.

Sitting at his feet and staring up at him with obvious distrust was a grey tabby cat. Not just any normal sized cat. *Nooo.* Leave it to *her* to have a giant of a cat. The chubby feline had to weigh at least twenty pounds. *What a freak of nature.* He'd never seen a cat so big before.

The cat's hackles rose and it started hissing and spitting. *Oh, hell.* Maybe the damn thing was rabid or something. Hell, he didn't know squat about cats.

Ever so slowly he started retreating. For every step he took backwards, the cat took one forwards still hissing and spitting. He grabbed his phone and punched in a speed dial number.

"Ross here."

"Ross! Get your ever lovin' ass over here right *now*! There's a psycho on the loose in here." Chance's distinctive Cajun accent became thick and more prominent.

"*Cruz* is there?" His partner squeaked in disbelief.

"No! A freaking humongous crazy assed cat! I swear it's as big as a mountain lion!"

"Pull it together, rookie. We'll be there in ten. I'm sure you can handle one small kitty for ten minutes."

"I'm telling you, it's huge and vicious! Make it five." He ended the call.

He was trying to talk the fierce looking animal down to no avail when a distinctive and familiar sounding click split the silence. He froze in place and lifted his hands in surrender as a deep male voice reverberated through the air.

"You just continue to hold the pose, asshole."

Chance lifted his eyes. He and the stranger were about the same in stature, which meant this guy wasn't wimpy looking Cruz. The only difference between Chance and *this* guy was the shotgun pointed directly at Chance's forehead.

Standing a couple of inches taller than Chance, the huge guy was dressed in a beige muscle shirt showing off massive shoulders and bare biceps. His bald head gleamed with beads of sweat. A familiar looking tattoo was on his right bicep -- a Special Forces Army Rangers tat. Chance should know. He had one just like it on his own arm. Which meant one thing. He was in deep trouble. His muscles twitched as he made a slow move toward his gun.

"I said hold the pose, shithead!" the guy yelled.

"Whoa, man. Just chill. Let's calm down here, all right?"

"Who the hell are you?"

"You know, I could ask you the same question."

"Maybe, but I'm the one with a gun aimed at your head, so I'll ask the questions. One more time. Who the hell are you and what are you doing in Tara's apartment?"

Figuring he'd better be straight up with this guy, Chance spoke calmly. "My name is Chance Anselmi. I'm FBI." He pointed down toward his belt to his badge. "If you give me a chance, I'll get my ID out my back pocket."

"Stop! I'll do the getting. Do not move a muscle, dickhead."

The guy walked over to him and gingerly reached around to Chance's back pocket pulling out the ID. He backed up a few steps before glancing at it. Only then did he lower the gun though he never lost his shooting stance. Chance relaxed a little... only a little.

"Why are you here without Tara and where is she?"

Before Chance could answer, the cat, who'd been eyeing the show, meowed and took off toward the front door of the apartment which swung open.

"Logan?" A tiny female voice trailed through the air. "What's going on here, Logan?" Tara crossed the living room while Ross now stood in the doorway behind her.

The gunman swung toward her and laid down the weapon. He took off flailing his hands in the air.

"Oh, Tara, Tara, my little cookie. Are you in some kind of trouble? Has someone hurt you? Why is the FBI here? What do they want with you? Are you sure you're all right?" He ranted while hugging Tara and patting her down like a mother checking her child for injury.

"Calm down, Logan. I'm fine. I'm not hurt, and the FBI's here because of Cruz."

"*Cruz*? Don't tell me the son of a bitch is out of the nut house?" Tara nodded. "Oh, cookie. How horrible. What? Is he coming after you or something?" She nodded again.

Putting his arm around her shoulders, he guided her to the couch. "Don't you worry now, girlfriend. Nobody's going to get to you without going through me first. Don't you dare be afraid now, you hear me?" He sniffled.

Chance felt his brows furrow. *The dude was crying?* This huge, menacing looking, full of bulging muscles man who'd just scared the crap out of him was now talking awfully funny, kind of... *girlish*? And was tearing up... like a *female*?

Tara told Logan about the FBI placing her under protective custody until Cruz could be caught and the fact she'd be gone for a while.

"Protective custody. Ooh. How Law and Orderish."

"Yeah. Well it's not like I have a choice here."

"Don't you worry your pretty little head about anything." He patted her hand in a reassuring way. "I'll look out for your apartment and your plants."

"And the cat," Chance chimed in quickly.

"Not no, but *hell* no!" Tara huffed. "Where I go, Timmy goes. We've been over this once already, Anselmi."

"She has a point," Logan interrupted, his voice more animated and higher pitched. "Timmy's not used to anyone except cookie. Why, he tries to bite my fingers off every time I come over here to feed him and he knows me."

Chance looked at his partner for help. There was no way in hell he was taking the monstrosity with them to a safe house. No *freakin'* way.

Derek rolled his eyes. "Now, Tara. Be reasonable here. There's no way we can keep an eye on you and the cat."

Tara folded her arms under her breasts, which drew his attention there. She straightened her spine. "No cat, no go. Final answer," she said like she'd just answered a question on *Who Wants to Be a Millionaire.*

Chance looked over at Derek again who just shrugged his shoulders and was looking amused. Frustrated, he threw his hands up in the air and gave in.

"Fine. Just freakin' fine. The cat comes with us, and I guess you want your plants, too."

"Don't be ridiculous, Anselmi." She put her hands around Logan's huge tattooed bicep. They didn't come close to meeting. "My dear friend and neighbor here will take care of them for me, won't you, sweetie pie?"

Chance cocked up an eyebrow. *Cookie? Sweetie pie?* The way Logan was acting, all sweet and girly like, he figured the man dripped sugar in his veins.

"You know it, honey. You just go with the nice FBI men and leave everything to me."

Oh, brother.

"Enough of this crap," Derek intervened. "Tara. Take Logan with you so he can keep an eye on you and go pack some clothes. Rookie and I will get the cat's food and the cat."

Chance gave him a wicked look. "Bullshit. There ain't no way on God's green earth I'm touchin' that huge mongrel."

Tara leaned down and picked up Timmy who'd been guarding his master at her feet. "Don't worry about Timmy. I've got him. And just for your information, Timmy is a Maine Coon. They grow really big. So *his* size is *not* abnormal." She eyed Chance up and down. "And he's not a mongrel! Come on, Logan." She headed down the hallway followed by her friend, her nose in the air in triumph.

*****

"Tara, honey. Why aren't you packing this?" Logan held up a fire engine red piece of lingerie by one finger. "Just why do you think I gave you this teddy for Christmas? It wasn't for it to sit in your dresser drawer and gather dust bunnies. You know, you haven't had any in so long you've forgotten how to flaunt your stuff."

"I don't need to flaunt my stuff." She was defensive while she continued to pack.

"Well, maybe if you did you'd get some more often." He pulled out a tiny black lace bikini swimsuit out of a drawer, held it up, and glared at her. She ignored him.

He moved toward her and placed his arm around her shoulder. "Listen to me, cookie. There's one very hot looking FBI man out there whose eyes have been smoking every time he looks at you. Don't think I haven't noticed." He paused for effect. "Take both of them."

Sighing, she shut the suitcase. "Come on, Timmy. Let's go." She grabbed the cat from where he was stretched out on the bed and walked out.

*****

Everyone was now gathered in the living room. Chance couldn't help himself. His curiosity was getting the better of him and he needed to ask.

"Uh, Logan? Is the Ranger tattoo significant to you or just for show?"

The other man's demeanor lightened. "Eight years, Special Forces." There was obvious pride in his voice, then a moment of silence. A slow smile then emerged from Logan's lips. "I've got another tattoo. Want to see it?" He grabbed his belt buckle and started unbuckling it.

"*Whoa* -- no, no, no. Not necessary," Chance stammered.

Derek coughed trying to cover his laughter. It didn't work.

Logan sighed and did a quick finger snap in Chance's direction. "Well, you just don't know what you're missing, brother."

"Yeah, well. As a fellow Special Forces brother in arms, won't you reconsider keeping an eye on the cat?" Chance begged as he pointed toward his own tattooed bicep.

Logan moved over and put his arm around Chance's shoulder. "Look here, my Ranger friend. Do you really think the kitty's going to stay here without her? Besides, Tara goes nowhere without her kitty." He waggled his eyebrows.

Derek almost choked trying to stifle his laughter. Chance's eyes made a beeline for the implied spot between Tara's thighs. When he looked back up at her face, he noted how red it was and she looked pissed as hell.

"My *cat*!"

Derek held his composure and started toward the door. "Time to go."

At the SUV, Logan hugged Tara. "Stay safe, cookie. Keep in touch, you hear?"

"Will do." She got in the back seat. Derek walked around to the driver's side still chuckling while Chance slid in the back on the opposite side of Tara. She pushed a button lowering the window. "Logan!"

He turned to look back at her. "Yeah?"

"Good luck with the contest. And help yourself to any of my makeup you might need."

"Thanks, cookie." He fanned his face with his hand to dry tears.

"Okay. I'll bite," Chance said.

Tara gave Chance a puzzled look. "What?"

"What contest?" He heard his partner snicker.

"Logan's a body builder."

Well of course. He should have figured it out by himself. "Obviously, but you said he could borrow your makeup."

"Yes. In his leisure time, Logan runs the clubs in drag. They're having a drag queen contest this weekend."

Again, Derek sounded like he was hacking up a fur ball while Chance gave her his best I'm-so-not-believing-this look.

"He's favored to win. He's good friends with famous drag queens, you know."

More snickering came from the front seat. Chance held his breath for a moment and then let it out in a whoosh. "One more question." He tried to maintain some decorum.

"Shoot."

"Where does he hide it?" He was curious. Derek was smothering a laugh.

Tara squelched her own giggle and asked innocently, "Hide what?"

"You know. How and where does he hide... *it*? When he's in drag?"

She cocked an eyebrow and stared down at his crotch making him squirm. "Do you really want to know?"

He hesitated a few seconds. "Uh, on second thought, no. Not really. Yo, Derek."

"Yes?"

"Does the FBI have a shrink on call for its employees? Because after this case is over, I think I'm gonna need one."

Derek's composure faltered. He outright roared as they merged onto the interstate.

Chapter Ten

Derek was preoccupied going through papers. Chance watched Tara sulking at the rear of the plane. The huge cat was curled up on her lap all content looking like a throw pillow. It was a shame they had to usurp her life like this but it was an absolute necessity. Cruz was a full blown psychotic and too much for her to contend with alone despite the fact she appeared to be strong and independent. Besides, with his penchant for murder and lack of remorse, it would be a matter of time before he found her, and if she refused him, she'd end up dead too.

Maybe if he talked to her she'd be more comfortable with him and he might gain some insight into Cruz's behavior while at it. He got up and walked toward the back of the plane.

"Mind if I sit here?" He looked down at her small curled up figure. She lifted her head and met his gaze. *Damn, but her eyes were luminous like fine cut emeralds.*

"Knock yourself out." She looked back down at the sleeping cat and stroked his fur.

Chance eased into the seat facing her not wanting to wake up the cat. "So, Tara. What got you into your line of work?" She didn't even look up at him. She just shrugged a shoulder.

Okay. That went well. Maybe a different approach might work.

"How long have you had Timmy?" She picked up her head and gave him a small smile, her affection for the animal evident.

"It's been quite a while now. Timmy was a family pet. He was a little kitten when..."

She didn't have to finish the sentence. He knew she meant when she lost her family. Well at least now he had her attention. "So. Is there anything you could tell me about Cruz which would help us track him?"

Her expression soured as she sighed. "Alvin and I were classmates in high school. For about six months, he tried every day to get me to go out with him. I kept refusing, but he's one of those people who can't understand the word 'no.' Sometimes he'd show up at our house uninvited and beg me to go out on a date. My dad, a retired vice cop, didn't like the look of him. He warned me all the time to stay clear of the lowlife because he said Alvin wasn't right in the head. Whenever Alvin came to the house trying to get me to go out with him, Dad always came up with an excuse to force him to leave."

"So what do you think set him off to make him hurt your family?"

"Alvin's a very self-centered person. I think he's always thought of me as his prize, a possession. He wants what he wants and no one else is going to have it."

"Did you ever go out with him?"

"No, no way. His aggressiveness always creeped me out. And even though Dad could sometimes be a stubborn, mule-headed man, he was usually right in his assessment of people. Twenty-two years as a cop tends to make you wise to things."

Chance nodded in agreement. "Have you had any contact with Cruz since the trial?"

"Once. I got curious, you know, wondering what set him off to do such a thing. About a year after he was committed, I went to the psych hospital to see him." Her beautiful eyes glassed over with a memory. He saw the pain of the memory reflected in them.

"What happened?" His voice was soft.

Taking in a deep breath, she told him the story. "It was a Sunday afternoon. I remember seeing a football game being broadcast on television in what they told me was a recreation room. Alvin was there with a bunch of other patients."

Chance's brows drew together in apprehension. "You didn't go there alone, did you?"

"I know. Not a brilliant idea, huh."

"No. It could have been a dangerous situation."

"I wasn't thinking so straight back then. I did ask a guard to accompany me before I showed my face to him. I may be an idiot sometimes but I don't have a death wish."

Chance's mouth quirked up into a grin. "Go on," he urged.

"Nothing happened. He wouldn't talk to me, wouldn't even look at me, nothing."

"It doesn't make any sense. His profile suggests he's obsessed with you. So why do you think he wouldn't even acknowledge your presence?"

She shrugged her shoulders. "I couldn't figure it out either. The only thing I could come up with was he didn't want to deal with me in front of an audience. The room was packed with other patients."

"Hey, rookie."

Chance leaned over the side of his seat and peered down the aisle at Derek who motioned with his fingers for him to come forward.

"Duty calls," he said in way of an apology. He rose and went back to the front.

"What's up?" His tone was hushed so Tara wouldn't hear their conversation.

"Scott just called about a hijacked vehicle belonging to a couple vacationing in LA. Their bodies were found in a ditch along South Central Avenue, their luggage and wallets missing. Both their throats were slit like the workers at the psych hospital."

Chance frowned. Cruz appeared to be hell bent on getting to Tara, and it looked like nothing was going to get in his way. Great. Just freaking great.

*****

Cruz milled about around the pool area at *Party Hard* trying to blend with the crowd as he scanned the grounds looking for her. There was no sign of his woman.

Initially he thought she was on her day off, but he'd already been to her apartment. After taking out the FBI agent watching the apartment in an unmarked vehicle across the street, he ransacked the place. It was locked up tighter than a drum, her car and the cat in all the pictures on the wall were gone.

After arriving at *Party Hard,* he located her car in the employee parking lot. She had to be here somewhere. Pulling out his cell phone, he hit speed dial.

"Yeah."

"Where is she, Junior? I've been hunting her down and can't find her anywhere."

"Haven't a clue. I do know the FBI picked her up and they're stashing her away in some safe house somewhere. The location is being withheld as confidential."

"Then get off your ass and find the location! I need her." He slammed the phone shut and cursed again.

*****

Exhausted from work and the trauma of being usurped from her home, Tara stretched out across two seats on the plane and instantly slept only to fall head first into her nightmare.

Dragging her unwilling body, Alvin led her into the family kitchen. Tara's eyes widened at the sight of her mother strapped to a chair, arms and legs bound tightly, her mouth covered with duct tape. A plea for help flickered in her eyes.

He whispered next to her ear as he forced her to sit down in a chair across from her mother. "See, baby? Mommy's fine." Grabbing duct tape stuck to the edge of the table, he bound her hands behind the chair and secured her feet to the chair's legs. He then strode around the table and stood behind her mother. Leaning down close to her mom's face, he rubbed his cheek against hers while he kept his eyes trained on Tara.

She watched as her mother's eyes closed, then re-opened filled with revulsion and fear. Alvin stood up straight and rubbed his right hand over Melanie's hair while he stared at Tara, his cold icy blue eyes flickering with madness. With calculated accuracy and without warning, he pulled on her mom's hair until her head tilted upward. He brought the already bloodied blade of his knife across her throat. A muffled scream came from Tara's own throat as she watched her mother die.

Gasping for breath, Tara became aware of something nibbling on her ear. "Timmy! Quit biting my ear! I'm awake now." She fussed her feline friend as she tried sitting up but couldn't under the weight of the Maine Coon.

"Are you all right, Tara?" A burly voice called from above.

When she looked up, Chance Anselmi was standing as tall as the Sears Tower hovering above her. "I'll live. Biting my ear off is just Timmy's way of waking me up."

Chance knelt beside her. "Were you dreaming?" His voice was soft. The cat reared up and hissed at him making him back up a little.

"Timmy! Behave or I'll put you in your pet carrier." Tara fussed again at the huge feline. After licking her face, the cat hurdled himself over the nearby arm rest and plopped down on the seat beside her. He was asleep in an instant.

Chance stood and moved to the seat across from her. "Was it a dream making you scream?"

Tara sighed. "I have them often."

He was disturbed by her announcement. "How often?"

She shrugged her shoulders like she was trying to pretend it was no big deal. "Every time I fall asleep." Tears shimmered in her eyes.

Now it *really* disturbed him. "The dreams frighten you." It was a statement, not a question. His tone held a hint of anger. "Why don't you tell me about them?"

"I'd rather not. Reliving the nightmares once a day and in weekly counselling sessions is enough for me."

She worked hard to appear normal. She held two jobs and maintained a household filled with plants and a cat, all well cared for.

"You know, sometimes talking about it helps," Chance told her sounding like he knew this on a personal level which made her wonder if he'd suffered loss as well.

She looked down at the floor, sighed, and looked back up at him. "The dream is about that night. Each time it's different, coming in bits and pieces. Sometimes it's Dad, sometimes Mom, sometimes one or both of my sisters. It's always a different scenario, and that's what gets to me. I never know which family member I'll have to watch die all over again."

The plane dipped downward as it started its descent. Chance looked toward the window. "We're here," he informed her.

Tara sat up grabbing Timmy off the seat. "Where exactly is here?"

"Columbus, Ohio. We're taking you to a safe house. Everything will be just fine as soon as we get you there." He stood and walked back to the front of the plane.

Chapter Eleven

They disembarked the plane in silence. The tarmac was well lit providing much needed brightness to the inky black night. Two dark SUVs were parked nearby, five agents standing at attention next to them. Derek met up with Agent Travis Dean.

"Everything secure?"

"Yes, sir. Surveillance and recon are complete. The area has been cleared. Just waiting for delivery of the package. Agents Bordeaux and Wright will go to the airport. Agents Robinson and Talbert will cover train and bus terminals. Navarro is at the safe house."

"Good. Scott and his team are tracing Cruz's trail. He should be contacting me within the hour with an update, so let's get out of here."

Chance guided Tara still holding Timmy toward the back of the first SUV while keeping his eyes trained on their surroundings. He opened the door, helped her in, and then walked around sliding into the back seat next to her. Derek was in the front passenger seat while Travis took his place as driver.

"Do we have very far to go?" Tara yawned.

"It's a twenty minute drive," Travis answered. "You have time for a few winks at least. I'm sure you're exhausted."

"I'm bushed but I've never been to Ohio. I want to see all I can see."

Chance grinned. Despite everything the woman was going through being uprooted, she was still optimistic enough to want to sightsee.

Twenty minutes later the vehicles pulled into a garage in the suburbs of Columbus. The house was a modest one story brick home which could have been in any suburban area in America. Chance walked around to open the door for Tara. As she placed her hand in his, a frizzle of electricity just like the one he'd felt when she'd put her keys in his hand shot up his arm. *That's interesting*. She must've felt it too because for a second he saw her tremble.

Derek took up the rear of the entourage being led by Travis. They were met in the living room by Agent Navarro.

"Agent Ross. Everything is secure and in order."

"Excellent, Agent Navarro. Chance, I realize you don't know these guys yet, but I'm sure they'll introduce themselves."

Chance nodded as Navarro moved in his direction.

"Hi. I'm Jason." Chance extended his hand but Jason stopped short and gazed down at his own latex gloved hand and then at Chance's bare one.

Travis, who'd just walked in, started laughing. "Don't mind Jason.

He's not unfriendly, just germaphobic, and arachnophobic, homophobic, and any other 'phobic' known to man."

"Am not, Travis. I'm just acutely aware of the potential for germs." Jason unconsciously rubbed his glove encased hands together shooing away unseen germs.

"Are too," Travis muttered.

"Am not!"

"Gentlemen!" Derek ordered.

*****

"Hey! Anybody care to introduce *me*? I haven't met anybody yet." Tara chimed in. Seated on the couch facing an armoire housing a television, her arms were draped over the back of the couch while Timmy was adorned across her lap.

Tara took in the new suits. The character, Jason, looked just like the other one described him, afraid of everything. He was short and squat with a balding head, a paunchy little stomach and a look suggesting he might be short a few brain cells. She wondered how he could have made it through rugged FBI training.

Now, as for the one called Travis? Hmm. From the build of his body, he most definitely could pass rugged training. He was at least over six feet full of muscle bulging through his suit. No fat -- just muscle. Not picture perfect handsome, but not hard on the eyes either.

Even though this situation sucked big time, at least there were a few good looking testosterone filled men to ogle. Face it. She was female and enjoyed eye candy any time it was dangled in front of her. "This is the vic," Chance said interrupting her ogling.

"*Vic*? Can't you remember my name, Anselmi?"

He glared at her before taking a deep breath. His reaction amused her. "Excuse me. Dean and Navarro? This is Tara Roberts, victim extraordinaire. Roberts? Agents Travis Dean and Jason Navarro."

Tara pasted on a fake smile and wiggled her fingers at them.

"Damn," Chance uttered low enough no one should have heard, but Tara had.

"You say something, Anselmi?" Sarcasm dripped from her mouth.

"Yeah. I'm going to the car for our bags. Think you can behave for five minutes?"

"Well, I don't know," She mused as she checked out Travis's body from head to toes and back up again. "I'll try."

"*Merde,*" Chance cursed as he stormed out the door.

*****

Once everyone else scattered, Chance watched as Tara took in her surroundings. The furnishings were a bit eclectic but were decent. It would do. Timmy woke up with a start when she moved. Chance listened as she spoke to the cat. "Sorry. Didn't mean to wake you." She looked up and their eyes met. "Chance?"

"Hmm?"

"Do you think there's a place around here I could take Timmy so he could stretch his legs and wander around a bit?"

He straightened his stance. "Sure. Let me check out the backyard. I'll be right back."

Chance located the back door through the kitchen. He opened it slow and peered into the backyard but couldn't see with the darkness. He tripped a light switch on the side of the door frame and a flood light illuminated the yard chasing away shadows.

Stepping outside with gun drawn, he did a quick recon of the grounds. Satisfied no threat loomed, he holstered his gun and went back to the living room and found Tara curled up on the couch in a ball with Timmy nestled on the floor at her feet. A funny twinge hit his chest. He rubbed it. Maybe he was out of shape. It was a few days since he'd been able to complete a good exercise routine. Tomorrow he'd have to make time and hit one hard.

Derek walked into the room. "Poor girl's had a rough day, hasn't she?"

"Yeah. She's wore out," he whispered. "Which room are we putting her in?"

"First one on the right. You'll be on the left across from hers."

"All right. I'll get her settled. You need anything else from me?"

"No. Get some sleep. I'll be up a couple more hours with paperwork and phone calls. Dean and Navarro will take first watch from me when they get back. I sent them to the all night grocery to stock up and get cat food. There are two agents out of sight securing the perimeter until they return. See you at seven a.m."

Chance strolled toward the sofa where Tara slept.

"Chance?"

He turned toward Derek. "Yeah, boss?"

"Not a bad first day in the field for a rookie, rookie."

He smiled. "Thanks. See you in the morning." Derek nodded and walked out.

Chance looked down at Tara. Even through the mask of sheer exhaustion on her face, she radiated beauty. He wondered just how much damage Cruz had done to her. He knew her sassiness and sarcasm were just cover-ups for the pain still imbedded in her heart.

With a deep sigh, he leaned over and lifted her off the couch trying not to wake her. She was light as a feather. He could bench press twice her weight. She stirred just enough to slide her arm around his neck. *Damn, but this feels right.*

He walked down the hall leading to the bedrooms and stopped at the first door nudging it open with his shoulder. Her suitcase sat atop an old fashioned chest of drawers. The bed cover and sheet were turned down. He laid her down gently on the bed. She let out a sigh and grabbed for the pillow snuggling her head into the soft down.

Making as little contact as possible with her skin, he slipped off her shoes and pulled the covers up tucking them in at her sides. Her scent wafted up to him -- warm vanilla, sugar, and woman. He was momentarily stunned.

Tara's glossy hair fanned across her pillow giving her an angelic auburn halo. Her face relaxed in slumber, high cheekbones cushioned thick dark eyelashes. Her skin was tan from hours under the Vegas sun. Her lips were full, a cupid's bow adorning her upper lip. He watched her chest rise in a steady rhythm with her breathing. He thought she was pretty when he'd first laid eyes on her. Now, he realized he was wrong. She was so beautiful.

"Meow."

Looking down at his feet, he saw Timmy standing over his toes with a mean look on his furry face. "Meow, meow, meow."

He whispered, "Shh, be quiet, kitty." The cat looked like he wanted up on the bed. Extending his arms toward the feline, he got within inches before Timmy hissed and his hackles rose. Straightening back up, Chance put his hands up in surrender. "Oh, no you don't. You ain't gonna play a game with me. Either you want me to touch you, kitty, or you don't. What's it gonna be?" Timmy plunked down on the floor ignoring him. Tara moaned.

"Touch me," she whispered sleepily. Chance's head whipped in her direction. Was *she* replying to his question or did he imagine it? She looked like she was still asleep.

"Mmm. Touch my kitty cat."

Holy crap. He scrambled to get out the room before she woke and realized just what she'd invited him to do.

*****

Alvin paced the floor of the run down motel room anxiously waiting for his contact to pick up the phone. Relieved when he heard a coarse hello, he shouted into the disposable cell. "You'd better have a location!"

"If you'd shut up a minute and listen, you'd find out I do."

"About damn time. Where is she?"

"Ohio."

"*Ohio?*"

"Ohio -- somewhere near Columbus, but I don't have a physical address yet. It should be forthcoming soon."

"You just get me the address if you want me to keep your dirty little secret." There was dead silence on the other end of the line.

"Did you hear me, Junior?" Cruz shouted.

"I heard you."

"Good. You find the address and we'll be all set." He slammed the phone shut without waiting for a response.

Chapter Twelve

Tara's nose twitched. The aroma of fresh brewed coffee wafted beneath her nostrils. She took in a deep breath of the sweet nectar. "Mmm, smells so good."

With some difficulty, she opened her eyes and perused her surroundings. The memories of being on the plane and driving to the safe house came back in a rush. She groaned out loud.

Would she ever be rid of Alvin Cruz? God, she hoped so. With the FBI involved, maybe soon she would be able to return to her apartment and hectic but lovable jobs.

She closed her eyes again unwilling to fully wake. When she re-opened them, she was staring at a big ball of grey furry cat, his wet nose practically touching hers. She scrambled to sit up. Timmy pounced on her lap wanting to play. "Stop it, Timmy." She tried fending him off but he kept it up. The cat had a mind of his own when it came to play time. "Stop it, I said." She chuckled as he jumped up and nibbled on her ear. She gave up and played with him instead.

*****

"You think Cruz knows she's gone by now?" Chance asked Derek as they sat at the table discussing the case.

"More than likely. If I have his profile accurate, he'll seek out his obsession until he's acquired it or he'll die trying, and he'll destroy whatever or whomever gets in his way."

"So you think it's just a matter of time before he shows up to claim her."

Derek nodded in affirmation.

"Do I smell coffee?"

They both swiveled to see Tara standing in the kitchen doorway. Her hair sleep tousled, she was wearing the same clothes she'd slept in. To Chance, she looked like an angel.

"Coffee's on the counter. Muffins are on top the stove. Help yourself," Derek offered. "Rookie. I need a good run, so I'll do a perimeter sweep. Since the other guys are on down time, the package is yours while I'm gone."

"Sure thing," Chance acknowledged. Derek headed out the door.

Tara moved to the stove and picked up a muffin. Nibbling on it, she crossed the room and sat down in a chair at the table folding one leg under her. Chance got up, poured a cup of coffee, and returned to the table placing it in front of her.

"Thanks."

"Did you have a good night's sleep?"

"Yes. I was so tired I think I passed out. I don't even remember climbing into bed. Any news about Alvin?" She glanced at him over the rim of her coffee cup.

"No, nothing new. But don't worry, *chère*. He won't get near you. It's a guarantee."

"Humph. You don't know much about Alvin, do you? He's nothing if not persistent."

Anger now colored Chance's voice. "He's a psychotic dickhead. That's all I need to know. He'll make a mistake and when he does, his ass belongs to me."

"My, my. Mr. Big Bad FBI Agent is mighty sure of himself."

"I'm sure of one thing and one thing only."

"And what would that be?"

"You are one hell of a handful of woman who could get a guy in trouble in the blink of an eye without batting an eyelash."

Her laughter tinkled through the air. "I'm good, Anselmi, but not *that* good." She moved to the counter and rinsed out her cup placing it on the drain board then turned to face him.

He stared at her mesmerized by her beauty. Had he ever met a woman who was so unaware of her effect on man? None he could remember. Yes, he could get in deep trouble with her. No doubt about it.

She cleared her throat. "Well, I need a shower bad, but first Timmy needs food."

Chance gave himself a mental shake as she brought his focus back on the moment. "Oh, yeah. I forgot. His litter box, food, and water are over there by the door."

"But Timmy's very finicky; he eats a certain brand of cat food."

Chance walked to the sink, intending to wash his coffee cup but ended up nose-to-nose with Tara... more like nose-to-forehead. He could feel a pull coming from her. She craned her neck to look up and meet his gaze. Her pupils were dilated. Ah, so she felt it too.

His hand came up to her face. He tucked a wayward curl behind her ear before his hand snaked its way to the nape of her neck as he leaned in closer, their lips a mere breath apart.

He reluctantly released her and moved to the table turning his back. *Dammit*. How could he be so stupid as to almost kiss her? He knew better, but the impulse was so immediate, the attraction so strong. "If you would stop to look, you'd see he's got his favorite food in the dish. Go shower, *chat marron*. If you need anything, just holler."

"Shot what?" she asked, still looking bewildered from his actions.

He laughed and then headed out.

Chapter Thirteen

"What are you doing?" Chance's rough voice boomed making Tara jump.

"What the hell does it look like I'm doing?" She held her cell phone up as proof. In two strides, he was in front of her ripping the phone from her hand. He looked at it like it was a poisonous snake.

"Who were you calling?"

She put her now empty hand on her hip and cocked it sideways. "If you really must know, and frankly I think it's none of your business one way or the other, I was calling Logan."

He snapped the phone shut and glared at her. "No calls." He placed the phone in his right front jeans pocket.

The move brought her eyes down to his zipper. Huh. Unless socks were stuffed down his pants, he was sporting a pretty healthy erection. He couldn't be that big without one. *Could he*? She mused as to whether or not she was the cause of his current state. The thought made her smile. Then she remembered. He'd taken away her phone.

"Un, un, buster. You just hand it back to me right now. You can't take it away from me. I have rights you know. Just because you're big and bad and full of yourself doesn't mean you can go around giving me orders. I'll do what I please, when I please."

Tara could tell Chance was trying to ignore her as she watched him pinch the bridge of his nose between his thumb and forefinger. She placed her hands on her hips waiting for him to say something.

"Do you ever shut up, woman?" His Cajun accent grew thick.

"Oh, yeah? You want me to shut up, do you? Then you'd better hand the phone back to me. This is insane. What did you think I was doing anyway, calling Alvin up and inviting him to dinner? Do you think I'm crazy like him, or do you think I'm that stupid?"

Chance gently put his hands on her shoulders stopping the verbal assault. "He. Can. Track. Your. Calls." He punctuated each word with his heavy Cajun accent but still said it like he was talking to a child.

"Oh," was all she could say. She hadn't thought of that.

Tara watched as Chance brushed his hand through his thick mane of hair while he started pacing back and forth in front of her. A rapid fire explosion of French flew from his mouth. He was rattling it off so fast her head was spinning. She listened while he ranted and raved in a language she just couldn't quite grasp.

"Maudit diable a mad."

Ooh, now that just sounded like something dirty.

"And furthermore..." He continued in English and was switching back to his own French when Derek walked in.

"Hey you two! What's the problem?" He stepped in between them. Mixing his Cajun French with bits of English, Chance continued airing his opinions.

"I'm telling you, Derek. She's wild like a mountain lion, quick as a fox, and more stubborn than a jackass."

"Ha! You're calling *me* a jackass? Well then you're the king of the jackasses, mister."

"Okay, Okay! Go to neutral corners. We're going to be confined in this house for several days so I suggest you two do your best to try and get along. What started this latest round of World War III anyway?"

Tara gave him a sheepish grin. "I guess I did. I was calling Logan on my cell and..."

"She didn't connect, did she?"

Chance shook his head giving Derek an I-told-you-so look. "No, but only because I took the phone away from her before she could connect the call."

"Now wait just a minute here, bozo. Granted, I made a little mistake, okay? I didn't realize I was doing a bad thing. The least you yahoos could do is tell me what the ground rules are or at least provide me with some secret FBI manual like '*Rules for the Clueless Entering Protective Custody*' for heaven's sake. I realize I've been stuck in a safe house before, but it was when I was still a kid. There wasn't anyone left I could call then. No family, no friends..." Her voice broke toward the end of her tirade, tears brimming her eyes.

"It's all right, Tara. Everything's cool. It was a simple mistake. Nobody is blaming you for anything." Tara saw regret on his face for his harsh response.

"So, Tara. Why don't you relax? Go read a book or something," Derek requested.

The thought of books had her tears drying up. Reading was her favorite pastime. She could escape the harsh real world for a few hours. "Ooh. You have books here? What kind? How many? Any romance novels? Murder mysteries? Chick lit? Vampire books?"

Chance rolled his eyes. "Unless you brought all that garbage with you, the answer is no. We have nothing on your wish list."

Disappointed, Tara dropped to the couch. She had really hoped for something she considered normal. She was a book nerd through and through, normal for her.

After a few moments of silence, Chance blew out what sounded like an exasperated breath."All right, for Chri'sake. Derek. Things are kind of slow over here. Do you think maybe you could do without me for a while? Could Travis and Jason handle the package with you for an hour or so? I can run into town to the bookstore and get her something to keep her occupied."

"Whoa. I'm not letting you pick books for me. You're likely to come back with a Road Hog biker magazine and ten copies of Playboy. Nope. I'm going with you."

"No!" Chance and Derek both yelled at the same time.

Tara looked at both of them like they each had two heads. "Yes! I am," she declared. "And stop freaking referring to me as an inanimate object!"

"See? I told you, Derek. As stubborn as a damn jackass!"

"Come on, Tara. Please be reasonable," Derek begged. "You're the one who's in danger here, not Chance. He can get whatever your heart desires without your help."

She moved over and planted her body in front of the door. Folding her arms over her chest, she lowered her bottom lip in a pout.

She saw Chance's eyebrows rise. "That pretty pout isn't going to help you."

Tara had a sudden revelation. "So, Chance." She grinned. "If I need tampons, you'll get me tampons? And Midol?"

If looks could kill, she wouldn't have to worry about Alvin because he gave her that look, the one saying he'd take her over his knees and blister her ass for the little taunt, but then again, maybe she'd use her pouty little lip action again.

*****

"Derek. Conference please?" Chance asked.

They moved out of earshot from Tara. Chance lowered his voice so only Derek could hear him. "Look. We know Cruz doesn't know her whereabouts, right?"

Derek nodded. "I'm afraid to ask, but where are you going with this?"

"Before you gripe, hear me out. I know this is against protocol, but what if I take her with me and have Travis dog us? Its twenty minutes there, twenty minutes back, and twenty minutes in the bookstore. It should be safe enough, and maybe she'll start being more cooperative."

Derek took in a big breath looking wary but he was nodding his head. "She's your responsibility. Anything happens to her, not only will I have your freshly minted badge, but I'll have your ass too. Got it?"

"Got it." They both turned to face Tara who was still in front of the door maintaining her pout. Derek delivered the verdict.

"Okay. You can go."

Tara's face lit up like a Christmas tree and she started bouncing on her toes.

"But!" Derek interjected pointing a finger at her. She stopped bouncing immediately.

"If Chance says jump? Don't bother asking how high -- just jump. *He* is in charge, not you. *You* make one move, on purpose or accidental, jeopardizing your safety, he'll jerk you out of there in a heartbeat, and when you get back, the only things you'll be seeing are the four walls of your bedroom. Do you understand, Roberts?"

She stood erect and saluted him. "Understood, Captain."

"Grab your purse and let's hit the road," Chance told her.

"*Woohoo*!" She broke out a wide grin. Chance couldn't help but smile too.

Chapter Fourteen

The popular bookstore in Columbus advertised thirty-two rooms of books -- they weren't kidding. Now exploring room number twelve, Tara was in seventh heaven.

"I thought Travis was coming with us?" she questioned Chance as she scanned yet another set of bookshelves.

"He's here."

Her eyes darted around the room, but she didn't see hide nor hair of the agent. She'd looked for him in all the other rooms too but she hadn't seen him there either.

"Then how come I haven't seen him anywhere?"

"You're not *supposed* to see him."

"Oh." She realized Travis was supposed to be incognito. Her arms were loaded down with books, book covers, and bookmarks.

"You about ready yet? I promised Derek twenty minutes. We've been here almost two hours and I've lost you at least four times in this maze of rooms. He's going to skin us alive."

"Well he'll just have to deal with it. I'm trying to decide. You can't rush an important decision like this."

"Time's up." He grabbed her arm, dragging her away from the shelf.

"All right, already." She tugged her arm loose. "I'm ready to go now."

Plopping her bounty down on the counter, she pulled her credit card out of her purse and handed it to the sales clerk. She heard Chance mumbling something to someone making her turn her head to see him. Was he talking into his shoulder?

"That'll be forty-two fifty," the clerk announced.

"*No!*" Chance yelled as he made a grab for the credit card. The sales clerk shrunk back at his aggressiveness. Taking out his wallet, he slipped her credit card in it and plunked three twenty dollar bills down on the counter. Tara glared at him.

"Hey! I can pay for my own stuff, you know. I'm not a charity case just yet. And give me back my credit card!"

He leaned in close to her. "Sweetheart. Let's not make a scene now."

"Sweet... just where do you get off calling me that?" She swiveled her head to glare at him over her shoulder.

Pulling her in close and wrapping his big arms around her, he whispered in her ear.

"Credit cards can be traced."

She stilled and whispered, "Sorry."

"Here's your change, sir."

"Keep it. Let's go, honey." This time Tara obeyed his command without another word.

*****

Four hours later, Chance stood in the doorway of the living room watching Tara. She'd settled in curled up on the couch, her nose buried in a book. Timmy was next to her, four paws in the air, snoring away.

"What are you reading?" His voice sounded huskier than normal, even to him.

She jumped at the sudden intrusion into her peaceful silence. He could see the pulse point in her neck pick up a quick beat.

"Sheesh, Anselmi. You keep scaring the crap out of me." She clutched her chest. "Can't you put some taps on those big shoes or something?"

He chuckled. "Oh, yeah. It would be real effective trying to sneak up on a bad guy."

She shrugged. "At least the poor fool wouldn't have a heart attack."

"You didn't answer my question. What are you reading?"

Before she could answer, he reached out stealthily and plucked the book from her hand.

"Hey!" She made a swipe trying to get it back but he held it out of reach. She gave up.

He examined the book cover she'd slipped on to protect the book's binding. Plain white with just a few words boldly imprinted on the front, Chance read from the cover. "This is not a trashy vampire novel." He opened the book and read a passage from it. He couldn't stop grinning as he snapped the book closed and waved it in front of her.

"But this *is* a trashy vampire novel."

"So?" She leaped up and snagged the book out of his hand. "Nobody else needs to know." Her reply made him laugh.

"Listen, Chance. I'm really sorry about the credit card thing. I wasn't thinking as usual."

His laughter died. He sat down on the coffee table in front of her and grabbed her hands. "It's all right, Tara. I know this is hard for you, *chère,* but you need to remember we're here to protect you. You're not alone in this."

"I know, I know. And although I don't act it, I do appreciate everything you guys are doing for me. I just don't like it."

"Well, like I said. It's our job."

"Chance?"

"Yeah?"

"Do you think he'll find us up here?"

The fear he saw lurking in her eyes combined with the skepticism seeping in her voice made his gut clench. She couldn't mask the fact she was afraid. Leaning forward, he placed his elbows on his thighs and his hand on her knee.

"Listen, *chère*. It doesn't matter one way or the other if he finds us. I'm not gonna let him touch you ever again. I promise."

Chance hoped Tara would hear the truth in his words. She let out a deep breath. "I trust you, Chance."

"Good. You need to trust me, *chat marron*."

He saw her pupils dilating, and this time she was the one who made the first move. Her body leaned in closer to his. Their mouths were now a mere inch apart. Her sweet breath fanned his face. He closed his eyes relishing the feel of it. The faintest whisper of her lips brushed against his. His blood was boiling and sank southward.

"Shift is over, Anselmi."

The echoing sound of Travis's voice in the otherwise empty room was like a bucket of ice water had been poured over him. Tara's eyes flew open as did his own. He closed his once more sucking in his breath on a groan.

Travis plopped down in the chair nearest them. "So what are you guys doing in here?" He popped a huge bubble with the gum he was chewing.

Tara rose. "Think I'll take a nap. Come on, Timmy."

"Yeah," Chance said as he rose. "Think I'll go take a shower." He walked out after Tara covering his groin with his hands hoping his discomfort wasn't obvious to Travis. He swore when he heard Travis say, "I wonder if those two think they're fooling anybody but themselves." As he headed toward his shower, Chance definitely heard Travis's hearty laugh.

*****

"Found the girl, Cruz."

"Excellent. Is she still in Ohio?"

"Yes. I've booked you on a red eye. Your plane leaves at one a.m. Pick up your ticket at the check-in counter. You're booked under the name on the ID I gave you. They'll hand you an envelope I left for you with directions on where to find her."

"'Bout time you come through."

"You just better remember how much trouble I've gone through to help you."

"Yeah, yeah, yeah," Cruz grumbled as he hung up.

*****

He packed away his surveillance equipment and monitoring devices. The gadgets always fascinated him which was why he was so proficient at their use. He could hide away across the street out of sight and still be able to clearly hear both ends of the conversation going on in Cruz's hotel room.

He wanted to nail the stupid psychopath to the wall by giving the Feds his location, but if he leaked the information too soon, his prime target, who had been helping Cruz, would get away which was the last thing he wanted happening. After all, Junior was the one he wanted nailed to the wall. The man cost him big time and he'd see to it Junior paid for his indiscretions in spades.

He stowed away the gear, revved the engine on his Harley, and sped down the highway.

Chapter Fifteen

Tara awoke with a start, beads of sweat rolling down her face. The darkened room grew hot and stuffy. She could barely make out the grey furry lump which was Timmy at the end of the bed. She leaned over and clicked the lamp switch on the night stand. Nothing. Maybe the bulb was burnt?

Looking down at her watch, she mashed a button on the side sending a glow of illumination over the dial. *Three-thirty a.m.*

Sheer silence in the room loomed in front of her. There wasn't a single sound stirring the air. No hum of air conditioning, no night sounds from outside, nothing.

An eerie feeling crept upon her. Was the electricity out? She opened the drawer on the night stand searching for a flashlight or something to guide her. Again, nothing.

Slipping out of bed and patting the air in front of her so she wouldn't bump into anything, she felt the hair at the back of her neck stand on in like static electricity. Though she could barely make him out, she saw Timmy stand up, hackles raised. He hissed vehemently.

A quick flash of white-hot light lit up the entire room followed by a crack of thunder so loud it vibrated the floorboards. She let out a high pitched squeak of fear as she grabbed her own arms and pulled them in over her chest as protection.

A thunderstorm, which must be what took out the electricity.

A shrill scratching sound like fingernails raking across a blackboard came from the window. She whipped her head toward the noise but saw nothing but drawn curtains.

The offensive noise came a second time. Fear started climbing up her spine making her heart race. *Was someone trying to open her window?*

Her feet moved quickly but silently to the door. Just as she reached out to turn the doorknob and make a run for it, the knob started turning on its own.

Holy crap! Someone was trying to get in her room!

Not sure she was headed in the right direction, she started feeling her way toward the closet. As she found the doorknob and twisted it, her bedroom door squeaked.

She jumped in the closet and pulled the door shut leaving a tiny crack so she could try to see her intruder. A beam of light swept back and forth across her darkened room. Someone was definitely in there. Fear ratcheted up another notch all through her body.

Wishing she had a weapon, she felt around the interior of the closet until she found purchase on some sort of metal stick which felt like a small piece of light pipe. She couldn't believe her luck! Wrapping her fingers around it, she lifted it in anticipation as she watched the beam of light grow stronger and nearer her location.

She could now see a shadowy figure holding what looked like a flashlight in one hand. Hovering in the other hand above it was a gun.

A gun! Oh, hell.

Her breath was suspended from fear, her heart was pounding out a brisk rhythm. All sorts of scenarios scooted through her brain, the worst of which was Alvin found her location, he'd murdered her FBI protectors, and now he was gunning for her. With one hand still on the doorknob, she felt a sudden pull on the door. Her heart jumped up in her throat. Not strong enough to counter the force, the door flew open.

Oh, God. This was it. Her life was going to end tonight right here in a damn closet.

Without further thought, she swung the metal stick over her head with both hands and struck the intruder on the head -- *hard!* The thud of metal meeting skull made her shiver.

"Hell!" A gruff voice blurted out as the shadowy form hunched over and grabbed his head with his arms, the beam of light from his flashlight dancing wildly about the room.

With him momentarily folded in upon himself, Tara dropped the metal bar and seized the opportunity to sweep her foot out behind his forcing him to tumble backwards. He hit the floor with a loud thud as the flashlight flew in the air landing on the bed next to Timmy who protested with a loud hiss at being disturbed.

Curse words rang in the air. Adrenaline rushing through her body gave Tara momentum. She hurdled the man's downed body to flee while he was incapacitated, but before she took her second step, a hand reached out grabbing her ankle. She screamed and fell face first to the floor.

"Stop it!" he yelled as Tara twisted in his grip and wound up in a sitting position facing him. She kicked with her feet and tried to scoot away with her elbows.

"Stop fighting me!" he yelled once more.

"Leave me alone!" she shouted as she kicked and clawed trying to get away. Hell if she'd let Alvin win again.

"Dammit, stop fighting me, Tara! Look at me!"

Somehow, he managed to pin her to the floor with his body. She shoved her hands against his chest but couldn't budge him.

"Tara! Look at me!"

Her fear kept his words from reaching her ears. "Get off me!"

"Look at me, dammit!"

"No!" she screamed, still struggling to get out from under his siege. Her fear was escalating second by second. Her heart was about to burst through her chest. She didn't even recognize his voice, she was so scared.

"Look at me, Tara!" he yelled even louder. She swung her head to the side toward the bed avoiding his gaze. The last thing she wanted to do was see Alvin's crystal blue haunting eyes. "The storm knocked out the power. You're safe, *chat marron*."

Her body stilled. Wasn't that what Chance called her? That "shot" thing?

"Tara, look at me. It's Chance. I'm not going to hurt you." His voice softened.

Her gaze swung toward his face. Those deep brown semi-sweet chocolate eyes were focused in on hers. There was a playful twinkle in them. *Son of a b...!* He'd scared her out of her wits and he was *amused*? She'd show him funny.

Pounding her fists into his rock hard chest, she spit a string of curses at him while he held up his hands trying to ward off her blows. She swung until her arms ached and she couldn't swing any more. She stilled and looked up once again. He'd managed to corral her wrists into his big hands, and the arrogant SOB had a grin on his damn face. He was *enjoying* her struggle.

"Stop or you'll regret it."

He laughed. "Oh, yeah, *chat marron*? And just what is it you plan on doing to me?"

She let her body go slack beneath his surrendering in defeat. His teasing smile disappeared. Those deep brown eyes dilated and darkened.

Dragging her wrists above her head, he leaned down and covered her mouth with his, and it wasn't a soft or gentle kiss. He was punishing her lips, molding them to his own with a sense of urgency and hunger. At first she was so stunned she couldn't respond, but liquid heat infused her body consuming her. She surrendered to the onslaught of lust gripping her senses and she kissed him right back.

His taste was a mixture of coffee, a hint of mint, and delicious man. He teased her bottom lip with his tongue until her lips parted. His warm tongue invaded her mouth. A sigh escaped her lips. She felt her thighs clinch, a wave of arousal suffusing her body creating dampness between her legs. *God, but he tasted good.*

A primal groan came from his throat. He withdrew his tongue and his kiss became gentler, softer. Breaking contact, he lifted his head sending her a piercing glare like she'd done something wrong.

How dare he? She seized the opportunity once more as his body weight shifted. Swinging her knee upwards, she struck him square at the juncture of his balls and rock hard erection.

With a loud grunt, he fell to her side grabbing his now injured body parts. Rolling away from him, she scrambled off the floor. Placing her hands on her hips, she peered down at him from above, a triumphant grin splitting her face.

"Son of a bitch, Tara! That hurt!"

"Well, it's what you get for scaring me, you ass!" She turned and stalked out the door leaving him on the floor moaning and writhing in pain.

*****

Rolling back and forth a couple of times, Chance started to laugh. She was one hellacious wildcat woman. A loud hiss sounded close to his ear. He froze in place. As he turned his head to the side, he came face-to-face with Timmy inches from his face.

Crap.

"Know what, Timmy? That's the best damn kiss I've ever had."

Timmy hissed at him one more time and pounced smack dab in the middle of his stomach. It had the effect of someone dropping a bowling ball on his abs from five feet up. The air whooshed from his lungs as a bright light hit his eyes.

"What the *hell* happened to you?" Derek asked, holding a flashlight down toward his face and peering at him from up above.

Chance shoved the cat off his stomach and gulped in some air. He looked up at Derek and managed a shaky laugh. "I don't think you really want to know."

Chapter Sixteen

Bright morning light filtered through the kitchen window. Chance peered out and took note of a few small tree limbs strewn across the lawn downed from the ferocity of last night's end-of-summer storm. An uneasy feeling was creeping up his spine. Something besides the weather was changing. The temporary serenity which settled in on him the past couple of days was gone. In its place, warrior instincts were kicking in, and from past experience, he knew damn well to trust those instincts. They saved his ass on many occasions. Derek sat at the table brooding. Chance turned to face him.

"You feel it too, don't you?"

Derek looked grim and nodded. "Oh, yeah, I feel it. Something tells me Cruz is nearby. We'd better keep a sharp eye out. Don't let her out of sight while you're on watch. This guy's a freaking bomb waiting to go off and he's itching to get his hands on her."

"Well just let him try. I'll scratch his itch for him until his skin bleeds."

"I'll alert Travis and Jason. Four sets of eyes will be more effective than two. I also need to call Joe and see if he's found any trace of Cruz heading this way." Derek headed down the hall toward the bedrooms of the two other agents.

Chance grabbed a cup of coffee and leaned against the counter, ankles crossed, sipping the warm brew. Last night's encounter with Tara replayed in his mind. The poor girl was scared to death. Her body trembled with fear. When he'd leaned down and kissed her though, her body became soft, supple, and pliant under his own.

He closed his eyes and inhaled remembering the sweet scent of vanilla, sugar, and woman shimmering around her. *And those lips.* They were warm and sweet as honey.

Without making a conscious effort to do so, he compared Tara to his ex-girlfriend, Lacy. Where Lacy was clingy, self-absorbed, and untrustworthy, Tara was independent, mindful of others, and didn't come off as being anything but trustworthy. When he gave it some real thought, there was no comparison. Tara was head and shoulders above Lacy no matter what the subject. Not to mention, she was a knockout in whatever she was wearing.

The mere thought of her made his blood run hot and heavy. He brought his hand down to adjust and ease the sudden ache he felt. The sound of a feminine voice froze his hand in place.

"Got a problem this morning, have we?"

Chance looked up into those amazing emerald eyes and saw them trained on the hand still cupping the area of his discomfort. Rarely did anything make his Cajun blood rise to his tanned cheeks in a blush, but she did things to him he'd never had done to him before. He felt the heat of his blood rushing to his face, at least what blood was left which hadn't pooled down south. He straightened his stance and cleared his throat.

"Good morning, Tara. Some storm last night, huh."

A bemused looking Tara walked to the counter and poured herself a cup of coffee. He stood head and shoulders above her height. She barely reached him mid chest. She was so close, he could feel the heat radiating off her body. He inhaled her clean and sweet scent.

This was not helping him one bit, but he just couldn't bring himself to move away from her.

Tara made the move and sat at the table breaking the sexual tension wavering between them. "What's the latest on the psychopath?" she asked.

Chance couldn't pull his eyes off Tara as she brought the cup to her full lips. When a drop of coffee remained on her bottom lip, she licked it with her pretty pink tongue. He stifled a groan at seeing her tongue wet her full lips, and then she blew softly into the cup of steaming brew. He imagined her warm breath caressing his own skin. A finger snap broke into his daydream.

"Hey, Cajun man. Want to get with the program here?"

Chance looked into her eyes and saw them twinkling with humor. Damn but she had the ability to make him lose his common sense. "Nothing's new. Status quo."

*****

Nodding her head, Tara could feel the zing of tension return. She met lots of big, burly types like him at work but none made her sexually aware like him. Just one seductive look from those dark eyes and her body hummed all over.

His strong chiseled features, sun bronzed skin, and dark brown eyes made a girl weak in the knees. Warmth spread through her body at the mere thought of running her fingers through his mass of thick wavy hair.

A hand waved in front of her face. She brought her eyes up to see him standing over her.

"Are you going to answer my question or continue daydreaming?"

She gave herself a mental shake and refocused. "Sorry. I didn't hear the question."

The corner of his mouth lifted. "I noticed. I asked if you'd like some breakfast. I'm fixin' Cajun omelets."

"You *cook*?" She squinted in disbelief.

"Don't be so damned surprised. I am full blooded Cajun, and we're infamous for our cooking skills not to mention a few other things we're known to be quite good at." His eyebrows waggled.

"Good Lord, Anselmi. Get over your big manly self, will you? I'm just surprised is all. Most of you brainy G-men don't exactly have reputations as gourmet chefs."

"But *I'm* the exception. Poppee always told me a smart man learned how to fend for himself without the help of a woman."

"Who's Poppee?"

"My grandfather... and you didn't answer my question. Want some breakfast?"

She smiled. "Sure. Why not?"

"You'll love it."

"This should be interesting. I've heard Cajun cuisine is great but have never eaten any."

"You've got to be kidding. *Chère,* you don't know what you're missing."

He set about the kitchen like he knew what he was doing. She lost herself watching his toned muscles move while he prepared a sweet smelling concoction. After turning off the burner, he slid two huge fluffy omelets onto separate plates and set one in front of her along with a fresh cup of coffee and a glass of OJ.

"Wow. This looks good. What's in it?"

He sat across from her and stabbed a fork into his omelet. "Just a few odds and ends."

"Wait. I'm the kind of person who likes to know what she's shoveling in her mouth before doing the shoveling. What exactly did you put in here?"

He chuckled and took a big bite without answering, chewing around his smile. Closing his eyes, he sighed. "Mmm."

The omelet sure did smell like heaven, she had to admit. What the hell. No guts, no glory, right? Cutting into the flaky mixture, she stuffed a bite in her mouth. A punch of spicy flavors she never before experienced burst on her tongue while the egg melted in her mouth. Mimicking his reaction, she closed her eyes and relished the twist of unique flavors.

"Oh. My. God. This is divine." When she opened her eyes, Chance was grinning like the Cheshire cat.

"Just how in hell did you learn to cook like this?" she mumbled in between bites of the scrumptious dish. "I've eaten omelets before, but this one is just so yummy it's... indescribable."

"I told you, *chat marron*. I'm Cajun. We're natural born cooks."

Tara dropped her fork onto her plate and cleared her mouth of food. "Stop right there. You just called me that shot thing again and I don't understand. What does it mean?"

"What? I don't know what you're talking about." His expression was pure innocence.

"Don't play dumb with me, Frenchie. You've called me that 'shot' thing before. What does it mean?"

Chance just looked at her with a solemn face. The corner of his mouth lifted and a twinkle crept into his eyes but he remained silent.

"This is so not funny, Anselmi. For all I know, you're calling me something dirty. Give. What does it mean?"

Chuckling, he stood next to her and tipped her chin up so she would look up at him. When their eyes met, his smile disappeared as he lost all his mirth. He placed his hand against her cheek and held it there for what felt like an eternity singeing the skin beneath his fingers. Without another word, just when she thought he'd lean down and kiss her, he left.

Her heart pounding, it took several moments before she regained her senses. Once she did, she realized once again he'd avoided the meaning of his strange words.

Moving quickly to the empty entrance of the kitchen, she yelled at him.

"Come back here you big chicken and tell me what it means!"

She heard his far away laughter ring through the air.

Chapter Seventeen

Everyone remained on alert throughout the day as all four agents alternated between perimeter checks and guarding Tara. As morning turned into late afternoon, the air grew heavy with tension. Derek paced in the living room wearing a new path into the already worn carpet. Chance sat in an arm chair, one ankle crossed over his other leg, his laptop perched upon his lap. Tara watched both men from underneath her lashes.

Something was going on. Both men's bodies were stiff and rigid. The tension they were exuding was as thick as a one inch porterhouse steak. Was Alvin getting closer, she wondered? If so, why were they hiding information from her? The thought of them keeping her in the dark just served to piss her off. If Alvin was getting closer, then she should be the first one to know. After all, *she* was the one who stood to lose if he found them. Slamming her book shut, she straightened her back and spoke up.

"Okay. Out with it, both of you. What the hell is going on?"

Derek stopped pacing just long enough to glance at her for a moment. He shifted his eyes toward Chance who was playing the I-haven't-a-clue game as he shrugged like he didn't know what the hell she was talking about and then Derek resumed pacing without a single word passing his lips. Tara stood and put a hand on her hip.

"I've got news for you two. I'm not a fragile little woman nor am I an idiot. There's something going on here neither of you want me to know about. Well, I'm not playing the game. One of you needs to clue me in. What the hell am I going to do when this stuff breaks loose if you keep me clueless, huh? Do you expect me to cower in a dark corner, be silent, and do nothing? That is *sooo* not going to happen. I will not be treated like a child. I'm all grown up in case both of you haven't noticed, and I've been taking care of myself most of my life. So far I've managed to do quite well on my own, thank you very much."

She'd said all that without taking a breath and needed to suck in some air before continuing her rampage. "And just because I'm a girl, it does not mean I can't carry my own weight around here. I don't need a damn Y chromosome to be able to take care of myself. You guys are starting to get on my very last nerve here."

She glared first at Chance, then at Derek. Neither one opened their mouth to agree or disagree. She exhaled an exasperated breath and waved her hands up in the air in defeat.

"Great. Fine. You both just be that way."

Heading toward the door, she mumbled on her way out. "Damn hard-headed, arrogant, self-righteous, egotistical, pig headed men!"

*****

A few more expletives flew from Tara's lips as they watched her disappear.

As soon as she was out of earshot, Chance stood and grabbed Derek's arm. "We'd better tell her something soon or she's liable to do something drastic."

Derek nodded just as his cell phone rang. Pulling it out his pocket, he answered. "Ross here. What have you got, Joe?"

Chance saw Derek's face change, the seriousness of the one-sided conversation evident.

"Thanks for the intel. We'll keep in touch. It was Joe Scott. He's tracking Cruz."

"What's he got?" Chance shut down his laptop, the fine hairs on his neck tingling.

"Cruz paid a visit to her apartment. He murdered the agent watching her place. When he found the apartment empty, he got pissed and trashed it -- plants and all."

"Damn. How long ago did *that* happen?"

"Last night. He'll just get angrier as time goes by and he can't find her."

"Let him. He'll screw up. When he does, it'll be his undoing."

Derek nodded just as his phone rang again. He flipped it open. "Ross." He listened while he ran his other hand through his hair. "What time did *that* happen? All right. Notify Joe Scott and brief him. The package is on the move. I'll call you all as soon as it's delivered to a new location."

"What is it?" Chance stood up, nerves ticking in his jaw. He knew trouble had arrived.

"Lucien and Kat spotted Cruz leaving an airport terminal in Columbus twenty minutes ago. He made a stop at a car rental place. They tried apprehending him there but he got away." Derek's face became a mask of concern. "He knows we're here."

As Chance started for the door to find Tara, he was stopped when Derek grabbed his arm. "Here's the plan, rookie. Get her packed and ready to go in ten minutes while I get Dean and Navarro rolling. I don't think it's wise to let her know how close he is."

"Derek. You just heard her. If we don't level with her, there'll be hell to pay. We need her cooperative, not belligerent."

Derek muddled it over. "You're right. Use good judgement and be tactful."

"No problem. Let's just get her the hell out of here and safe again."

"Right."

Chance hurried down the hallway and rapped lightly on Tara's door.

"Come in."

When he entered, he found her propped on the bed with her vampire book in hand. Timmy was vigilant at her feet eyeing his every move. He hated upsetting her again but couldn't do anything about it. They needed to move her and quick. From the look on her face, she knew the news wasn't good.

Shutting the book, she sat upright. "What is it?" A hint of worry crossed her face.

"Pack and be ready to move out in ten minutes. We're out of here." He wanted to tell her how serious the situation was, but it just wasn't in him to give her more bad news. He turned to leave but she halted him with her next words.

"You no good. There *is* something going on, isn't there?"

He turned back and looked her square in the eyes. "Yes, Tara, there is. Alvin's in Columbus and is headed this way." He saw the blood drain from her face. "Get a move on. We've only got a few minutes to get you out of here." She stood next to the bed, unmoving, immobile. "Move it!"

Tara jumped and started grabbing the few things not already in her suitcase and throwing them in haphazardly. Chance left to get his own gear.

Chapter Eighteen

Joe Scott called to let them know Cruz was once again in the wind. They headed out of town with Tara in tow.

Leaving Columbus far behind, the SUVs were traveling down I-54 toward some destination known only to Derek who was driving and not talking. Chance sat in the back with Tara who hadn't spoken either since they'd left Ohio. Travis and Jason were keeping a safe distance behind them in the other vehicle.

Watching twilight morph into darkness, Chance's mind raced. How did Alvin find their location? As far as he knew, no one outside the bureau had an inkling of where they were or why they were there. Somehow Cruz knew and found their hideout within days.

He made a mental note to discuss it with Derek first chance he got. He glanced over at Tara. Her tiny body was scrunched up against the door in a fear filled posture. He couldn't blame her. If not for their eyes in the field, Cruz would have caught them with their guard down and her life might have been in jeopardy.

"Tara," he spoke softly. She turned those emerald eyes toward him. A shimmer of unshed tears veiled them. "You okay, *chère*?"

"Oh, I'm just peachy." Her reply was acerbic. Her wall of self-preservation was back up making him unsure how to approach her. He wanted... no... *needed* her to understand. As long as he was here, Cruz wouldn't get near her.

"Anybody hungry?" Derek asked. "I think we're safe to pull into a fast food joint."

"Can I get down and take a bathroom break?" Tara's voice was so tentative, Chance's heart squeezed a little.

"Sure, Tara. Anselmi. Stick to her," Derek ordered.

Chance nodded knowing Derek could see him in the rear view mirror. He too must be asking himself the same question as Chance -- how Alvin knew where to find them.

Ten minutes later during their stop at a burger joint, Chance and Tara stood side-by-side watching the gray tabby drink from a water dish on a small patch of grass next to the building. The other agents were inside ordering for everyone.

Watching the cat reminded him of what Logan said about Tara going nowhere without her beloved cat. He understood now why she insisted on taking him along. Timmy was the only living being left to love so she doted on him and protected him with everything she had inside. The thought made his heart ache. She didn't deserve to be alone.

Out the corner of his eye, he noticed her shiver. "Cold?"

She gave him a weak smile. "A little."

Chance moved behind her and placed his hands on her shoulders rubbing her arms. The friction from his touch warmed her, the shiver he'd seen traveling through her calmed. Without hesitating, Tara leaned back and rested her head against his chest. He felt her sigh. He took a deep breath of his own and wound his arms even tighter around her body. She rubbed her head against his chest like a cat soaking up the warmth friction created.

Her head turned and he was leaning down to kiss her. Her lips were like a drug, all consuming. His bigger body enveloped her small frame as he turned her to get a better angle.

Their tongues did a primal dance as they both became caught up in the sudden flame of passion flaring between them. As his hands slid down her back toward her rump, she moaned. A loud, grizzly meow rent the air just before the cat pounced on them trying to break them apart.

"*Maudit*! Crap!" Chance pulled away. "Your mangy fleabag just clawed my arm!"

"Hey! Don't yell at him. He didn't mean to do it; he's just protective, and he's not mangy and doesn't have fleas!"

"Could've fooled me. He isn't protective. He's possessive... and mean... and a freak of nature, and he's a damn cat, *chat marron,* not a person!"

"Well, you just leave him alone, do you hear me? Do not come near him if you can't treat him better. And what the *hell* are you saying when you say that shot thing, anyway?"

"If I can treat him better? What about if he can't treat me better? The damn thing's been after me since the minute he laid eyes on me."

Derek turned the corner of the building. "Hey, both of you! Ti me's up. Back to the car before you do bodily harm."

Tara picked up her cat and stalked past Chance. He glared at her back.

Derek cocked his head to one side and eyed Chance.

"What?"

Raising his eyebrows and chuckling, Derek turned around and headed back to the vehicle leaving his partner frowning and dismayed.

*****

An hour after stopping for food and fuel, the second SUV whipped around the first.

"Where are they going?" Tara asked.

Derek glanced up at the rear view mirror to see Tara. She was huddled next to the door again looking lost and alone. There was an ocean of empty space between her and Chance.

"I've sent Travis and Jason on ahead so they can secure the premises. This way, we'll be able to enter the safe house without concern."

She didn't reply. It bothered him a bit because he was coming to think of her like a little sister. It wasn't a professional thing to do, develop feelings for a person involved in a case, but he couldn't help it. He liked her which made him understand his partner just a little bit better. It appeared his partner like her too... *a lot.*

He knew he should pull Chance off this case or at the very least keep him away from Tara, but he didn't think it would do Tara any good. For as much as Chance and Tara fought, he could see how much Chance's presence was helping her cope with the situation.

"Tara. Are you all right? I'm worried about you."

Surreptitiously, he saw Tara glance at Chance who was leaning back in his seat, head cocked back, eyes closed, and arms folded over his abs like he was asleep. A muscle ticked in Chance's jaw. So he was waiting to hear her reply. Derek saw her grin. She knew Chance was faking it too. Her eyes were trained on the big Cajun.

"I'm fine, Derek. Thanks for asking. I appreciate your concern. Unlike some men around here, you're secure enough in your manhood to voice such an emotion. Some men are so insecure they can't express a damn thing when it comes to what they feel."

Her comment hit its mark. Chance's jaw muscle twitched again and his eyebrows drew together. Tara was trying to stifle a giggle. Derek chuckled.

Chapter Nineteen

Chance led Tara up the steps to the cabin as his eyes searched the dark night blanketing the area for anything out of the ordinary. The Great Smoky Mountains of Tennessee were a far cry from Las Vegas but after the first fiasco in Ohio, nobody was taking chances.

"Derek. Were the premises searched?"

"Yes. Travis and Jason have been through it. They're out putting up surveillance equipment. This particular cabin was chosen because of location. From the deck in back, you can see every road, path, and trail surrounding it. No way is anyone going to find her here without us catching a glimpse of them first."

"Good." Chance opened the door to the cabin, gun drawn. There was silence, but again, no chances. He peered around each corner taking in their surroundings. Everything appeared in order as Tara followed him in.

"Nice digs," she remarked. "Oh look! There's a huge hot tub big enough for eight!"

Chance glanced out the double doors leading to the deck. Sure enough, there was a large hot tub. Tara started to open the doors. He covered her hand and stopped her. She scowled. Even though they hadn't spoken to one another since leaving the burger joint, he felt the now familiar zing of sexual tension flow between them and wondered if she felt it too.

"Not until we're sure it's secure," he warned.

She sighed and stalked off. "Party pooper."

It made him grin.

"The monitoring equipment is in place and all is secure."

Looking up, Chance saw the two men entering, their FBI badges secured to their waistbands. Both Derek and Chance moved toward the two agents.

"Anyone follow us, Travis?" Derek asked.

"Nope. Nothing via highway, and we scouted the trails and paths leading up here too. We have surveillance cameras posted at each entrance. I've set up the bedroom at the far right side of the cabin with the monitoring equipment."

"Excellent. Same routine as before. You and Jason team and we'll alternate shifts. It's been a long drive. Get her settled and meet out on the deck for a briefing in thirty minutes. Jason, man the monitors for a while and I'll brief you in private later."

"Fine. We've got to check and make sure everything's working right anyway," Jason remarked as he and Travis exited the room.

"I think you should put your things away before we meet, Chance. Take the bedroom nearest Tara's," Derek advised as he turned to exit the room.

Chance stopped him by placing a hand on his arm. "Derek, we need to talk. Alone."

"Not now, rookie. Stow your gear and check on her first. We'll talk later."

Derek walked away dismissing Chance's concerns.

Although most of his gear stayed within the confines of his bag, Chance did unpack a few items. He wasn't taking another chance. If an attack came, he'd be able to grab and go.

Pausing in front of the door across the hall, he turned the knob. Even though the room was blanketed in total darkness, he made out her figure sprawled across the bed. She'd been so tired she didn't even take the time to undress. Lying face down with her arms extended and her feet dangling off the side of the bed, she was out like a light.

He crept toward her and heard Timmy hiss.

"Shut the hell up. You'll wake her up," he whispered.

The cat, for once, obliged and remained quiet. Carefully taking off her shoes, he moved her enough to pull the spread out from under her body without waking her. After he straightened her up and covered her, he leaned down and placed a gentle kiss on her forehead.

"Sleep tight, *chat marron,*" he whispered, then exited the room.

*****

Derek and Travis were sitting in lounge chairs near the covered hot tub when Chance stepped out onto the deck.

"We've got a big problem, don't we?" Chance wasn't hiding his anger or worry.

"What are you talking about, rookie?"

"Cruz. He found the safe house in Ohio. The only people who knew about the location were our own. This is starting to smell, Ross."

Derek noted the angry tone of Chance's voice and the tenseness in his body. Sometimes body language gave away a person's true feelings. Chance was like an open book and Derek was far from blind. He picked up the fact Anselmi cared about the girl. His body language was speaking volumes the last few days, but he was a rookie on his first assignment.

Although Derek was starting to know Chance quite well and believed him to be forthright and trustworthy, he wasn't above suspicion, not in Derek's book anyway. It just wasn't in his nature not to suspect everyone no matter the blatant show of attraction. There could always be ulterior motive.

"I agree, rookie. It is starting to stink from where I stand. I believe we have a mole amongst us."

Derek watched as Chance's eyes sought out Travis at the mention of a mole.

"Just in case you're wondering, Anselmi, I've known Travis since his arrival at the bureau years ago. Reggie has known him since he was a kid. In fact, Reggie commanded the task force which investigated the murder of Travis's mother."

Chance's look was now riddled with guilt. "Sorry, man."

Travis nodded. "No problem. This stuff bothers me just as much as it bothers you."

"What happened to your mother?" Chance asked.

"I was young. Reggie could tell you more about it than I could."

Derek stepped into the conversation. "I trust Travis implicitly, Chance."

"But do you trust the rest of the team?" Chance asked the question on everybody's mind. He watched as something passed between Travis and Derek.

"Normally, I'd say yes, but our faith in each other has been shaken. So the answer is no. Joe and I have been together since the beginning of the team and he's my second in command. I would have no problem leaving the team in his hands, but everyone else? Right now, I can't afford to trust anyone else."

Travis reacted immediately to Derek's statement. Shaking his head and looking quite aggravated, he jumped up and paced near the deck railing. In a fit of obvious anger, he slapped the railing with his hand.

"I still don't think the kid's involved." He was upset.

"Travis. You know my specialty is profiling, and even though he didn't fit the profile, the evidence against him is overwhelming."

"Damn the evidence, Derek! It was all circumstantial. You know he is innocent."

Chance jumped back into their conversation. "What the hell are you two talking about? Is it something to do with the Maguire guy? You know what? Never mind. The important thing is right here and now." Chance turned toward Derek. "So, team leader, what are we going to do about this situation?"

"*We* are doing nothing. *I* am catching the next flight out of here and heading back to Quantico in the morning. What I need from you two is complete silence. Do not, I repeat, do not let Navarro know where I'm going. Give him some excuse for my absence, and keep Tara in your sights at all times. I'll be gone a couple of days."

"So you definitely think we have a snake among us?" Travis inquired, a little calmer now.

"I don't think, Travis. I know. Someone's passing information on to Cruz and it's got to be one of our own. I'll be taking one of the SUVs in the morning. You should be able to do with just one. Keep your mouths shut and your eyes wide open. Trust no one but yourselves. Remember. Right now, only the three of us know what's going on. I'll handle the rest of the team when I get to Quantico. Do not trust anyone but yourselves. If one of the other members contacts you trying to extract information, play dumb."

Both agents nodded.

"We'll contact you if the situation here changes," Chance added.

"Good. In the meantime, keep her safe." Derek walked back into the cabin.

*****

Travis turned in Chance's direction. "Look, Anselmi. I realize we haven't known each other long, but I've known Derek a long time. If there is someone leaking information, I guarantee you he'll ferret out the bastard and won't stop until he finds the leak and plugs it."

"I sure hope you're right, Dean, because if he doesn't, I will, and I don't care if I have to do it legal or not."

Chance stalked off leaving Travis a little dumbfounded and alone on the deck.

Chapter Twenty

His office was small compared to those of others who'd been with the bureau forever, but Derek was content with it on a day when he was alone and ensconced in a case file. Today was not one of those days. His team of agents minus Anselmi, Dean, and Navarro, were huddled within the confines of his little space having been called back to Quantico for this very meeting.

Katrina Wright, Lucien Bordeaux, and Joe Scott were old timers just like Dean and they'd been with his team for quite some time. Eric Robinson and Steven Talbert were not new kids on the block like Anselmi and Navarro, but they weren't with him as long as the others.

"Let's get this meeting started." Everyone grew silent. "As you all know, we moved the Roberts girl yesterday after Cruz was sighted in the area. We don't yet know how he found out about the location, but because he did, the rules are changing.

"As of this minute, nothing on the Roberts case leaves the confines of this room. No one outside this office will be privy to this case except the three agents absent from this meeting."

"Are they still on guard duty with the woman?" Lucien's Canadian French accent was thick.

"I'll get to it in a minute, Lucien." Turning, he faced Joe. The man's blood ran FBI blue. He came from a long line of law enforcement. He was the agent Derek trusted the most. "What's the latest intel on Cruz, Joe?"

"M.I.A. again. Two of my guys are trying to locate him at this moment. So far, no luck. Last known whereabouts was the safe house in Ohio. He cut phone wires and disabled the security system before leaving us a calling card."

Derek balked. "What calling card?" He had no knowledge of this new piece of evidence.

"He pinned a picture to the living room wall of the Roberts girl leaving a bookstore in Columbus with one of our men shadowing her. Cruz used a bloody home-made knife which was placed in the middle of the agent's forehead on purpose. Forensics identified a little bit of DNA on the knife from all of his victims since his escape as well as some of his own."

Damn. Derek realized he should never have allowed the excursion. Normally he wouldn't have, but he liked the girl because she reminded him of his little sister. As for Anselmi, he wasn't worried about what this intel meant to him. His partner could handle whatever Cruz threw his way. He refocused on the new information.

"And why the hell am I just learning about this now? Didn't anyone here think I might need to know since I'm heading this task force?" He searched everyone's face for telltale clues. No one flinched under his wrath, but the majority of them held guilty looks.

"I don't appreciate getting intel after the fact nor will I tolerate being left in the dark. We communicate on everything. Does everyone understand?" he bellowed.

A chorus of murmurs and "yes, sirs" filtered through the room. He extracted a piece of paper from his suit pocket and passed it to Lucien who was standing to his left. "The new safe house is at this location. Pass it around and memorize the address."

The note went from hand to hand until it landed back on Derek's desk. He picked it up and shoved it through the paper shredder.

"Here are your new assignments. Lucien and Katrina will stake out the airport nearest the new safe house just like you did in Columbus. Scott? Keep on your assignment as is but replace your other two agents with Eric and Stephen. I want you guys to locate Cruz."

"Got it. One question though."

"What?"

"Is the girl already at the new location?"

"Yes, and there are still three agents there with me on guard duty. All right, lady and gentlemen. Let's find this psychotic asshole and move on to bigger and better things."

As the agents started leaving the room, Derek kept his eyes trained on each of them. Whoever was supplying information to the enemy was bound to slip up and make a mistake, and when this happened, he would put his size twelve and a half shoe up the agent's ass and twist it. One thing he abhorred was a crooked law man or woman as the case might be. As far as he was concerned, the worm of an agent should be put under the jail instead of in it.

*****

Derek waited patiently seated in front of the Deputy Director's desk. He'd been working for Reginald Lyons since his first day with the bureau. The man was a twenty-five year seasoned veteran and was the most trustworthy person he'd ever met. As Reggie entered the room, Derek stood giving respect to his colleague and mentor.

"Derek. Good to see you." Lyons shook his hand. "Fill me in on the case."

Derek gave him the up-to-date details and confided his suspicion one of his team members was turning mole.

"Hmm, sounds fishy and all too familiar to me too. How are you handling the situation?"

"Simple. I just gave them all the address of a fake safe house. The only five people who know the real location are Anselmi, Dean, Navarro, me, and you. Those three are with me at the real safe house and are unaware we've established a fake one."

"Good plan. If the Tennessee safe house gets hit, we'll know it's one of the guys you have assigned there. If the fake safe house gets hit, then you've eliminated the agents with you as suspects and have narrowed down the list."

Derek nodded and smiled at him.

"So, Ross. What is it you need from me?"

"What I need from you, sir, is another team of agents for the fake safe house. A few agents and a decoy who looks like the Roberts girl would do. The decoy team needs to report directly to you and you only. You can keep me informed if you don't mind, sir."

"I know just the team. They aren't FBI so we won't have to worry about them leaking anything."

Derek watched Reggie move to a file cabinet behind his desk and unlock it. He opened the top drawer and pulled out a SAT phone. Now Derek's curiosity was peaked.

"Sir, are you sure this team will be willing to help? If they're not FBI, then what exactly are they, and are you sure we can trust them?" He couldn't help but let his skepticism about this so-called team bleed through his words. Besides, if it got out SIU7 was compromised, he could lose everyone.

Reggie raised an eyebrow. "I have known their team leader for years, plus he owes me a few favors." He put the phone to his ear and looked directly at Derek. "I'll call you when they arrive." His tone was dismissive. Derek didn't have to be told twice. He nodded and left.

*****

Derek stepped out the SUV in front of what looked like a deserted warehouse. When Reggie called asking him to meet here, he began worrying about this mystery team Reggie was pulling in. He didn't want to be pulled off this case because someone thought his team was compromised. Whatever SIU7 started, SIU7 finished.

Derek walked over to a group of people standing next to two other SUVs. One vehicle he knew belonged to Reggie. The other was a huge Humvee -- definitely military. Reggie was easy to spot within the group of four men and one woman.

Reggie reached out to shake his hand. "Derek. Glad you found the place." As he shook Reggie's hand, Derek eyed the others who were eyeballing him.

The guy standing closest to Reggie looked about the same age as Reggie but this guy had a larger build and a shaved head. He looked like someone who'd seen and done too much.

The biggest of the lot was a guy with shoulder length blonde hair and a pretty boy look.

The woman who was standing next to pretty boy could easily pass for Tara Roberts. She was quite petite with curly red hair, but where Tara looked sweet, soft and innocent, this woman was rough, hard and looked like she could hold her own with the men. The combat boots and colorful full sleeve tattoo on her well defined arm finished the look.

The last guy was the smallest but was also the tallest of the motley crew with shaggy dark hair and a definitive five o'clock shadow happening. What stood out most about him were his eyes; they were a striking blue.

"Derek. This is the team I was telling you about. This gentleman is Stryker, leader of this team and an old friend of mine." Reggie slapped the man on the back. "Next to him is Reno. And this lovely young lady is Jax." She gave him an almost shy little wave which didn't go with her appearance. "The one who needs to shave is Hunter." Hunter smirked at the introduction.

Derek took in a deep breath and addressed the group. "Thanks for coming out and helping us on such short notice." He made the round and shook everyone's hand. When he reached Stryker, the man let loose with a grin and spoke.

"Not a problem. We are in between assignments at the moment. So what's going on that the FBI needs help from us?"

Derek looked in Reggie's direction for approval before he answered. Reggie nodded.

"First, I need all of you to understand something. This is my team, SIU7's case. I don't know anything about any of you, but Reggie's been my boss since the day I joined the FBI. I have no trust in your team, but I do have trust in his faith in your team. Just remember, this is my show." He looked at Reggie to make sure he hadn't overstepped his boundaries, but Reggie was eyeing Stryker simply backing up what Derek just laid forth.

Stryker shrugged. "It's fine with us. We don't exist on the books, so we can't take the case even if we want to."

That surprised Derek. He knew Reggie had some pull but he never imagined something like this. They were obviously a ghost team. Derek just couldn't help himself.

"Which books?"

Stryker smiled. In fact, the whole damn team was smiling. "All of them."

Derek's brows rose. He had no choice but accept the line which was drawn. "Okay. So here's what we have so far." He started filling them in on the plan.

*****

"Got her again, Cruz."

"Hot damn! Where is she, Junior?"

"Same deal as last time. Your ticket and directions await you at Gate B. Your plane leaves in forty-five minutes, so you'd better get your ass in gear."

"No problem."

"Cruz? Do the job right this time."

"You just worry about your end and I'll worry about mine."

Chapter Twenty-One

Chance, along with Travis and Jason, had decided to rotate ten hour shifts on monitor watch with two hour overlays for perimeter checks during Derek's absence. Jason and Travis were having a lively discussion about the schedule. Chance seated himself on the couch with a book in hand. He glanced up as Tara walked through the open doorway.

He couldn't help but react to the sight of her. His eyes roamed every inch of her body. They fixated on a little silver belly button ring glistening in the slit of exposed skin between the white tank top and black shorts she wore. When her head went down as if to check her own appearance, the motion stopped his perusal.

"What's wrong? Is something vital showing?" Tara inquired.

"Quite the contrary," Travis quipped. "Everything is showing just fine."

Chance growled low at Travis's comment as Tara moved to the opposite end of the couch away from where Chance was sitting, her own paperback book in hand.

From out the corner of his eye, he saw her head bend to the side as she appeared to be looking at the cover of his book. He glanced up and gave her a quizzical look wondering just what it was she was trying to accomplish.

A mischievous grin emerged on Tara's face. "I didn't know you knew how to read. You snubbed your nose at my books so I thought maybe you weren't much into reading." Leaning toward Chance and still trying to get a glimpse of the book, she said, "So what does Chance Anselmi read for fun?"

He turned so his back faced her hiding the book from her sight. She stood up and sat in the arm chair across from him. He realized she now had a better view of his book, so he turned back in the opposite direction once again hiding the book from her view. His shoulders shook with laughter.

Tara marched over to him making him sit straight once more. She climbed in his lap and snatched the book out of his hand.

"Hey! That's mine!" he protested.

She looked triumphantly at the cover. Her eyebrows knitted together.

He gave her his own mischievous grin. "Disappointed it's not a vampire novel?" The book was his behavioral science textbook.

"Sort of. I didn't realize you like heavy reading."

"It's a textbook, Tara. Just because we do field work doesn't mean we stop learning. I take classes all the time. When I'm not in the field or have some down time, I'm taking a behavioral science course online."

"And what does that mean exactly?"

"It's about profiling. You learn how to get into the mind of the criminal. It's very similar to the TV show. Derek is an expert profiler; it's his specialty."

Chance looked down at where Tara was still straddling his lap. Unconsciously, he held her hips in place. When he glanced at the other two agents, he suddenly became aware that they were both watching them, Jason a little harder than Travis. He looked up. "Uh, Tara?" He looked back down where their bodies met in an effort to draw her attention to their compromised position. He knew the minute she realized their situation because she hopped off his lap amidst laughter from Travis and Jason.

Jason stood. "I think I'll go keep an eye on the monitors," he announced and walked out the room. Travis didn't look anxious to leave. Instead, he moved to the opposite end of the couch from Chance, grabbed the TV remote, and turned on the set.

Tara was back in the armchair with her own book in hand, her nose buried within its depths. Chance continued to read. After ten or so minutes of silence, Travis broke the spell.

"Hey. I'm lost here. Anyone know what the date is?"

Chance glanced down at his watch with a calendar feature on it. "It's the fifteenth."

"Wow," Travis exclaimed. "Time flies. I think I lost the whole first half of the month."

Tara slammed her book down on the end table and walked out the room.

Chance looked at Travis a little dumbfounded.

"Did I say something wrong?" Travis speculated.

"No, but something set her off. I wonder what's got her tied up in knots."

"Think we should go find her and see if we can help?" Travis asked.

"You bet. Let's go."

*****

Tara walked in her room and went straight to her suitcase. Flipping it open, she dug under her clothes until she found what she was looking for. Wrapping her arms around the item, she headed outside for the deck needing a moment alone. She was browsing through her family album when Chance and Travis showed up.

"Tara. You know better than being out here all alone. Haven't I told you time and again you need one of us to go out ahead of you in case there's danger? You can't go traipsing about outdoors without an escort.

It's not safe," Chance scolded.

She looked up at them, her eyes brimming with tears. Both he and Travis rushed to her side.

"*Chère*, you're crying. What's wrong?"

Travis spoke, "Was it something I said? If so, I'm sorry."

She gave him a half smile. "Stop worrying, Travis. When you asked about the date, it reminded me Meagan's birthday is in a couple of days. She was my baby sister."

She turned the album sitting on her lap so they could see a picture of Meagan. Blonde hair and blue eyes, she was cute as a button but looked nothing like Tara. There was, however, a gleam in the child's eyes which matched her big sister's look when she was in a happy mood.

"She was eight years old. It's hard to imagine but she would be turning sixteen on her next birthday -- the same age I was when I lost them all. She was always in a hurry to grow up. She used to tell me all the time how she wanted to be just like me." Her voice cracked with emotion on the last statement.

"You know, it breaks my heart I'm going to miss visiting their grave sites this year." She thumped her chest over her heart with her fist. "I've never missed any of their birthdays before."

"I know how you feel," Travis interjected. "It's been years since I lost my mom, but since I've been old enough, I've always tried to make it to her grave site for every birthday. With work there have been more than a few times when I couldn't get back home in time. Those years were the hardest."

"I missed going to my parents' graves nine years in a row," Chance added to the conversation. "I couldn't get time off while I was in the Army. My grandfather used to tell me it wasn't my fault I couldn't make it back there, but I always felt guilty about it even though I knew he was right. Just like it's not your fault you can't go this year, *chère*. You've got to believe Meagan knows the situation and wouldn't want you putting yourself in harm's way."

"He's right, Tara," Travis chimed in. "If anyone knows how you feel, it's us. My mother was taken from me when I was just a little boy. It makes it harder to miss one of her milestones. Like Chance said, Meagan wouldn't want you to be in harm's way on her account."

Tara studied the two intently taking in their advice. Travis and Chance were like kindred spirits who could empathize. They'd both lost loved ones at young ages too.

They were right, of course. She couldn't let emotions overrule her actions. She needed to be strong and independent. Wiping the tears from her face, she gave them a smile.

"Thanks, guys. Guess I needed some brotherly advice, and since I don't have a brother, you guys are a pretty darn good substitute."

When she looked at Chance, he was frowning. Travis looked like he was trying to hold back a laugh.

"Brother? You look at me like I'm your *brother*?" Chance sounded incredulous.

She could feel the heat travel to her cheeks. Unable to figure a way out of the spot she'd put herself in, she got up, pecked Travis on the cheek with a mumbled thanks and did the same to Chance lingering a little bit longer. "Thanks again, guys." She took her album and went inside.

*****

Chance was still frowning long after Tara had gone back inside. Travis thought of leaving him in his misery but couldn't.

"Chance. If you believe for one second she looks at you like a brother, then you're insane my friend. The woman is hot for you."

Chance came out of his stupor and gave Travis a quick grin.

"You think so?" He sounded like a teenager excited by a bout of puppy love.

"Come on, man. Be real here. Neither one of you can hide it. You two have chemistry overflowing."

"We do kind of have something between us, don't we?" He smiled. Then he frowned and asked, "What is the FBI going to say if I start a relationship with her?"

"Well, it may be a problem, but I'm sure Derek would smooth it out or something. Come on. It's time for some shut eye. I've got the next watch. You go get some sleep." They both got up and went inside.

Chapter Twenty-Two

Just before daybreak the next morning, the doors to all the bedrooms opened at just about the same time. Jason, Travis, Chance, and Tara all stood in the hallway eyeing one another. Tara was stunned to see everyone in the hallway so early in the morning. She just wanted to get to the bathroom and didn't expect to run into anyone in the hallway.

"What's everybody doing up?"

Jason was the one brave enough to speak up.

"Holy *crap*, Tara! You look hot!"

She looked down to note she was still in sleepwear -- a tight little tank top and a pair of tiny booty shorts. She felt the blood rush to her cheeks from embarrassment.

Travis's eyes twinkled. "Now, Tara, honey. You really shouldn't tease like that."

Chance growled low and menacingly. "Don't you guys have work to do or something?"

"Not me," Jason chimed. "I'm off duty. It's time for your shift, Anselmi." Jason's eyes remained trained on Tara.

When Chance spoke, his voice was rough. "If I were you, Navarro, I'd high tail it into my room right now, and put your damn eyes back in your head!"

"Uh, Jason? I wouldn't push him if I were you," Travis added on a suppressed laugh.

With wide eyes, Jason grabbed the doorknob leading to this room and ran in slamming it shut leaving the rest of them gawking at each other.

Travis cleared his throat. "Think I'll go check the monitors." He forged down the hall leaving Chance and Tara alone.

Chance held up a finger to her and went back into his bedroom. A few seconds later, he emerged with one of his shirts in his hand. He threw it in her direction.

"Put this on before you go parading around out here." Still embarrassed by her sleep outfit, she did as he said and donned the shirt. As she started walking toward the bathroom, he grabbed her by the arm and pulled her in close to his body. He looked deep into her eyes searching for something. "You don't have a clue, do you?"

"About what?"

He eyed her from head to toe with scorching heat in his eyes. "About what your state of undress can do to a man."

She took in a deep breath to steady her nerves, pulled out of his grip, and walked away.

*****

Chance stared after Tara who'd disappeared into the bathroom. *What in the world am I doing here?* Shaking his head, he walked into the kitchen to find Travis.

"Hey, man, I'm going out to check on the grounds."

Travis looked at him over the rim of his coffee cup. "Okay. I'll hold down the fort."

Chance headed for one of the more difficult trails. He broke into a light jog down the path around the cabin. About half done, he stopped by a small creek. *I don't have any idea what the hell I'm doing with her. I'll be out of a job and will screw up whatever is happening between us in the process.*

Leaning back against a tree, he watched as the water ran downstream. *Maybe I just give too much of myself to my job and there isn't enough of me for someone else.* He shook his head. *My ex is probably right -- I'll end up old and alone.*

Pushing off the tree and breaking into a run, Chance tried shoving the thought out of his head. All he ever wanted was to find love, true love, real love like his parents and grandparents, and he wanted the family which came with it as well.

With the cabin now in sight he stopped, bent at the waist bracing his hands on the top of his thighs, and gulped in short breaths of air. *Dammit! I shouldn't have run the last three miles so hard.* He was wearing jeans and a polo shirt, not workout clothes, and work shoes didn't help either. But he knew he just needed to get this out of his system. Or as his grandfather, Poppee, would say, he was trying to run from his problems but they were back now.

"Why can't I have love and a family with a career I want?" He kicked a pinecone out of his way.

"What the hell did that pinecone ever do to you?"

Startled, Chance found himself within steps of the back deck of the cabin. He didn't realize how far he'd run or how close to the cabin he'd stopped. He saw Travis standing on the deck with a smirk on his face. Embarrassed, Chance tried pushing past Travis but Travis stopped him short.

"Go shower, and while you're in there, get your head on straight. And to answer your question, I'll tell you like another agent told me years ago. If you want it bad enough and you love her hard enough, you will move heaven and earth to make it work. So while you're in the bathroom, you need to decide if she's worth fighting for because all I see you doing is fighting against her." Travis moved aside to let him pass.

Chance nodded in understanding. "Thanks, man." He made his way inside the cabin. When he reached Tara's door, he stopped and stared at it, emotions at war within himself. *Yeah, she's worth it,* he decided and headed for the shower.

*****

In midafternoon, Tara paced the floor in front of him venting her frustration. "I've got to get out of here, Chance. I'm going stir crazy with cabin fever."

"You know you can't, Tara. I'm sorry you're cooped up like this, but you know it's important you stay inside. With Derek gone, we only have three sets of eyes to watch over you." She stuck her lower lip out. "Tara. Pouting won't get you anywhere," he warned.

She moved to the couch where he was sitting and plopped down leaving a full foot of empty space between them, still in full pout mode.

Chance's brows rose. The woman was going to play him like a fiddle and he was probably going to let her do it.

"Tara." Inch by inch, she scooted closer until a mere six inches separated their bodies. She was so close he could feel the heat radiating off her in waves. A bead of perspiration popped out on his brow as a small groan slipped from his throat.

He shifted his body into more of a slouch to accommodate the growing bulge behind the zipper of his jeans. Her lip was still sticking out looking so pink and moist. If she didn't cease and desist soon, he'd be a goner.

She kept her eyes lowered and her body straight ahead. Every couple of seconds, she shifted her gaze his way beneath lowered lashes.

When his resistance was strained to the max, he gave in letting a loud groan escape from his lips as he reached over and grabbed her by the shoulders. He planted a kiss on her he meant for her to never, ever forget. The heat coming from his lips was scorching. She turned her body flush with his so she could run a hand through his hair. It took several moments before his lips left hers. Without moving a muscle other than his mouth, he yelled out Travis's name.

"Dean! Do a perimeter sweep right now... and take Jason with you!"

Travis yelled back, "Why?"

"Because it needs to be done. Go. Now!"

"All right. All right! Hey, Jason!"

"I heard. Meet you out on deck."

Chance looked down into Tara's glazed eyes. "Where were we? Oh, yeah."

He locked his lips with hers once more. It took mere seconds for heat to spread throughout his body. His brain was overloaded with lust.

Chance was placing soft kisses behind her ear, along her jawline and down the column of her throat. Her head fell back giving him better access to her sensitive skin. When his lips stopped moving, she looked deep into his eyes. He knew she would see the want and need in them.

Without hesitation, she hopped on his lap straddling his hips with her legs. A more ragged groan emanated from somewhere deep inside him. She hooked her arms around his neck and began the same trek behind his ear and along his jawline. She sought out his lips and nibbled over the lower one before she covered them both with her own. Their lips parted and their tongues parried in a mimic of what was really on their minds.

When she came up for air, she started a new trek down his chin toward his Adam's apple. Stopping at the hollow between his collar bones, she gave him an open mouthed kiss and sucked gently at his skin.

"Good God." He moaned as he shifted his body causing his pulsing erection to rub against her. Her thighs clinched in response. Her own lustful groan sent him sputtering a mixture of English and French, the words flying from his lips.

"*Mon Dieu.* You're so hot, *mon petit chat marron.*" He tried saying something else but she hushed him with her mouth, her tongue seeking out his once more.

It took a minute of intense focusing on his part, but Chance allowed reality to slap him silly. Grabbing Tara around the waist so she wouldn't fall, he stood up locking his knees in place. She was so taken aback by his sudden movement, her head jerked backwards causing her balance to falter. Had it not been for his strength wrapped around her waist, she would've landed head first on the floor.

"Oh, no you don't, *chat marron*. You are not going to distract me like this again." He sounded like he'd just run a marathon.

Ceremoniously, he peeled her hands off his neck and planted her feet back on the ground, her tiny wrists still encapsulated in his bigger hands.

"Distract you? I distracted you? I don't think so," she huffed.

"You did so distract me with the damn pouty pink lip sticking out."

"I did no such thing! You're the one who leaned over to play sucky face, not me!"

"Sucky fa... why you little tease. You purposely stuck out the pretty pink lip so I'd feel sorry for you being locked in this cabin without fresh air and all, but it's just not gonna work this time, Tara. You are not going outside. That's it! Final answer."

"Ooh, you stubborn, pig headed, ego-maniacal jackass... and what the hell does that French thing you keep calling me mean anyway?" She was shouting.

"Uh, what's going on here?"

They both turned to see Travis standing in the doorway, his hands on his hips and a silly grin on his face.

"Nothing!" Their shouts were simultaneous.

Taking one last look at him, Tara huffed and exited, knocking

Travis against the shoulder on her way out.

Running a hand through his already mussed hair, Chance spouted a string of Cajun and English expletives a mile long before he stopped and glared at the man standing before him. Travis let out a little laugh and held up his hands in surrender.

"Perimeter check was clear. Jason's maintaining monitor watch. I'll be in my room if you guys need a referee."

Travis turned and headed down the hallway, his laughter peeling though the air. Another string of mixed English and French curses poured from Chance's mouth and he was addressing them all to his *chat marron.*

*****

Thirty minutes later, Chance rapped softly on Tara's door. After a few moments, she opened it roughly banging it against the side of the dresser in her room.

"What?"

She looked so cute when she huffed. Yes, sir. She had played that fiddle quite well.

"If, and I do mean if, you do exactly as I tell you to do and don't complain -- and if you swear to me if any one of us shouts out an order to drop, run, or whatever, you'll do as you're told without hesitation..."

Her mouth opened to speak but he clamped two fingers over her lips before she could utter the first syllable.

"And, last but not least, if you agree to one hour and one hour only -- no extensions, no begging, no pretty pouty lip, no nothing?"

She propped her little hand on her hip as she was inclined to do and breathed deeply through her nose, eyes scrunched down awaiting his ultimatum.

"We can go in the hot tub."

She nipped at his fingers covering her mouth forcing him to let go with an "ouch." She jumped up in the air and grabbed onto his neck, her body dangling in front of his, her toes almost a foot off the floor. She kissed him silly for a minute or so before coming up for air.

"I knew you were good for something, Frenchie." Her smile was radiant.

"One hour. No more. I mean it, Tara, and you will listen?" She nodded. "No back talk?" She shook her head.

"All right. Get dressed. Just wear a tee shirt and shorts. I'll let Travis know what we're doing. Do not go out unless one of us is out there first. Got it?"

"Aye, aye." She saluted with one hand while hanging onto his neck with the other. Chance swatted her rear and dropped her down on her feet.

"Ow!" She barked, rubbing her offended bottom as he walked out smiling.

"Fifty-nine minutes and counting!" he yelled over his shoulder as he crossed the hallway to his own room.

*****

Ugh! "I'm coming!" Tara yelled back at Chance as she turned toward her suitcase and withdrew the black flimsy bikini she'd found stashed in a side pocket along with the red teddy Logan wanted her to pack. She had only one thought.

God bless Logan's little bi-sexual romantic heart.

Chapter Twenty-Three

Tara tip-toed to the double doors leading to the back deck and the hot tub. She saw Travis sitting in a lounge chair in cotton shorts sipping on a bottle of water. Chance was nowhere in sight. Making a crack in the door, she poked her head out and spoke to the agent.

"Is the coast clear?"

"Sure is. You can come out now. Jason's watching the monitors."

Taking in the tall pines lining three sides of the cabin and the mountain peak glistening with fresh fallen snow, Tara sighed. "God, this is beautiful country." The cabin was built into the mountain side which provided a panoramic view from the back deck. The air was a bit cool showing early signs of fall, but the sunshine made things toasty.

"It sure is. Why don't you sit here with me while we wait for Chance?" Travis patted the seat next to his own. She sat so her towel remained wrapped around her torso.

"Here you go." He handed her a glass filled with an amber liquid.

"What's this?" She reached out for the glass.

"White wine. Chance asked me to get some for you when we went shopping."

She took a sip. "Mmm, delicious. How does he know I like wine?" Travis just shrugged.

She put the glass down on the table between the two chairs and leaned back. Now this was much better. Fresh air and sunlight. She was in her own element once again.

A buzzing sound around her ear startled her. Some kind of bug was being busy around her head. She swatted at the thing trying to keep it from landing on her, but it flew into her eye.

"Ow, ow, ow! Bug in my eye," she yelped helplessly and stood trying to get the unwanted bug out from under her lashes. Travis stood and grabbed her by the shoulders.

"Hold up, Tara. Stay still. I'll get it for you."

She tried but couldn't stop wiggling. He bent her head back into one of his hands and moved in for a closer look. The bug was somehow tangled in her lashes. Gently, he plucked and released it from its grip.

"Okay. It's gone." He had a grip on her head with her back bent. Her eyes fluttered open making sure they were clear. She didn't feel any residual effect from the bug.

"Ahem!" Chance cleared his throat standing in front of the door on the deck, arms at his sides and fists clenched. His eyebrows were drawn together in a menacing look.

Nearly dropping her, Travis let her go. Her mouth was agape at the sight of Mountain Man. He'd shed his rugged duds and donned a pair of workout shorts which hung low on his hips. His bare chest had a few soft looking dark curls trailing down over rock hard abs into a fine line ending at the edge of the shorts. All in all, he had a body to die for.

Travis took his index finger and placed it under Tara's chin, then lifted it effectively closing her yawning mouth.

"Holy Mother of God," she murmured low.

"Why, Tara," Travis droned with a hint of humor. "I didn't know you were religious."

She let loose a sassy grin. "Yeah, well, sometimes it's the only thing to fit the occasion."

She walked toward Chance stopping a couple of inches in front of him. She glided one finger over a two inch scar which ran horizontally across his throat. She trailed the finger over to another scar across his right pectoral muscle. While rubbing the scar, she caught sight of another low on his hips near the edge of his shorts. Her finger ran up his shoulder and down his arm. She traced the edges of his Ranger tattoo and felt him shiver.

*****

Taking a deep breath, Chance walked to the edge of the hot tub and settled in sliding down until he was completely immersed. Travis followed on the opposite end of the tub.

When Chance resurfaced, he came up trying to clear water from his face. Tara stood at the edge of the tub right in front of him. Standing as rigid as a board with tense muscles, she loosened the towel tucked in around her body letting it fall to the ground. His hands froze over his face when he caught sight of her sexy little black bikini.

"Sweet Jesus." Chance let his eyes roam over her body. The black highlighted her tanned skin. She was so beautiful. The halter top hugged her chest which was just the right size for her frame. His eyes rested on the swell of her breasts making him want to bury his face there. Her waist was tiny, not sickly tiny, just perfectly small. He could see some definition to her muscles, the start of a six pack abs set, but she still looked soft and feminine. His gaze moved to the curve of her hips which had him all but drooling. He shifted trying to gain some relief for his erection while trying to hide it from the other agent in the tub.

"Great," Travis droned again. "Two religious converts."

Chance managed to regain his composure once she dropped down into the water where the miniscule bikini couldn't affect his senses. She looked more relaxed once she hit the water.

The three faced each other. Chance kept his back to the cabin so he could see out in each direction. Travis positioned himself so he could see over Chance's head.

Chance cleared his throat. "Tara, where did you get the swimsuit? I didn't think you would have packed one."

Tara was looking at him from beneath lowered eyelashes, a smirk on her face. "I guess Logan thought it would come in handy."

"Well remind me to thank him." Chance smiled.

Timmy came out on deck with his master. As soon as she took her position in the hot tub, the cat took his own position on the edge of the tub to her right. With his head on his paws, he stretched out in all his glory. The extra weight he carried hung over the side of the tub only an inch above the water line.

Tara struck up a conversation. "So, Travis. What place do you call home? You didn't mention it before."

"Maine. I worked with my father on the docks and boats while I attended school. Dad was a lobsterman. He died some years ago."

"Sorry to hear it. Your mother, how'd she die?"

"She was murdered."

Tara gasped, her voice filled with empathy. "Oh, Travis. I'm so sorry. I didn't realize she died from violence. What happened?"

"I don't know. I was twelve. The case went cold. I decided to go into law enforcement of some kind so I could hunt down her killer and maybe keep someone else's kid from experiencing the grief of losing a parent."

The mood grew somber for a good ten minutes without another word.

"Hey! How come you guys didn't wait for me?"

All eyes, including Timmy's, swung toward the door. Jason stood there shirtless, his milky white skin glistening. He wore a skimpy banana yellow Speedo which was partially hidden by his paunchy stomach.

Timmy meowed at him and, in slow motion, fell into the hot tub.

"Timmy!" Tara screeched. The cat was so heavy he sunk straight to the bottom.

"I've got him!" Travis shouted as he reached down and came up with the cat sputtering, flailing his paws, and squawking. "Here you go, Tara." He handed over the agitated feline.

She looked at both Travis and Chance, glanced at Timmy, and then looked over at Jason who was walking toward the hot tub skipping like a kid. He landed in the tub with a splash.

"I've got to get Timmy dried off." Tara tried not to laugh. She struggled while climbing out with the water-logged cat.

Chance leaped at the opportunity to follow suit. "Let me help you, Tara."

"Me too." Travis chimed in.

All three grabbed towels and made a beeline for the doors leaving Jason alone.

"You guys coming back?" Jason asked ten minutes later. No one answered.

*****

A few hours later sitting in front of the monitors, Chance watched for signs of intrusion from the cameras strategically placed around the cabin. With Derek gone, they decided to take watch in four hour shifts so no one person would grow too tired to be vigilant.

It was nearing the time for his second shift to end. Jason would be relieving him soon. Although his eyes were focused on their surroundings, his mind strayed. He could no longer deny the chemistry between himself and Tara. Sparks flew whenever they were within arm's length of each other.

Over the years, he'd been with his fair share of women, but none affected him like she did. He realized their constant bickering was a defense mechanism to keep the sexual tension between them from exploding.

It was against regulations to fraternize with a person in protective custody. He knew it all too well, and besides, as far as he could tell, her entire adult life was filled with fear, misery, and grief. The fact she was so much younger than he rang another warning bell in his head. Hell. He'd been able to lead his life on his own terms, but not Tara.

She was stymied from the tender age of sixteen by ever present fear, and now, with Alvin hunting her down, her life was ruled by forces beyond her control.

He couldn't help but think she deserved a life where she could make her own choices free from restraint, free from grief, and most of all, free from fear. Maybe he could help with her new life after this was all over. He shook his head. *You're getting ahead of yourself old boy.* He grunted. She had him talking to himself again. Maybe ignoring the sexual tension until this was over would be best. Maybe then he could pursue her. *Yeah, right. Good luck with that, buddy.*

"Hey, Chance. Ready for me to take over?"

Chance looked up and saw Jason. "Yeah. More than ready. Where's Travis? Is he watching Tara?"

"He's out on the deck. I just left Tara in the living room. We were playing cards. She beat the crap out of me." Chance smiled. "I was thinking, Chance. There's a barbeque pit on the deck. Could we light it up and grill some steaks for dinner? One of us can go to the grocery store and pick up what we need."

"Sounds like a plan to me. I'll check with Travis and see if we can do that." He stood and left the room

*****

Travis sat staring at the mountain, his thoughts far away. The fact there was someone consorting with the enemy ticked him off. Over the past few years, they'd had enough trouble amongst themselves to last a lifetime.

As it is, their trust was shaken to the core. It wasn't something he liked thinking about, but this business about a mole brought back memories he would rather forget, memories of friends and co-workers who'd betrayed them all. He hoped one day his unit would be back to its former self where complete trust was a given.

The doors leading to the deck opened. Chance sat down next to him.

"So how's our little package doing this evening?" Travis grinned.

Chance smiled back. "She just finished playing cards with Jason and she beat the crap out of him, the dumb idiot. She lives in Vegas. She probably knows every card trick in the book."

"Well it serves him right then."

"Yeah. Listen. He just asked if we could fire up the grill over there with steaks. One of us could go get the stuff while the other two keep an eye on her. I told him I'd run it past you."

"Sounds good to me. Want to draw straws as to who gets to go pick up the groceries?"

"Doesn't matter to me one way or another."

Travis outright laughed. "You lying son of a bitch. But it's okay. I'll cut you some slack on this one. It won't take but twenty minutes to go there and back. So how about Jason and I both go? Or do you need backup here?"

Chance gave him a killer look which only fueled Travis's laughter. "All right. We'll be back in a flash."

Travis stopped in front of Chance's chair and looked down at him. "All kidding aside, Chance. Keep your wits about you, all right?"

"Sure thing." Now alone out on the deck, he watched the sun set in peaceful silence.

Chapter Twenty-Four

Chance turned from his position next to the railing and smiled as Tara asked, "Do I have permission to go out there?"

"Yes, *chère,* you have permission."

His smile faded as soon as she came into full view. She still wore the sexy black bikini from the afternoon but she'd covered it up with a short, lacey black wrap which did nothing to hide her curvaceous figure. *Now just how the heck am I supposed to maintain my self-control when she walks out looking like that?*

"What are you up to out here?" She leaned over the railing gazing at the scenery.

"Just chilling. What about you? I heard you beat the pants off Jason."

She laughed. "A fourth grader could beat Jason at cards. If he's smart, he'll never try to beat the odds in Vegas. Where did boy wonder and his faithful sidekick go anyway?"

"They're headed to the store to pick up steaks. We're going to fire up the grill tonight which means you're off the hook for having to cook."

"What? You didn't like my cooking?"

"Well you do live alone, and often people who live alone tend to make do with fast food instead of cooking. Besides, you live in Las Vegas, the capitol of the all night diner and cheap buffet meals. I figure the meal you cooked last night was a fluke."

She punched him on the arm right over his Ranger tattoo. He feigned injury and yelped, laughing in the process.

"You making fun of me again, Anselmi?"

"Sorry, *chère*. You just make it so easy for me to pick on you. I'm just teasin' is all. The meal you served was damn good."

She looked appeased with his answer as she leaned against the deck railing surveying their surroundings. The warm Tennessee sunshine was long replaced by an inky black blanket with millions of stars shimmering underneath its dome.

"Wow. The stars are so beautiful. You don't get to see them in Vegas with all the bright lights blazing. I don't think I've ever seen such a beautiful sight."

Chance stood next to her leaning against the railing too. "It is a beautiful night. In Louisiana when we'd all go to the camp and the weather was hot and steamy, we'd throw a few blankets on solid ground near the camp and lay back gazing at the stars. When the weather was clear, you could pick out a slew of constellations. We even learned to navigate by the stars."

"I can't imagine how nice it would be to see this every night. Even in California you can't see stars like this."

"No, you can't. Big city lights obscure this beauty."

The night air was becoming a bit cool. He noticed her shiver. Without a word, he stood behind her wrapping his big arms around her waist blanketing her tiny body with his. Placing his lips to her ear, he whispered, "Cold, *chère*?"

She snuggled against him, Chance letting his warmth seep into her body.

"Not anymore."

He let his breath fan across her ear and neck. She shivered again, but he knew this time it wasn't from the cold.

Without warning, he spun her around so they were face-to-face. For just a moment, he thought he could see down into her soul. His desire for her was out in the open now, blatant and evident.

He was seduced by the depth of emotions shining in her eyes. He leaned down and kissed her. It took two seconds to feel her heat, the kiss turning from gentle to steamy and hot. He was lost in the sensations taking over his body.

Chance let his hands roam freely until he reached the front of her cover up. He pulled back asking for permission to remove it. Tara showed her impatience as she ripped it over her head so fast her arms got caught in the material. They were up in the air, half of her face covered, the lower half free from the confines. Chance couldn't help but laugh at the sight which caused Tara to huff in annoyance.

"Help me. I'm stuck!"

"Sorry, *chère*. You look too cute all tangled up like that, and I kind of like you like this -- blindfolded and restrained." He bent down and kissed her. Even though she looked surprised, he could tell she was pleased.

Leaving a trail of open mouthed kisses down her neck to the top of her chest, Chance looked up at a helpless Tara who was breathing just as heavy as he was. She stopped struggling and was all flushed with lust... for *him*. God, she was so beautiful.

He smoothed his hands down over her bikini covered breasts. He was rewarded with a little whimper from his captive beauty.

"Chance, please." She was begging.

"*Mon chère*, you don't ever have to beg for anything from me. Just tell me what you want and I'll do it."

"Touch me, Chance. Please."

He ran a finger just beneath the bikini top making her squirm. "Like this?"

"Mmm. Yes. More."

He slid the top up exposing her breasts to the night air. The coolness made her pink nipples tighten. He palmed each breast loving the feel of her smooth skin.

"Oh. It feels so good." Her head was tilted back.

Chance moved one hand to her waist and replaced his hand with his mouth. Tara was moving so much trying to create friction, she got loose from her cover up.

He looked up at her from his kneeling position, her nipple still in his mouth. He let it go with a *pop* while smoothing his hand down to the front of her bikini bottoms. He slipped a finger into each side of the bottoms like he was going to remove them as he planted wet kisses along her lower stomach.

Chance gave the bottoms a little tug and started to lower them as he ran his tongue along her newly uncovered flesh. He could tell she was about to explode.

"Ahem! We're back!" Travis blurted with pealing laughter.

Chance jumped up and blocked Tara from Travis's view while she straightened her clothing. "Damn, Travis. You've got rotten timing." He heard Travis laugh a little harder.

"Yeah, I know. You guys about ready to fire up the grill?"

Chance looked at Tara. Leaning down, he whispered in her ear, "You'd better go change or I'll be forced to hurt them if they comment on how you look."

Tara glanced down. Her bikini was askew and her skin was flush from his kisses.

"I'll go change real quick. It's getting chilly." She took off toward the doors.

Travis walked up to Chance and slapped him on the back. "Sorry we made it back so quick, buddy. I'm sure you could've used a few more minutes -- or hours." He smiled.

Two hours later, they were sitting around the deck in jovial conversation when Chance's mood changed for no reason at all.

"Tara. I think you'd better get back inside now. It's getting late and it isn't safe for you to be out here."

She gave him a funny look as if not understanding his sudden shift in demeanor. He couldn't help the fact that he'd suddenly experienced a sense of dread.

She got up and headed for the door but stopped midway turning to face them, smiling. "Dinner was great, the company was great, and most of all, thanks for treating me like one of your friends." She turned and walked in the cabin.

Chance rose scratching his chin. "Well. My shift's about to start, so I guess I'll leave the cleanup to you guys." He smirked and walked out the door.

*****

"I've got to do a perimeter sweep, so I guess I'll leave the cleanup to you," Travis smirked and left.

Jason looked around the now empty deck. He frowned. "I wonder why I always end up being alone." He donned fresh gloves and started cleaning up the mess.

Chapter Twenty-Five

The next morning, Derek walked into the kitchen and grabbed a cup of coffee. Tara and Chance had just finished breakfast and were having their own coffee.

"Hey! The happy wanderer returns," Tara mused. "You have a nice vacation?"

"I've only been gone a few days, Tara. Just how much trouble did you manage to get yourself into?" He teased.

She gave him an I'm-such-an-innocent-person look. "Me? I've been an angel."

Chance choked on the sip of coffee he'd been drinking.

"What's wrong with you, Anselmi? Anything out of the ordinary you'd like to report?" Derek inquired.

Chance's eyes were glued to Tara's, and Derek could tell his agent was definitely relaying a don't-you-dare-say-anything look before he turned an innocent gaze Derek's way.

"Nope."

"Yeah. Figured that." Derek took his coffee and sipped it while he walked to the doors leading to the deck. He stopped mid sip when he looked outside. "Who's on watch?"

"Travis is on monitors. Jason's on perimeter."

"Why is the cover off the hot tub?" When no reply came, he turned toward the two culprits sitting at the table trying to pull off looks of innocence. He wasn't buying it from either one of them.

"I don't think it was covered before, Derek," Tara answered with a little too much sweetness dripping from her voice. "Do you remember it being covered, Chance?"

He shrugged and shook his head. Derek was about to tear into both of them when Travis walked in saving them both.

"Derek! Good to have you back. Where have you been?" he asked like he didn't know.

Derek's mood shifted. "Get Navarro. Meet us in the living room in ten minutes. We need to go over security measures. Tara? Take a break and go read one of those books you hauled out here." He turned, put his cup in the sink, and walked out.

*****

"What the hell's his problem?" Travis asked.

"Well." Tara jumped out of her chair looking like she'd just been fully chastised. "Guess I've got a book to read." She slinked out of the kitchen and out of Derek's range of fire.

*****

Derek paced as he watched his three agents enter the living room.

"What's going on, Derek?" Chance sat in an arm chair in the living room. Travis and Jason were seated on the couch.

"I have reason to believe Cruz may have knowledge of our current location."

Chance shot out of his chair, fists at his side. "And just how would he know?"

Derek took in a deep breath and focused on Jason, the one person in the room who knew nothing of their suspicions concerning a mole. "He's being fed intel by an unknown within the bureau."

"What?" Travis voice innocently, also standing.

Jason was the only one still sitting. "Wait a minute. How do you know what's happening? Is there proof of a mole?" he asked the obvious useless question.

Travis looked at him like he was crazy. "Derek. Want to trade rookie for rookie?"

Derek grinned. "Not in a million years, Travis."

Chance bellowed, "Who gives a crap about proof? He found us in Ohio. What more proof do you need, dipshit?" He addressed Jason.

Derek's tone grew serious once more. "Chance and I will take first watch tonight." He dug in his jack pocket and retrieved several car keys passing one to each agent. "I've hidden a vehicle on the western mountain path about a half mile down the trail. Keep your key on you at all times. If crap breaks loose here, whoever's closest to the girl gets her out of here and to that vehicle. There's a bag of clothes in there for her as well as a pet carrier for the cat. No matter what happens, she gets out. Understood?" Everyone nodded.

"And if you're the only one left standing, don't look back. Two of us will be up and awake at all times tonight. Tomorrow, we move again. Get to it."

Everyone started moving at once. "Wait up, rookie." Chance turned back. Derek waited until the other two agents were out of ear shot to speak, his voice low. "I've got a really bad belly ache right about now, Chance. Cruz knew when and where to hit in Ohio, and I think he's making his way here as we speak."

"What makes you think that?"

"Reggie and I set up a fake safe house on the west coast yesterday morning. We even had a look-alike decoy of Tara there. I met with the rest of the team and passed on the dummy location. Reggie called me half an hour ago. Cruz hit the fake location at four this morning. He got his hands on the decoy but she managed to get away. We were fortunate no one got hurt. Cruz slipped out of their grasps. You three here were kept out of the loop so we could narrow down the list of suspects. But even though the rest of the team is unaware of this location, I've got a funny feeling the mole will find out and leak the info to Cruz real soon."

"Any clue as to the identity of the traitor?"

"I've got my suspicions, but until I can confirm it, we stay status quo. And, rookie?"

"Yeah?"

"I know your feelings about this girl. You do realize regulations forbid fraternization?"

Chance looked away before speaking. "I know the regs."

"Can you remain objective or do I have to replace you?"

Blood roared to the Cajun's face as his anger obviously cranked up a notch. "No freaking way. I'm not leaving her here."

"We'll have her covered. We can accomplish this mission without you."

"Dammit, Derek. Don't do this to me. I can handle it."

Derek looked into Chance's eyes. What he saw there was a look of determination. Sighing in resignation, he caved. "Look. If something goes wrong, I need you to step up to the plate. Get her out of here as fast as you can. Contact no one except Lyons. He's the only one you can trust."

"So Travis and Jason are cleared?"

"Yes. So are you, but someone's fighting against us. Reggie's working on flushing out the mole. In the meantime, I've got your back and you've got mine, right?"

Chance nodded. "Right. One more thing, Derek."

"What?"

"If he finds her this time, I quit taking chances. You can fire me if you want. I'm going to get her to a place where I know neither Cruz nor the mole can find her and to hell with the bureau. She'll be safe if I have to die to accomplish it."

"Now wait a minute, Chance. You know I can't sanction a rogue action."

"I don't give a damn whether you sanction it or not. It's what's gonna be."

Derek swiped a hand through his hair in frustration. "Whatever happens, you keep her safe. I'm beginning to like the crazy little woman."

Chance grinned. "Just so happens, so am I."

*****

"Where the hell are you going, Navarro?" Travis whispered in the dimly lit hallway. It was approaching two a.m. Chance, Derek, and Tara were ensconced in their bedrooms.

"I told you before, Travis. I've got to take a load off. My stomach's been queasy since dinner. We do get bathroom breaks, don't we?"

"Shh. Lower your voice. The others are sleeping."

"If you need me in the next ten minutes, you give a shout." He headed down the hall.

Travis shook his head in dismay and headed toward the kitchen. His cell phone sounded an alert to an incoming text message. He retrieved the phone from his pocket and clicked until the text came into view: Find Junior and you'll find Cruz.

Travis's brows sunk. The message made no sense. Who the hell was Junior? Curious to see who sent it, he clicked a few buttons to retrieve the sender's identity, but to his dismay, the sender's name was blocked and was more than likely untraceable.

He put the phone back in his pocket and made a mental note to talk to Derek about it in the morning. Grabbing a cup of coffee, he peeked out the doors onto the deck. The full moon was bright and illuminated most of the shadows. Everything looked peaceful, but just to be sure, he opened the doors and stepped out. The cool, crisp Tennessee night air whistled briskly through the massive pines.

Without warning, the fine hairs on the back of his neck stood on end. Before he could put the cup down and grab his weapon, gun fire rent the air. The cup flew as pain shot up his arm into his shoulder. Within seconds, bullets ripped through his stomach, his side, and his leg. He was on the ground and unconscious before he knew what hit him.

*****

"Travis! What the hell's going on out there?" someone yelled from the door to Alvin's right.

He flung the door to the bathroom open, a satisfied smile on his face at finding one of the agents in a compromising position. The last thing the agent sitting on the commode saw was the barrel of a gun as Alvin pointed it toward the agent's forehead and fired two rounds right between the eyes. The agent's pants were still folded around his ankles.

"Two down -- two to go," Cruz mused to himself.

Hunkered down near the bathroom door listening for movement, Alvin tried to slow his breathing. Adrenaline spiked through his body from the kills. He needed to calm himself and focus. Knowing there were two more agents loose in the house made his blood pump too rapidly in his chest. The thrill of the hunt always provided him with an adrenaline rush. If he picked off the two remaining agents one at a time, he'd have her right where he wanted her -- all alone.

He crept around the corner leading into the living room, his body hugging the wall. Hesitantly, he peered around the door jamb into the dark gloomy room, gun drawn at his side.

A shot rang out. He retreated pulling himself back to cover. From his peripheral vision, he saw a spot on the door jamb where the bullet nicked the wood as it flew past his head. Sweat broke out across his brow. He wasn't sure if he was facing one or both agents.

Taking a deep breath, he jumped into the open doorway and fired a shot at the same spot where the previous one came from. A loud grunt sounded as the distinct sound of a weapon hitting the floor echoed through the air. Next he heard a thump like the sound a body might make hitting the floor.

"Gotcha!" he exclaimed with delight.

*****

"Tara! Grab Timmy! Let's go!" Chanced urged in a loud whisper. So far he'd heard seven shots. The bastard would have to reload soon. They only had a few seconds to spare. Tara, who'd dressed quickly when she'd first heard the gun shots, sat frozen on the edge of the bed clutching Timmy with all her might, her eyes ablaze with fear.

Leaning down in front of her, Chance forced her to look into his eyes. "I've got you. He won't get to you, I promise. Now let's go!"

She picked up her book from the night stand and tucked it in the back pocket of her jeans as Chance led them into the darkened hallway, gun drawn. He forced her to stay at his back. If they could make it to the deck, he stood a chance of getting her out of harm's way.

Keeping their bodies crouched down low, they hugged the wall until he was able to see the entrance to the living room. "Follow my lead," he whispered.

They entered the dimly lit room. Slight shadows were cast across the darkened floor. With his excellent night vision, he could see someone slumped on the floor near the arm chair. A muffled groan came from the direction of the body. Instinct told him it was one of the good guys.

"Follow me and stay low." With her free hand clutching the back of his shirt, they reached the fallen man. Chance caught sight of Derek's gun peeking out from under the chair.

"Derek." Tara let out a muffled gasp. Chance bent down and turned the agent over. Derek grunted. He was conscious but was in a lot of pain.

"Where'd he get you?" Chance examined him for wounds.

"Shoulder. I'll live. Get her out of here, rookie." He grunted in pain.

"We can't leave him here, Chance," Tara whispered, her voice trembling.

Derek pulled on Chance's shirt with his good arm and forced him down within earshot. "Follow instructions, rookie. Do what you have to do. Get the hell out of here. Now!"

Chance nodded, picked up Derek's gun, and placed it in his good hand. He grabbed Tara's hand and they sprinted toward the kitchen heading for the doors leading to the deck.

Opening them slow, he allowed his eyes to adjust to the dim moonlight and saw no threat lurking but caught sight of Travis's prone body. He prayed Tara wouldn't see him.

Grabbing her by the arm, he hugged the wall of the cabin until they were to the western most corner where he knew there was a foot path beneath the deck leading down the mountain side. He stepped over the railing and turned back toward Tara.

"Hand me Timmy." She did so reluctantly. The feline showed no disapproval.

"Come on," Chance urged. He helped her hurdle the railing. When they'd gone about ten feet down the path, a bullet whizzed past his ear. Tara let out a scream.

"Run!" He pushed her in front of himself so he now stood between her and the gun fire. They set out in a full blown sprint down the mountain.

*****

Finished sending the text message to his old friend, Travis, he tucked his cell phone in his pocket and smiled. One way or another, he'd get his long awaited revenge on Junior.

Chapter Twenty-Six

As they hit I-65 heading south out of Tennessee, Chance pulled out his cell phone and punched in a number on his speed dial.

"Lyons."

"Reggie. The safe house has been hit," Chance reported.

"I know. I got a distress signal from Ross's cell. A task force has been dispatched to the house as well as local fire, police, and medical personnel. Is the girl safe?"

"Yeah. She's with me. We're on the road. Derek's been shot, Reggie. He was alive when we left. I didn't see the others."

There was silence.

"What is it?" Chance was leery of Reggie's hesitation.

"Derek took one to the shoulder but will be fine. Travis is touch and go. He took four rounds but is hanging in there. Jason took two to the forehead."

"*Dammit!*" Chance hit the steering wheel with his hand.

Tara flinched. "What happened?"

"Anselmi. I need to know where you're headed."

He shook his head. "Un, un, no way. Two freaking safe houses and still she's not safe. I'm taking her somewhere no one can find her."

"You know procedure demands you give me the location," Reggie admonished.

Chance thought for a split second. "Screw procedure. I'll be in touch." He slammed the cell phone shut.

"Chance, what happened?" He glanced at her fear-filled face knowing the news would hit her sensitive heart hard. He relayed the info about Travis and Derek's injuries. With some trepidation, he told her about Jason. Silent tears streamed down her face.

"Tara. Don't cry. Please." He reached a hand out to comfort her. She backed herself against the door as far away from him as she could get.

"No! Don't touch me! Don't get near me. I'm poison."

"No, *chère*. Don't do this to yourself. This is not your fault."

"Isn't it? Jason would still be alive right now if not for me. Whose fault is it if it isn't mine? It certainly isn't yours."

"That's where you're wrong. It *is* my fault. I should've pulled you out of there the minute I realized Cruz had a contact in the bureau feeding him information. This could have been avoided if I'd just reacted sooner."

Her sniffling ceased. "What do you mean, Alvin's got a contact in the bureau?"

"There's a mole on the task force, an agent gone bad. We suspected such since we left Ohio. It's the reason Derek went to Quantico, to ferret out the mole."

"Did he find out who it is?"

"If he did, he's not talking and rightly so."

"But it couldn't be you." She sounded incredulous to the very thought of it being him.

"Thanks for the vote of confidence, but it isn't me, Travis, or Jason."

Chance pulled into a gas station and drove to the back parking under a street light. "Stay inside for now. I have to remove the GPS tracker on this car. It will only take a minute."

He watched her nod and lean back into the seat before he went about disabling the tracker.

Chance opened her door. "Okay. I need to go into the store, so I'll drive to the front and we'll both go in together. Stay close to me."

Once in the store, Chance bought a prepaid cell and minutes, snacks, and drinks for the trip as well as food for Timmy. After he loaded important numbers into the new phone, on the way out he tossed his personal cell phone in the trash. They headed back out on the road.

Inhaling, Tara leaned against the head rest. Chance knew she felt safe with him, but the news of someone within the FBI leading an obsessed murderer straight to her door had to make the grip of her fear quadruple. He pulled out the new phone and dialed.

"Who are you calling now?" Her voice wavered with uncertainty.

"Remi Dubois, an old friend of mine."

"Why are you calling him?"

"I need help, Tara. This is gonna take help from someone I can trust."

"What makes you think he can stop Alvin when the others couldn't?"

"Damn. It's going to voice mail." He ignored her question. "Remi? It's Chance." He left a lengthy message in his Cajun French. He hung up and looked at Tara's disbelieving eyes.

"I hate when you talk that French crap. I can't understand a damn thing you're saying."

He smiled. "Sorry. Old habit. Remi and I grew up together, and Poppee only spoke to us in French. So if we wanted to communicate, we had to learn to say it and understand it."

Chance saw the twinge of loneliness cross her face as she listened to him speak of his youth. From her records, he knew her grandparents all died by the time she was six. She had no aunts or uncles, cousins, brothers, sisters, or parents left -- no family whatsoever, and she made it clear a family of her own who could love her as she wanted to love in return was the one and only thing she ever wanted out of life.

"So what's this Dubois character got the others didn't?"

Chance couldn't help but grin when he spoke of his friends and family. "He's got everything we need."

"Such as?"

"Such as cunning, alacrity, and muscle. He's the best damn shot with a pistol or rifle I've ever seen and he can track a man through the woods without a stick of trouble. He's a damn bad ass to beat the band, and despite all that, he's the only person on the planet I'd trust with my life without question besides Poppee." He glanced her way. "And your life too, *chère*."

His phone rang. He checked the incoming number before answering the call. "Remi Dubois, you old goat. *Comon sa va, mon ami*? How is everything?"

Chance saw Tara roll her eyes as he continued to speak to his childhood friend in their native Cajun tongue. The real reason he'd switched to French was because he didn't want her to know just how tricky this move was going to be.

"Great, Remi. I'll give you a call when we get closer. Thanks for your help, bud." He listened for a moment and started laughing. "No, I can't stop in Georgia and pick up a brunette peach for you." He laughed again. "No, no Mississippi queen either. You'll just have to stick with the local fare. Yeah, yeah, I know. I'm no damn fun and you're nothin' but a dog. See ya soon, Remi, and thanks again." He turned off the phone.

"Uh, brunette peach?"

"Yeah. Remi Dubois is a consummate connoisseur of fine wine and even finer women."

"Great. I'm going to put my life in the hands of a womanizing wild Cajun man."

"Tara. All kidding aside. Remi is the best of the best. We've been lifelong friends since we were knee high to a grasshopper and were sneaking out of school to go crawfishin' in the swamps. I do trust him with my life and everything I own."

"Well, I guess we'll see just how trustworthy he is, won't we?"

*****

Tara felt like they'd been in the car for days instead of hours. Her body was jet lagged having bounced around the country from one coast almost to another and now down to the Deep South. She caught a glimpse of a highway sign which read *US 90 West* and realized they'd left the city of New Orleans in Louisiana behind.

"Why are we by-passing New Orleans? I thought there wasn't anything further south?"

"Whatever gave you the idea there was nothin' south of New Orleans, *chère*?"

"What? Have you looked at a map lately? There's New Orleans and below it the Gulf of Mexico. There's nothing in between."

"That's where you're wrong, Miss West Coast Sunshine. There's a heck of a lot south of New Orleans you non-southern people don't even know about."

"Well I sure hope you're right since we don't have a boat attached to this vehicle."

He let out a little laugh. "We've got another hour's drive before we get to Poppee's place. Why don't you try and catch a few zz's. I'll wake you up when we get there."

"Not a bad idea. I am a little tired."

Timmy, who'd been taking a nap of his own on the backseat, meowed. She turned to look at him. "You want up front, sweetie?"

She went to her knees and stretched over the seat to reach for him. She felt Chance's breath fan over her butt which made her realize it was up in the air just inches from his head.

He grumbled in French as she straightened up in her seat and put Timmy on her lap. "*Mon Dieu,* please give me strength."

"What did you say?" She giggled.

"Oh, nothing... nothing at all."

*****

"Tara. Wake up, *chère*. We're at Poppee's."

She slid up in the seat rubbing her sleep-filled eyes. They were in the driveway of a two story house exuding southern charm. Its shutters were midnight black and the vinyl exterior was a pleasant light grey. No garage was evident but a covering was attached to the frame of the house which accommodated two cars and a pick-up truck.

"Your grandfather lives here alone?"

"Yes. Grams died six years ago. The house is too big for him now but he refuses to sell and move into something more manageable. I've asked him to move in with me, but he flat out refuses. Remi has tried the same so he could keep an eye on him, but it didn't work either. He says he'd rather pay someone who needs the money to come in and clean for him than sell the house he and Grams built from the ground up with their own bare hands."

"What a sweet sentiment. He must be a loveable character."

Chance laughed out loud. "Character? Hell, yeah. Loveable? Up for debate. Put it this way. Don't believe a damn thing he tells you. He's got a shitload of stories running around in his big old head and he'll try to make you believe them all if you let him... so don't let him."

"Come now, Anselmi. He can't be that bad."

"Yes he can. Come on. They are probably chompin' at the bit to meet you."

"They? Who else is there with him?"

"Remi."

"He's the friend you called earlier?"

"Yeah. We grew up together, remember? He used to spend more time at our house than he did at his own." He walked to her side of the car and helped her out. When he shut the door, he pinned her up against it not letting her move. She looked up at him, curious.

"What?"

"I need to warn you about Remi."

Her eyebrows shot up. "What about him?"

"Remi's a womanizer. He makes a pass at every pretty woman he meets, and he has a silver tongue when it comes to sweet-talkin' the ladies, but all in all, he's got a good heart. Just don't believe anything he says either."

Tara smiled when she realized his warning held a note of jealousy. "Is there anybody around here I *can* believe?"

He pretended to think about it for a moment. "Nope. Nobody but me." He put his arm around her shoulder and they headed for the house.

"Thought so," she murmured under her breath.

Chapter Twenty-Seven

"Hey, Poppee! Where are you? We're here." They entered the kitchen through the side door beneath the carport as Chance shouted for his grandfather.

"Where da hell you think we would be, t-boy?" Someone shouted back at him. "Come in da livin' room an' bring dat little woman in here so we can meet her."

Chance leaned down and whispered in Tara's ear. "Warning. You are about to meet one cranky-assed full blooded Cajun. His accent is really thick and he'll pretend he can't hear a thing you say, but trust me. He hears everything within a mile radius of where he stands."

"Chance! Git your sorry ass in here, boy!"

Chance and Tara walked through the kitchen and stood in the open doorway leading to the family living room. An elderly gentleman stood to the right of a fireplace. He stood no taller than five-eight, five-nine. His darkened skin was leathery and wrinkled from over exposure to the southern sun. His hair, what little he had left, was snow white and cut short. Round wire-framed glasses were perched atop his nose. He peered over the glasses at Tara.

"*Bon Dieu*! *C'est joli*!"

The French didn't come from the old man; it came from the younger one standing to the left of the fireplace with his arm draped across the mantle.

This man, as tall as Chance but leaner, was almost as good looking. Tara eyed him from head to toe in female appreciation of a fine male physique. She noted where Chance was big and full of muscle, this guy was lean and muscular. His skin was bronzed to a golden hue, his jet black hair thick, a little shaggy and wavy. His classic chiseled features sported a well-groomed mustache and goatee. Sky blue eyes were taking in the sight of her body without shame.

With those looks, she could understand how women fell under his spell. Glancing Chance's way, she saw an angry look flit across his face.

"What did he just say?" she asked Chance.

"He said you're very pretty, and if he opens his mouth again, I'm gonna stick my right fist in it and shut him up."

That set the guy laughing. The older man limped over using a walking cane. Propping the cane against his thigh, he pulled on Chance's shirt forcing him to bend down. When Chance leaned in, the old man whacked him on top his head.

"Mind your manners, boy, and don't you talk to Remi dat way. I done taught you better than dat." Chance straightened up and smiled.

"Thanks for the welcome home, Poppee." The old man ignored him and smiled at Tara grabbing her hand and ensconcing it between his own arthritis ridden ones.

"I'm Chance's Poppee. You must be Mizz Roberts."

"Tara." She nodded. "How do you do, sir?"

The old man smiled. "For once in his life, Remi is dead to right. You sure are a pretty little thing. Don't you go mindin' dat grandson of mine. He got the manners of a bullfrog, dat one, and I taught him better, too. But he don't listen to his elders."

Tara's lips quirked. "It's a pleasure to meet you, sir."

"Poppee. Call me Poppee. All da young folks do."

Her smile widened. "Okay, Poppee."

Remi sauntered over to where they stood and grabbed his buddy by the neck pulling him into a big old man hug. "Welcome home, brother. Good to have you back."

"Thanks," Chance replied. "And before we go any further, keep your damn hands to yourself, Dubois. Got it?"

Remi laughed hard. "Now, bro. Come on. Give me some credit. Why don't you introduce me to your pretty little friend here?" He gave Tara one of those looks a man gives a woman to let her know he likes what he sees.

"Oh, brother." She rolled her eyes.

Without taking his eyes off Remi, Chance made the introduction. "Remi? Tara Roberts. Tara? Remi 'playboy' Dubois.

Chuckling, she extended her hand. With true southern charm, Remi took her fingers and bent them placing a gentle kiss on top of her hand. He spoke with a lovely French accent not quite as heavy as Poppee's but not as light as Chance's.

"*Enchanté, mademoiselle.* Remi Dubois at your service."

Tara looked up at Chance. "Is he for real?"

Chance laughed. "He thinks he is."

A loud bark ripped through the room. Tara flinched just as a set of paws landed smack in the middle of her back shoving her right into Remi's strong arms.

She looked up at him and he wiggled his eyebrows. Then she felt Chance's hand pulling her arm as he yanked her away from his friend.

"What was that?" She heard another woof. Looking down at her feet, she caught sight of a fully grown basset hound, floppy ears and all. He was panting, his tongue hanging out and spittle drooling from the corner of his mouth down onto her foot.

"Hey, buddy. How are you?" She knelt down to his level and petted him on top of his head. The dog put his head in her lap. "Awe, you're so cute."

"He's so bad," Chance remarked.

"So what's your name, buddy?" As she asked, the dog barked again.

"Buddy," Chance replied.

She looked up. "No. I called him buddy, as in pal or friend. What's his name?"

"Buddy," Chance repeated. She gave him a confused look.

Bending down to their level, Chance whistled. "Come here, Buddy." The dog ignored him.

With a scowl, he stood up and whistled again. "Buddy! Heel!" Chance commanded him. The old dog turned his head toward his master lifting his droopy eyelids, gave him a quick look, and dropped his head down into Tara's lap. She snickered at the dog's reaction.

"Buddy, you traitor. Come tell me hello."

Finally the dog lifted himself up and scampered toward Chance who leaned down to pet his friend. "You miss me, big fella?" He scratched the dog behind his ear. Buddy barked once and headed back to Tara who giggled.

"Well, I'll be. Dat dog sure does know a pretty female when he sees one. Seems he likes her a lot more than he likes you, t-boy." Poppee grinned.

Chance frowned. "I'll just go to the car and get Timmy."

"Timmy?" Poppee and Remi chanted at the same time.

"My cat. You brave enough, Anselmi?" She bit her lower lip to keep from laughing outright.

"I think I can handle one damn cat."

Remi grabbed Chance's shoulder. "I'll go with you, friend. For protection."

Chance twisted Remi's hand. "You're so askin' for a whuppin', Dubois."

Remi laughed and escaped Chance's grip as they headed out the door side-by-side.

Once the men left the room, Tara turned toward Poppee. "Is there a bathroom somewhere I could use, Poppee? It was a long drive."

"Sure, t-sha. Jus' go down dat hall to da right. Da bathroom is on your left two doors down. When they come back, I'll have 'em put your things in da first bedroom on da right."

"Thank you." She smiled and headed down the hall.

*****

Chance and Remi came back loaded down with luggage and a pet carrier. Setting them down in the living room, they both stared at the old man.

"What?" Poppee looked perplexed.

"Where is she? What did you do to her?"

"Now what in tarnation makes you think I did somethin' to dat pretty little thing, Chance? She needed a bathroom for heaven's sake."

Feeling a little guilty and much too over protective, Chance apologized. "Sorry, Poppee. Listen. Would it be okay if we stayed here tonight and take off for the camp in the morning?"

The old man squinted and looked up. "Just how much trouble is she in, son?"

Poppee had an uncanny ability to see things for what they were. "How do you know she's in trouble?"

Poppee smiled. "Pretty little filly like dat here with you? Only means she's in trouble and needs some help."

Damn, but the old goat knew him well, and Chance knew he wouldn't get by with feeding him a bunch of lies. "I shouldn't tell you anything, but I know you. You'll just hound me until I fess up and tell you the truth. Sit down and I'll tell you." He motioned to the couch.

All three sat while he recounted Tara's troubles. Remi and Poppee listened intently. Remi sat with a dumfounded look on his face while Poppee shook his head in dismay.

"Dat poor girl. To see her parents and sisters killed like dat right in front of her own eyes, and at such a young age, too. Must've been real hard on her living without a family. Sort of like you, t-boy. You was real young too when you lost your family."

Chance smiled down at the aging man. "I didn't lose my whole family, Poppee. I lost my parents. You, Grams, and Remi are my family too. At least I had you three to fall back on. She has no one."

The wise old man nodded and smiled in appreciation of his grandson's wisdom. "Of course you two can stay here. I wouldn't have it any other way, but the cupboards are bare. I didn't get to make a bill at da grocery today. What are we gonna feed dat poor child? Do I have time to run to da store?"

Chance furrowed his brows. "You haven't been driving around by yourself, have you?"

His grandfather took up a defensive stance. "Sure 'nuff have."

"Poppee. You shouldn't be driving by yourself. It's dangerous."

"You listen up, boy. I done served my country, worked thirty years in da shrimpin' business, and paid my dues. I will do as I please, when I please, and dat includes gettin' behind da wheel of my own truck and goin' wherever I want to go."

Chance looked at Remi who'd just been taking in the conversation. "You're supposed to stop him from doing crazy crap. So why haven't you?"

Remi shrugged his shoulders. "*You* try stopping the old cuss from doing what he wants. See how far you get."

"I should jus' put you both over my knee and give y'all a whuppin'," Poppee countered.

Chance busted out laughing. "Don't think you could anymore, old man."

Remi chimed in. "I wouldn't goad him if I were you. You haven't been around in a while. Lately, he's been more ornery than ever. You know he'll do it too. Better yet, he'll wait until she comes back out and do it in front of her just so he can embarrass you,"

"Look. One way or another, we have to feed dat lil' woman. She's so tiny she's probably never eaten a decent meal in her life," Poppee interjected.

"Remi. Why don't you go get some groceries?" Chance suggested.

"But we were gonna go to Miss Joanne's place for supper. Can't we all go there?"

Chance shook his head. "We're in hiding, numb nuts. I can't take her out in public with a psychotic killer after her."

"Hold up," Poppee said. "I got an idea."

Chance and Remi looked at each other as the old man headed down the hall.

"Oh, brother. This could be dangerous," Remi muttered. A few moments later, the old man returned with some clothing in his hands.

"Let's put this on her. Dat would camouflage her looks. Besides, Grams would be happy to know she helped da girl out."

Chance took the clothing and examined them. They weren't bad. He recognized them. They were clothes his Grams wore toward the end after she'd lost weight from the cancer. "Okay. The clothing might work, but her face? How would we disguise her face?" Poppee handed him another item: a long haired bleach blonde wig.

Both Chance and Remi's eyebrows shot up. "Poppee. What the hell are you doin' with a woman's wig?"

Without an ounce of shame, the old man answered. "What? You two think me and Grams didn't have sex? I'll have you both know we were very active and we shared some pretty wild fantasies, let me tell you. In fact, this here wig brings back some very fond memories for me." Remi almost choked with laughter.

"Whoa, whoa. Stop right there, old man," Chance ordered trying to mentally shake the image of his grandparents doing the dirty, his precious, oh so reverent, Grams sporting the flaxen wig. He held up his hands trying to hold back a laugh. "*Way* too much information for me."

Remi laughed even louder. "For me too, Gramps."

"What's so funny?" Tara stood at the entrance to the living room, a hand propped on her hip looking bewildered.

"Either one of you damn young'uns want dat whuppin' right now like I done promised?" Poppee asked, a wicked little grin on his aged face. Both Chance and Remi shot through the front door, their laughter echoing in the air.

Chapter Twenty-Eight

Chance told Tara about their plans. Remi and Poppee were changing clothes.

"We're going to a restaurant? Really?" She must be stymied by the possibility of going out in public for a meal since they were supposed to be hiding.

"Here. Try on these clothes. If we can disguise you enough, we'll go out and have ourselves a decent meal for a change."

Tara appeared totally into the prospect of role playing. "Ooh! Wait up." She ran to her room and when she returned, a little white box sat in the palm of her hand.

"What's that?"

"Contacts."

"I didn't know you wore contacts."

"I don't."

"Then why do you have a pair of contacts with you?"

"I like to change my eye color when I go out."

"And that would be because?"

"Because I work in a bar, remember? When I go out, I don't want some loser who's seen me at work coming on to me, so I change my looks. But I don't have to when I go out with Logan. He keeps me safe."

"You go out with Logan?" Chance's voice sounded baffled even to himself.

"Hell yeah. Going out with a sometimes gay guy who looks like Logan is just like going out with a straight one except a lot safer. He keeps the losers from trying to get in my pants."

"A gay guy is trying to get in your pants?" Remi re-entered the room, his question showing he'd walked in mid-conversation.

Poppee walked in behind Remi. "Remi! Did you jus' say you're gay now? Since when? Dat would explain da revolving door in dat bedroom of yours."

"*Non*, no, Poppee! I'm not gay."

"I warned you," Chance told Tara. They both roared with laughter.

Remi thrust the wig into her hands. "Here. Put this on real quick-like before Poppee calls the newspaper and announces to the entire bayou that I'm gay."

"See. I knew it was you," Poppee chimed in. "But I don't understand. If you like men, then how come there are so many women hangin' 'round this place all da time?"

Remi twisted Tara around by the shoulders and gave her a gentle shove. "Go! Now!"

*****

"Where is she?" Chance glanced for the tenth time at his watch wondering how the hell he'd been talked into this crazy scheme. He always managed to lose his common sense when he came home and hung around these two. They were trouble personified.

Remi answered, "She's a woman in case you haven't noticed, dipshit. All women take their sweet time getting dressed."

Tara appeared and stood in the doorway awaiting their inspection. Chance's mouth flew open. The transformation was amazing. She looked like a different person. He peered at her eyes. They were... *purple*?

"Wow. What a switch. Just what color are your eyes now? Purple?"

She snorted. "They're not purple -- they're violet. Just like Liz Taylor's. So, how do I look?" She twirled around, the long blonde tresses swinging with her.

Both Remi and Chance cocked their heads to the side and gave her a slow once over from head to toe. Chance's heart thudded in his chest. If she was wearing burlap he'd still think she was beautiful. "I definitely prefer the real hair and eyes," Chance replied.

"I don't give a damn about real or not. She's just damn luscious," Remi added. Chance popped him on the shoulder making Tara smile.

"Revolving door," Poppee added. "Wait. We better give her a new name so we don't give her away."

Chance nodded. "Good idea, Poppee. So, Miss West Coast. What's your new name?"

Tara's smile disappeared and was replaced with a wistful look. She raised her eyes toward the ceiling then looked at them speaking softly. "Meagan."

Chance wanted to question why she'd chosen the name but he let it slide as they headed out the door.

*****

When they entered the restaurant, Poppee led the way. Evidently they all came here often and had a favorite table. Remi grabbed a chair and pulled it back allowing Tara to sit. Chance gave him a pair of eyes.

"What? I'm just being polite."

"Uh, huh." Chance pushed Remi away from the chair next to Tara's then sat down with a satisfied grin on his face.

Facing a large window, Tara took in the wonders of Louisiana. They were next to a body of water. Across from the restaurant, a huge boat was anchored to shore. It was different from any type of boat she'd ever seen. "Wow. Look at the boat. What kind is it? We're so close to the water. Does this place sit on a creek?"

All three men chuckled. Poppee was the one to answer. "No. Dat is Bayou Lafourche, and this place sits next to da bayou. If you look good, you'll see dat in daytime, you can have your meal out in da sunshine at those tables out there. And dat boat across the ways is a shrimp boat. Shrimpin' season just closed so most boats are inshore."

A pretty woman came from the back of the restaurant and walked up to their table. "Poppa Anselmi. So good to see you, my friend." She hugged him. Not knowing why, Tara had the feeling this woman was a grandmother. It was probably her sweet motherly smile.

"Good to see you too, Joanne. How's business these days?"

"Pretty good. It's been hard keeping up with all the workers and cleanup crews manning the oil spill. They booked up all the hotels and eat out a lot. And you, Remi Dubois. Why aren't you out on water patrol today?" She ruffled his hair like he was a ten year old kid.

"Miss Joanne." He nodded in respect. "I'm on my days off so I'm leavin' the work to someone else today."

She smiled and then noticed Chance.

"Oh my Lord! Chance!" she exclaimed. He stood and gave her a hug. "I haven't seen you since you left for the Army. You're looking good, and boy have you grown!"

"You're looking mighty good yourself, Miss Joanne. I'd like to introduce you to my friend, Meagan. She's from out of state and we thought we'd treat her to a fine Cajun meal."

The woman held out her hand to Tara. "Pleasure to meet you, Miss Joanne."

"Just Joanne, sweetie. Have you ever eaten real Cajun food before?"

"No, ma'am. Oh, wait. I guess I have. Chance fixed me a Cajun omelet the other day."

Remi couldn't hold his tongue. "You mean to tell me you actually ate something he cooked? On purpose?"

Chance gave him an irritated look. "You're pushin' me, Dubois."

Joanne interrupted their banter. "Well, Meagan. I'll bring you something special once you've had your meal." She looked at Remi, then Tara, then Chance. She leaned down whispering something in Chance's ear. She pointed toward Remi making Chance laugh. "I'll send Daphne out here to take your orders."

Chance lost his smile. He jumped up and shouted, "Wait!" But she had already turned toward the kitchen. "*Maudit!* Dammit!" he grumbled plopping back down in his chair. Poppee and Remi snickered.

"Who's Daphne?" Tara was guessing she was someone from Chance's past, hopefully not recent. He moaned just as a woman approached their table and let out a gasp.

"Chance! Honey!" She dropped her notepad on the table and put her arms around his neck. Tara's back stiffened. She was pretty enough but she wasn't a supermodel. There was a wild gleam in her eyes. Chance pried her arms off his neck and scooted his chair closer to Tara's draping his arm around her shoulder. He told the woman hello. Her exuberant demeanor changed the moment she spotted Tara.

"Who are you?" Her tone was aggressive.

Without hesitating, Tara rubbed her hand across Chance's chest as she eyed the woman. "I'm Meagan, Chance's lover." Poppee and Remi were giggling.

"*Lover*? No way. Chance and I have been dating for years."

"Uh, Daphne? We haven't dated since high school," he countered.

Daphne turned her attention from Tara to Chance with a piercing glare. "How dare you cheapen what we have? I've been patiently waiting for you to come back to me."

"It was two weeks! Two measly weeks! In high school! Which was... how many years ago?" he retorted. Remi and Poppee were giggling so much everyone in the restaurant turned to watch. Chance glared at them both. Poppee cleared his throat and spoke.

"Daphne, darlin'. We're getting mighty hungry. How 'bout you take our orders, sugar?"

The woman did an about face, a different persona emerging. "Why certainly, Poppa Anselmi. What would you like? The gumbos are great tonight."

Hmm. Split personality? Tara thought.

Daphne finished taking their orders and went back into the kitchen.

"President of your fan club?" Tara stabbed Chance in the ribs grinning.

"It was what, fourteen years ago? The woman's delusional. I haven't even seen her since I left for the Army."

Remi leaned across the table like he was going to tell them all a big secret. He spoke in a hushed tone so only they could hear. "Every time we come here, either me or Poppee, she asks about you, Chance, and every time we tell her you're out of state and might never come back. Every time she says she's waiting for lover boy to come back and claim her. I think she's obsessed with you and would stalk you if she could. You'd better stay away from her before she does something drastic."

Both Tara and Chance stiffened at his comment, the obsessed stalker implication hitting a bit too close to home. Poppee waved two fingers in Remi's direction calling him in closer. When Remi leaned down, Poppee took the hat off his own head and bopped Remi with it.

"What?" Remi looked perplexed and rubbed the spot where Poppee whacked him.

"Well at least your stalker hasn't gone psycho yet." Tara smiled at Chance but she knew it was weak.

"*Well*?" Poppee drolled. "Dat's not entirely true."

They all looked at him. "She did bust out da windows of his truck da last year y'all were in high school. If I remember right, dat was when you took Lacy to prom instead of her, t-boy."

Tara stiffened and gave Chance a disbelieving look.

"Who is *Lacy* and how many more women are going to pop up at this table?"

"Not a good subject, Poppee. Change it quick," Chance ordered.

"Yep. Guess I shoulda kept dat story to myself. Sorry, t-boy. But don't you worry none, Miss Meagan. Daphne? She's jus' not quite right in da head."

"Forget wonder woman. Who is Lacy?" She was a little more determined and direct to her Cajun protector himself.

He just groaned and sank a little lower in his chair. Another waitress walked past their table and stopped to take an order from a couple seated behind them. This one was wearing a semi-short black skirt which hit mid-thigh with a low cut white tank top displaying a generous portion of cleavage. The outfit maximized her hour glass figure and made her legs look a mile long. Long, dark wavy hair bounced across her shoulders. Remi's eyes lit up like a Christmas tree when he spotted her.

"Who's she?" Tara whispered to Chance.

"She's Candy. She serves drinks here. Once upon a time she and Remi were an item but, as with every woman he meets, it didn't last long."

Candy walked away from the other table and stopped in front of theirs. Remi grabbed her empty hand and placed a kiss on top of it.

"Candy, sweetheart. You're looking mighty fine tonight. How you been doin', honey?" His velvety sensual voice was humming.

"Just the same as I always am whenever you come in here, Remi. What can I get you?" He eyed her up and down and quirked up a sexy little grin.

"I don't think what I want tonight is on the menu. So how 'bout beer for the men and white wine for the lady?"

Candy rolled her eyes. "Sure, sugar. Anything for you." When Candy looked up and saw Chance, she smiled. "Chance Anselmi. Where the hell have you been hiding yourself, you big lug?" Leaning toward him, he semi-stood and they hugged.

"It's been a long time, Candy. How are the kids doin'?" He took his seat once more.

She shrugged her shoulders. "Don't know anymore. They decided to go live with their daddy in Texas. I don't hear from them very often. I'm a loner now."

"Sorry to hear it."

Remi straightened up in his chair. "So, maybe what I'm wantin' tonight is available after all, huh?" He gave her a sassy, sexy grin. She gave him the same in return.

"Not on your ever lovin' life, Dubois. Been there -- done that. Ain't gonna go there again. But thanks anyway." She tugged on his goatee.

As she turned and walked away, Remi slid down into his seat extending his long legs out straight under the table. "Too bad," he mumbled to himself.

Candy returned a few moments later with their drinks. When she placed Remi's beer in front of him, she leaned in causing her cleavage to be eye level with Remi's eyes. He kept them trained there until she straightened up.

"Enjoy." She smiled and rounded the table taking drinks to the couple behind them. Remi cranked his head around and watched her the entire time. He sunk down even further in his seat. As she passed him by, he bent his head back and smiled up at her. She patted his cheek and smiled back. As she moved on, he cocked his head to the side, sunk even further down in his seat and leaned down toward the floor.

"What the hell you doin', boy?" Poppee asked.

Holding up his thumb and index finger with an eighth inch space between them, Remi answered, "If only her skirt was this much shorter..."

Pop. He tried to cover his head as Poppee bopped him once again but he just wasn't fast enough. Chance and Tara both laughed.

Throughout the meal, a steady parade of woman showed up at their table to either hug on Remi, hug on Chance, or hug on both of them. A few even hugged on Poppee. Upset at the steady cavalcade of women, Tara clunked her fork down on her plate.

"Have you two been sharing women or something?"

Total silence ensued until Poppee roared with laughter.

"I done told you boys one day all dat womanizing would come back and bite you both on your asses."

Chapter Twenty-Nine

With nerves on edge and unable to sleep, Tara stepped into the kitchen hoping to find a coffee pot and grounds. She rummaged through canisters on the counter until she unearthed the coffee. When she finished setting up the coffee, she sat at the table with her feet on the seat of the chair waiting. Resting her chin on her knees, her thoughts wandered to happier times in her life when friends and family were in abundance.

She sorely missed Tracy and Meagan. Being a big sister was fun. The two girls tried to grow up too fast by emulating her every move. She happily accepted the responsibility of being a role model for them. She loved them so much. Now all she had was Timmy. He'd been a God send at a time when depression was trying to overtake her life. She loved him dearly too, but love for a pet just couldn't replace family love.

The coffee pot gurgled. She hoped it didn't awaken the others.

"What's the matter, t-sha? Can't sleep?"

Poppee's voice startled Tara. "I'm sorry, Poppee. Did I wake you?"

"*Non*, sha. I'm an old man who don't sleep worth a crap no ways. You made enough coffee for two?" He smiled.

She nodded as he walked to the counter. Grabbing two mugs out the cabinet, he filled them both and placed one in front of her. Turning a chair sideways, he sat down.

"So tell me, little one. What troubles you so dat you can't sleep?"

She pasted on a smile even though she felt more like crying. "I work nights. I guess my internal clock is messed up." He studied her face for a moment. She hoped she'd fooled him.

"Dat may be, but it's not what has you drinkin' coffee at four in da mornin'. You know, we Cajuns are known to be pretty good listeners. Tell me what's ailing you, sweetie."

It was a long time since Tara confided in anyone. With eyes beginning to mist, she bore her soul to the kind man.

"I was remembering my family. My parents were firm with us but fair. We got into our share of trouble as kids, but not once did they raise a hand to us. No matter what the big deal of the day was, we always had their support. I remember once when Tracy got into Mom's makeup. She was trying to act grown up like me. Everything I did, she wanted to do. Mom could have blasted her, but instead, she sat her down and showed her how to put the makeup on properly."

"How old was Tracy?" His voice sounded interested and kind.

"She was ten. Meagan was eight. He took them all away from me."

She couldn't control the wobble in her voice. Silent tears rimmed her eyes and she fought to hold them back.

Without hesitation, Poppee wrapped her in his arms. Her fight to maintain control ended as she caved in and wept openly for the first time in forever in the comfort of his warmth.

"You just let it all out, little one. It's not good to keep da bad things bottled up inside. Dat's what makes us crazy, you know. I think dat's why Chance is a little bit crazy. He holds everything inside ever since he lost his parents. Sometimes it makes him plum loco. Like da time when he was a young'un and he tried wrestling a cai'mon down at da camp."

Tara sniffled and looked up at him. "A what?"

"A cai'mon -- an alligator. Mind you, dat there gator was nothin' but a pup. But Chance, he don't care. He rolled all over the swamps with dat thing before he realized all he had to do was use his thumb and index finger to clamp dat gator's mouth shut and stop him from movin'."

Still in his arms, she was amused picturing the big guy being bested by a baby alligator.

"You tellin' wild stories again, old man?" Chance was leaning against the door jamb, his arms folded over his bare chest, ankles crossed.

While Poppee glanced over her head, Tara turned in his arms to see the man standing in the doorway, all six plus feet of him. Hair sleep tousled, chest bare, and unsnapped jeans riding low on his lips, he looked like a centerfold straight out of *Playgirl.* Her stomach quivered. When he caught sight of her tear streaked face, he rushed over and knelt down beside her.

"Tara. What's wrong? Why are you crying?" His voice was filled with concern. Before she could answer, Poppee intervened.

"She's a girl, you idiot. They cry jus' to clear out da eyes sometimes. Why don't you get me a refill if you gonna stay here and be a pest?" Poppee shoved his coffee mug in front of Chance's face. Chance took the hint and the mug and walked to the coffee pot.

While his back was turned, Tara leaned over and planted a soft kiss on the old man's cheek. "Thank you, Poppee."

"Anytime, t-sha, anytime."

*****

After filling Poppee's cup and filling one for himself, Chance turned with both mugs in his hands. His grandfather was gone. "Where did he go?"

Tara shrugged as she wiped tears from her face and eyes. He put the mugs down on the table and turned a chair around so he could face her.

With a very gentle touch, he tucked a wayward curl behind her ear.

"Why the tears?" She shrugged again while new moisture glistened in her eyes. "Come on, *chère*. Don't hold back. Please talk to me."

After fidgeting with her hands a few moments and keeping her eyes averted, she finally looked up at him. The pain on her face broke his heart.

"It's so much to handle, you know? For the last few years, the pain has been slowly subsiding. Sure, I think about my family every day, but the cutting pain which would come when I thought about them had begun to ease. Since the asshole escaped, it's back with a vengeance and hits me harder every time I remember."

A gleaming solitary tear fell from her eye. It took a slow trek down her cheek. Chance reached over and lifted the tear with his finger. Pressing it to his mouth, he kissed the tear away.

She took in a deep breath. "I feel safe here with all of you, but at the same time, I can't help but worry he'll find us just like before. I'm beginning to wonder if there's any place I can run where he can't find me."

Her words angered him. "No. Do not let yourself be fearful. I've told you before, *chère*, and I'll tell you once more. I will not let him hurt you ever again. We're leaving here in a few hours. My family has a camp in the swamps not too far away. We're going to hide out there for a while. No one knows where we're going except Poppee and Remi. My boss, Reggie, doesn't even know. From now on, no more fear. Trust me, Tara."

"I want to."

"Then do." He bent down and gently kissed her. It was a reassuring kiss full of promise. When they came up for air, he took a deep breath and touched his forehead to hers. "You do things to me, you know."

Tara lifted her head and stared back at him. Then she gave him the sweetest smile which unglued him. "I hope the things I do to you are good."

"The best. Now back to bed. We leave right after breakfast."

She stood up and nodded. Placing her warm hand against his cheek, she leaned down and kissed him. "Thank you," she whispered against his lips, then turned and walked away.

Chapter Thirty

The boat glided calmly through the murky swamp water like a hot knife slicing through butter. A dense layer of water lilies hugging the shoreline rolled with the waves triggered by the boat's passage. Tara was fascinated with all she saw along the way despite her uncomfortable state. Chance made her don a life vest. The adult one wasn't small enough, so she was wearing one meant for a large child. It was snug, confining, and aggravating the crap out of her.

All in all though, the trip through the wetlands was a sight to behold. As the boat turned right down one of the many canals which formed a maze through the swamps, a building slowly came into view on the right side of the canal. To her, it looked rather large. She'd never seen a "camp" before, so she had nothing to compare it to.

Slowing to an idle, the boat drifted into a slip in front of the camp. After shutting off the engine, Chance grabbed a rope and secured the vessel to a huge supporting pylon. Buddy leaped on the wharf and took off to play. Chance jumped up too after unloading the luggage.

Turning around, he put his hand out to help Tara get out of the boat. With Timmy in one arm, she looked down at the gap between the edge of the boat and the wharf. It looked huge though in actuality, it was probably less than a foot wide.

"You comin' with me or are you gonna sleep in the boat?"

She frowned. "You going to pull me up there or let me drop down into the ugly black water?" She tried to mimic his Cajun accent without much success.

He kicked up a grin. "You never know what a bad ass Cajun will do, *chère*, but have a little faith, will ya, woman?"

She took in a gulp of air and grabbed hold of his hand. He yanked her up in one swift motion. She squealed like a little girl as she landed hard against his broad chest clinging to him like he was a lifeline, Timmy meowing away on her arm.

"Comfy?" His eyes gleamed with mischief as he tightened his grip around her waist.

She swatted his chest and pushed away. "Get over yourself, Frenchie."

He lifted his head and laughed as she walked toward the camp, Timmy in hand and Buddy nipping at her feet.

"Thanks, Chance!" he yelled at her back. "You're welcome, Tara," he added. She gave him a one finger salute without turning around.

Grabbing the luggage, Chance followed Tara to the steps leading to the porch surrounding the camp. The building sat fifteen feet high in the air atop massive wooden pillars.

At the bottom of the steps she halted, her head tilting back as she read the sign attached to the overhang just above the entrance of the porch. She turned around and looked at him.

"Camp Fluffy?"

He nodded and smiled. "Fluffy was the family cat when this place was built. They never came here without Fluffy."

Tara grinned and looked down at Timmy in her arms appreciating his family's love for their own furry friend. She turned and walked up the steps.

As Tara placed a hand on the door knob, Chance pulled her back. "Have you listened to anything I've told you so far?" He was vehement.

She turned to face him, pouting. "What now?"

"I go in first. Always. Stay here until I give the 'all clear'."

Rolling her eyes, she took a step to the side allowing him access to the front door. He put the bags down and drew the .40 caliber Glock 22 tucked in his waistband. He opened the door and entered. After checking each room, he yelled the coast was clear.

The first room she walked in was the living room. To the right was a mantled fireplace with a couch facing it and an armchair was on the left. A second couch stretched along the far right wall. Two doors bordered each side of the fireplace. The room was spacious and airy. Although the furniture was far from new, it was well kept.

She spotted another door to the left of the room but couldn't tell where it lead. Straight ahead was the entrance to the kitchen.

"Quaint," she commented.

"It's not the Ritz, but it is the safest place on the planet." He slipped the Glock back in place behind his back.

Buddy was roaming through the place like he owned it. Tara let Timmy down and on the floor. After one rub against her leg, he plopped his big furry body on the area rug in front of the fireplace making himself at home. The new surroundings did nothing to impress him.

"The bedroom to the left of the fireplace is the guest room. As kids, Remi and I used to share the one on the right since it has bunk beds. The larger bedroom over there is the master. You can have that one."

"And where do you plan to sleep?"

He lifted a brow, grinned, and pointed to the guest bedroom. "There are a few things I need to tell you about the camp."

"What? The ghost of Christmas past lives here?"

He grinned again. "No ghosts but plenty of things I'm sure you're not used to."

"Such as?"

"First off, the stove. It's not electric. It runs on propane, so until I hook it up to the propane tank, it won't work."

"No sweat. You'll be doing all the cooking anyway, right?" She smirked.

"Yeah, right. Second. We have no modern plumbing here. The shower works with rain water from the cistern but we need to haul water from the canal to flush the toilet."

"And just what in the heck is a cistern?" She was distracted by her surroundings.

"Do you remember seeing the big barrel shaped thing sitting on the left side of the camp when we came in?"

"Yes. It's a cistern?"

He nodded.

"And what exactly does a cistern do?"

"Not much of anything. It holds fresh rain water. We use the water for showering and washing dishes."

She nodded like she understood even though she didn't. "Okay. What other unusual anomalies do we have here?"

"No electricity except when we run the generator. I'll go out and start it up in a minute. There's a light plant next to the generator which powers the lights and doubles as a tool shed."

"And?"

"No fridge. We have an old deep freezer on the back porch. If he does his damn job, Remi should bring us ice tomorrow to fill it up. It's where we store our perishable food. Until we get ice, we'll keep the perishables in the ice chest on the front porch. It's very important to keep the ice chest closed so critters can't get into our food supply."

"Is that it?"

"Not quite." He left and returned carrying a pair of white vinyl boots.

"What are those?"

"Shrimper's boots."

"They look awfully small for your big clodhopper feet."

He laughed. "They're not for me, Tara. They're for you. This camp sits on marsh land. Water pretty much surrounds the place making it a mini-island of sorts. If you wander off, keep your feet moving. You'll need these if you don't want to sink knee deep in mud and get stuck."

Tara took the boots from him, eyeing them like they had fungus growing inside. She marched into the master bedroom and placed them by the door. When she came back, she noticed him eyeing her like she was an oasis and he was a parched man. He straightened up shaking his head.

"One last thing."

"And what would it be?"

"Tomorrow, you learn how to shoot."

"Shoot? Shoot what?"

He looked at her with unbelieving eyes. "A gun. In case I'm not around, you'll be able to defend yourself."

"No freaking way. Don't like them, can't stand to see them much less touch them."

"Doesn't matter. You will learn how to shoot one tomorrow."

"Sure thing." She dripped a little sarcasm into her words.

"I'm gonna go start the generator and get some power goin'." As he got midway to the door, he turned and gave her a stern look. "You stay inside and don't come out unless I say so."

"Yes, sir, mister boss man, sir," she chided.

"I'm serious, Tara. Just because we're isolated doesn't mean we let our guard down."

She breathed deep. "I know. But damn, can't you lighten up just a little, Frenchie?"

He lifted a brow and put a hand to his hip.

"Guess not. All right, already. Go!" She shooed him away with her hands.

Moments later while exploring each room, she heard the whir of the generator float through the air. Evidently the man knew what he was doing as far as a generator was concerned.

She walked down a hallway between the kitchen and her bedroom. There was a door to her right. She opened it and found the bathroom. Nothing unusual there. Just as she was shutting the door, a strange noise sounded from inside the tub. As she peeked back in, an animal hopped out of the tub onto the floor. She shrieked and slammed the door shut. In what was a matter of seconds, Chance was standing at her back.

"What happened?" He was a little breathless grabbing her by the shoulders.

Her hand was still on the door knob shaking like a leaf. She gulped. "Animal in there." Her voice was vibrating with tension.

Prying her hand off the knob, he opened the door and peered inside. Quickly shutting it, he started laughing.

Tara whipped around and punched him solid in the chest. "You stop making fun of me right now, do you hear me?" she barked.

Still laughing, he grabbed her wrist to stop the assault. "It's just Bandit. It's a raccoon, Tara. He won't hurt you if you don't hurt him."

She huffed. "Well how the hell am I supposed to know that?"

"You could've asked."

"You weren't here!" she bellowed. "Are you going to get it out of there or not?"

"Yes, I'm going to get it out of there. I'd better set him free before you find a butcher knife and try to slash his throat," he chimed jokingly.

Immediately, he realized his faux pas. The slashing jibe was an inappropriate thing to say to a woman who agonizingly watched her family die by the knife.

His smile faded. He tried putting his arms around her. "Tara, I'm sorry. I didn't mean to..."

"Leave me be." She held up a hand as she walked to the living room.

"Damn stupid idiot, Anselmi." She could hear him chastising himself.

*****

After dinner they both settled onto the couch, Tara at one end, Chance at the other, and Timmy in between. Tara was reading one of her books. Chance had various gun parts on the coffee table along with a couple other weapons and was cleaning the guns.

"Just how many guns did you bring here? What the heck is this?" Tara's curiosity was evident with her words. Chance grabbed her arm stopping her before she reached the table.

"Don't touch it. It's a landmine."

Tara's brows rose. "Why do you have a landmine?"

Chance could tell by her face she was picturing herself walking around the yard and stepping on one or maybe Timmy or Buddy accidently tripping one. He saw her shiver.

"You aren't planning on putting them out in the yard, are you?"

Chance moved closer to her, as close as he could with Timmy playing guard cat between them. "No, *chère*. I have them just in case. As for the guns, I only brought my FBI issue, a .40 Caliber Glock. This one." He pointed toward the dismantled gun on the table he was in the process of cleaning. "Now the long, single barreled rifle is a .22 single shot we keep here and the long one with two barrels is a double barreled shotgun. This one here is a small pistol Poppee keeps here."

The look on Tara's wide eyed face, a mixture of a little fear and a lot of curiosity, had Chance smiling. It did make him realize she was clueless about guns.

"Don't worry about the guns until tomorrow. Okay, Tara?"

Tara looked up, then, reached and pulled his face down to hers, kissing him full on the mouth. She took him by surprise, but it didn't take him long before he was kissing her back. He could feel her hands wander over his chest. She started to unbutton his shirt. His skin burned wherever she touched it. She pulled away from his mouth only long enough to lay butterfly kisses on his chest. The touch of her mouth made him shiver. He was moaning, her name leaving his lips like a prayer. A searing pain ran down his arm. He jumped up knocking Tara back.

"Damn cat!" he hissed."

A bewildered looking Tara yelled at him, "Why are you fussing Timmy? He hasn't done anything wrong."

"He didn't? Then how the hell did this happen?" Chance held up his arm, the skin covering the side of his forearm scratched and quite bloody.

"Oh, my," she muttered, her gaze transfixed on his wound. She grabbed the arm of the couch wobbling a bit. And with that, she fell into his arms passing out cold. Chance looked down at his little wildcat. "Well this is not how I hoped tonight would end."

Chapter Thirty-One

The brilliant afternoon southern sun was shining its golden rays down on the camp ground. Chance adjusted a pair of aviator glasses over his eyes. He placed an empty soda can atop an old cypress stump then walked back toward Tara who was impatiently waiting.

"I told you. I don't like guns," she pouted.

"And I don't care if you do or don't. You're gonna learn how to shoot."

He thrust the butt end of the gun in her hand and closed her fingers around it. Taking her by the shoulders, he spun her around to face the northern edge of the swamp. Wrapping his arms around her shoulders, he slid his hands down her arms slow and methodical encompassing her tiny hands in his.

He placed her fingers around the butt end of the gun. She glanced at him over her shoulder, pinpoints of anxiety gleaming in her eyes.

"Eyes straight," he commanded.

She swiveled her head forward with a sigh.

"Now. Keep your hands wrapped around the gun like this." To emphasize his point, he repositioned her hands and fingers until she had a firm grip. The sensual feel as his fingertips slid over her creamy skin captured his attention. He gave himself a mental shake to try and focus on the task at hand, but it didn't help the cause any when she wiggled her little ass rubbing it against his groin. He moaned and tried again to refocus.

"See the can sitting on top the cypress stump over there?"

He saw her squint in the general direction he'd indicated. She nodded once.

"Okay. Aim the little notch at the end of the gun barrel about half an inch below the can, take a deep breath, and hold it. Then gently, very gently, squeeze the trigger."

He watched her focus her gaze on the end of the gun and aim it at the can. Dropping the sight down half an inch like he'd told her, she took in a huge gulp of air and held it in her lungs, and held it... and held it...

"Shoot, Tara!"

And held it...

"Dammit! Shoot!"

She flinched and the air she'd been holding in came whooshing out of her lungs. At the same moment, she closed her eyes and squeezed the trigger -- *hard*!

The gun's recoil shoved her back into his body. Had he not been behind her, she would've fallen flat on her ass.

She spun around and faced him. He could see her heart pounding against her chest at breakneck speed. "Did I hit it?" She was breathless. "Well, did I?" she asked again anxiously when he didn't immediately answer.

Chance looked down at his chest where the gun was now aimed straight in front of his heart. Ever so slowly, he put his index finger on the side of the gun barrel and swiveled its aim away from both of them. He pried her trembling fingers loose from the gun as he slid the dangerous weapon out of her hands.

"Well, did I hit the target or not?" she asked again, oblivious to the fact she'd aimed the gun at his heart.

He stepped around her and headed toward the target without speaking.

Chance made his way toward the cypress stump and soon spotted the can still in evidence on its perch. About five feet ahead of the target, he stopped and leaned down picking something up off the ground. Standing straight, he held up a furry animal by its hind feet.

"If your target was this, then yeah, you hit it," he yelled.

"Oh. My. God! I killed Thumper?"

Chance walked back with the rabbit's hind legs hooked between his fingers. "It's okay. You just snagged us supper."

With the rabbit dangling from his hand, he headed for the camp leaving her alone to freak out over her first and probably last practice shoot... and first kill.

Chance cleaned the rabbit Tara killed and put it in the ice chest along with their other perishables. Since evening was coming on soon, he wanted to wait and cook it the next day for lunch. So with twilight dangling on the horizon, they sat on the front porch swing having their meal consisting of bologna sandwiches, chips, and chilled sodas.

*****

Two hours after they settled in for the night, Chance heard Tara scream. With boxers on, he took off toward the master bedroom. When he opened the door, she was sitting upright in bed with her face in her hands.

Chance leaned against the doorframe eyeing her. "What's wrong, Tara?" He walked toward the bed and sat down beside her.

"Nothing." She pushed her hair upwards. A mask of pure disgust covered her face.

"You had a bad dream?"

"Yes."

The look of pain in her eyes was killing him. "Same one?"

She nodded. "I'm fine now, Chance. Go back to sleep."

"You want me to get you something to help you sleep?"

"No. Please, just leave me be."

She lay back down and hugged her pillow. Some undefined emotion tugged at his heart. He just couldn't figure out how to help her deal with the pain. He turned and quietly left.

*****

"Where's my son, Junior?" John Cruz yelled into the receiver. "You were supposed to deliver him to me and I haven't seen hide nor hair of him. Where are you hiding him?"

"I'm not. He's bound and determined to get to the girl. Twice already he's missed his shot at her. She's being hidden in a very secluded part of the country, but I've managed to find her. I'll be sending him on his way there soon. I've warned him, John. This is his last chance at getting the girl. From now on, I'm through playing his games."

"You can't skip out on me now. You've still got work to do."

"Like hell. I've kept the FBI off his ass like we agreed. I'm finished my part of this deal. Now, if you want me to set him up so he'll never be found again, just say the word. I'll get him and that damned wild obsession of his out of this country where no one will ever be able to find them. So, what do you say, my old friend?"

Cruz let out an exasperated breath. "How much is this going to cost me?"

"Another quarter mil in my bank account by noon. It will be your final payment."

"Do it."

"Then consider it done and them gone."

Chapter Thirty-Two

"*Maudit diable a mad*! Damn devil!" French and English cuss words flew as Chance frantically paced on the porch. The mid-morning sun began heating up the air and he was already hotter than a firecracker.

"Tara!" He paced in front of the ice chest. "The woman never listens, does she?"

Swinging the door open, Tara stepped out onto the porch. "What's wrong?"

"I asked you when we got here yesterday to do one little thing, didn't I?"

"What are you talking about?"

He pointed toward the ice chest which was now empty except for wet scraps of paper and a few small bits of food. "You were the last one to go in the ice chest last night. Didn't I ask you to make sure it was latched tight? Didn't I? I even said please, didn't I?"

Eyebrows furrowed in confusion, she peered down into the ice chest. For all intents and purposes, it was empty. Their perishable food was gone -- even Thumper.

"What the hell happened to the rabbit and the rest of our food?"

He gave her a stiff smile. "Why do you think we call the daffy *chaoui*, Bandit?"

"The what?"

"*Chaoui* -- raccoon. The one you found in the bathtub." He nudged the lid on the ice chest open. "Since *someone* didn't snap it tight like I asked her to, he ate all our food."

Tara put a hand over her mouth in surprise. "We don't have any more food? What are we going to do?"

"Oh, we have food all right." His voice was infused with sarcasm.

"I thought you said all our perishables were in there. Where's the rest of it?"

He pointed his finger to the canal in front of the camp. "Out there, and since you're the one who let Bandit get into the ice chest, *you're* the one who's gonna catch our next meal."

The total cost of food lost to Bandit: *maybe one hundred dollars.*

The look of shock on Tara's face when she realized what she would have to do to replace their food: *priceless.*

*****

"Just what is it you catch in these waters?" Tara was enthused about the prospect of fishing since she'd never done it before. Chance was sitting on the wharf, legs dangling over the water.

"We're gonna try to catch redfish and speckled trout. I have a line already set up for you. Come, *chère*. Sit right here and I'll show you how it's done."

She eased herself down next to him. "Okay. I'm ready. Shoot."

"First, you have to bait your line. We're using cacahoe minnows as bait."

She smirked. "What kind of minnows?"

He rolled his eyes and grinned. "Cock. A. Ho," he exaggerated each syllable. She giggled. "I'm gonna bait your line the first time since you're a rookie."

He pulled on a yellow plastic rope hooked around a pylon. With a whooshing sound, a black and yellow bait bucket surfaced on the water. After pulling it up onto the wharf, he opened the lid and pulled out a wriggling, fat minnow.

"Ew! It looks slimy," she squeaked.

"It is a bit slippery. Now take the hook and stab the minnow right here behind the eyes."

"No! Cruel!" She covered her eyes with her hands. Chance waited until she peeked through her fingers before continuing.

"See? He's fine. He's still floppin'. Now this reel is simple to operate. Put your thumb on this button here like this and keep it mashed. Then cast the line out over the water."

He demonstrated what to do like an old pro. The line sailed quite a distance before the minnow plopped in the water. "The most important thing to remember is once you bring the rod forward, don't forget to release the button so the line can flow freely. When the minnow hits the water, crank this lever right here forward. It'll lock the line in place. Got it?"

"I think so." She didn't sound very sure of herself. Chance reeled in the line and handed it to her. He stood and knelt behind her placing his arms over hers so he could help her cast. Involuntarily, he inhaled a deep breath of her scent. His groin tightened in delight from the sensual assault. Giving himself a mental head shake, he positioned her hand on the reel putting her thumb over the button.

"Ready?" She nodded. He helped her position the rod over her shoulder. "On three, we'll cast. One, two three!" The rod went forward but the tip hit the water right in front of the wharf. "Tara? What did I say was the most important thing to remember?" He tried to reel in his impatience.

"To release the button once I cast the line?"

"So why didn't you let it go?"

"I forgot."

He tried not to laugh. "All right. One more time, and this time..."

"I know. Let the button go."

"Yes. Let the button go. Ready? One, two three!"

The rod went forward and the translucent filament sailed through the air. The minnow plopped in the water a good distance away.

"Great! Now turn the handle like I showed you. Good. Now we wait for a bite."

"How am I going to know I've got one?"

"Depends. A trout tends to hit the bait a few times before swallowing it. It'll feel like a tug and release, tug and release. Let him pull it down before you lift it up. If it's a redfish, he'll chomp the minnow in one gulp and he'll pull it down fast. Set the hook as soon as you feel the downward pull."

"How long do you usually have to wait?" She was a might impatient.

"It depends on whether the fish are hungry. Sometimes minutes, sometimes longer."

He sat down next to her and threw out his own line just beyond where hers landed.

"Hey! That's my spot! Get your own," she complained. He laughed.

"There's plenty of fish in these waters, *chat marron*. It doesn't matter where you cast; they'll bite.

"You have got to tell me what that means, dammit!" Tara said. "Whoa!"

"Got a bite, *chère*?" He was amused at her reaction as he saw her rod tip dip a bit.

"Yes! At least I think so. It felt just like you said, a tug and release. What do I do?" Her enthusiasm was now in full bloom.

"Just hold on until he takes it. When you feel it going down, lean the rod down a little, then jerk it up quick to set the hook."

Right about then, he saw the tip of her rod bend again. Doing as he'd instructed, Chance watched as she lowered the rod a little then pulled up hard.

"Ah ha! I think I've got him! What do I do, Chance?"

The rod bent in half. He put his own line down and crouched down behind her.

"Pull up on it like this without reeling and then reel in while you're lowering it." He helped her through the process. "You've got a good one on there." She looked proud of her accomplishment so far grinning at him while she fought the fish.

"You think so?"

"Oh, yeah. You can tell by how hard he's fightin' you." After a few moments of reeling, the fish broke the surface of the water splashing about at their feet. Using a big net, he helped her snag it and lift it onto the wharf.

Once it was safely landed, she grabbed him around the neck and gave him a huge hug and peck on the cheek.

"My first fish! It's beautiful. What kind is it?" Her exuberance combined with their close proximity had him completely poleaxed. He felt emotion well up inside his heart. "Chance?"

"Uh, it's a speckled trout."

"How can you tell?"

They both bent down toward the fish. "See all these spots on the fish's body? It's the markings of a speckled trout."

"What do we do with him now?"

"I'll unhook him for you. He can stay out here on the wharf for a little while, but I'll have to fetch an ice chest in a bit to put him in."

"Oh, look! The minnow's gone." She was amazed. "Did the fish eat it?"

"Yep. You'll have to re-bait your line now."

"Me? All by myself?"

He grinned at her look of disgust. "Well, since you caught the first fish, I'll do it for you this time," he conceded.

They fished for a couple of hours while Buddy played in the yard and Timmy watched Buddy's antics from his perch on the bottom step. Tara caught four trout and two redfish. Chance had three trout and one redfish. She was out-fishing him, the natural born fisherman. When she made him aware of the fact, he muttered, "beginner's luck." They both laughed.

Chance was at the end of the wharf rinsing out the bait bucket when he noticed Tara standing proudly over her bounty of fish like a ten year old. The sight of her so happy made him wish he could take her picture.

She picked up the last fish she'd caught ready to put it in the ice chest when a big brown bird swooped down and snatched the fish right out of her hand. The sudden intrusion knocked her balance off kilter. With arms wind milling, her body tilted backward. She tumbled toward the water, yelling, "Chance! Help!"

"Tara!" He jumped up running toward where she'd fallen into the water. Scrambling to the edge of the wharf, he leaned down and reached out a hand to her. By the time he'd gotten there, she'd righted herself and was standing chest deep in the murky shallow water, her hands brushing the water soaked hair from her face. She sputtered and blew water out of her mouth.

"Give me your hand, Tara!"

She didn't move. "What the hell was that?" she asked, not making a move to reach for his hand.

"Tara! Give me your hand!"

Ignoring him, she pointed toward the shore at the brown pelican staring at them with her fish draped across his beak.

"That *thing* stole my fish!"

"Tara! Give me your damn hand! Gators roam these waters!"

Her eyes widened. With one swift jerk of her arm, she slapped her hand in his. He hauled her up onto the wharf in one quick swoop.

When she was steady on her feet, he looked down at her and roared with laughter. She was covered with muddy swamp water from head to toe. She pounded on his chest.

"Stop laughing, Anselmi. That damn bird stole my fish!" she griped.

He looked back at the shore and stared at the pelican still proudly displaying Tara's treasured catch.

"That's just old Blue."

"Old Blue? What? He hangs around here, too? What is this place, an animal refuge? I've never seen so many animals in one place at one time."

He laughed even harder as he once again took in her bedraggled appearance.

He watched Tara make her trademark move and put her fists on her hips. She stomped down the wharf toward the shore amidst his still bellowing laughter. She stopped short as Blue waddled to the wharf's entrance blocking her way.

The bird stared her down, her fish still hanging from his beak. She leaned in as if trying to get a closer look.

She turned back toward Chance. "Why is his beak blue?"

He stopped laughing and shrugged his shoulders, the heat of guilt rising to his face. "That old bird used to steal our fish when Remi and I came out here during the summers. We threw some blue paint at him to shoo him away."

Tara doubled over laughing.

The bird waddled past her and went stand next to Chance, fish flopping against his beak, rubbing its head against Chance's leg.

Tara cackled. "What? Now he loves you? And aren't brown pelicans a protected species? Isn't it a Federal crime punishable by law to harm them, Mr. FBI Man?" He could tell she was having a ball egging him on.

"Hey. We were young and stupid, okay? We weren't tryin' to hurt him, just scare him. We didn't realize we were breaking a Federal law. Anyhow, we paid our dues for the stunt."

"Really? What kind of dues?"

"Big ones. Grams liked to kill us both when she got hold of us. And Poppee's punishment hurt even worse than hers. When all was said and done, we'd spent the entire summer volunteering every afternoon at a local animal shelter. We felt so guilty about what we'd done, we didn't argue. Now, I just try makin' it up to the old bird by feedin' him some of my catch when I'm here."

"No wonder he stole my fish. You owe him." She laughed.

"Yeah. He probably figures if you're here with me, you'd be a sucker for him, too." Something red on Tara's leg caught Chance's eye. "Tara, you're bleeding." He leaned down to examine her leg. A two inch long gash was seeping blood onto her ankle.

"Ow." She winced when he touched the now tender area.

Without warning, he stood and swung her up in his arms, then started walking toward the camp leaving the pelican behind.

"What are you doing, Anselmi? It's just a little cut. I'm capable of walking on my own."

"You fell in swamp water. God knows what kind of bacteria are in there."

"And that has what to do with me walking on my own?"

"Not a damn thing. Now shut up and let me get you in the camp so we can clean out the wound and you can take a shower."

*****

After setting Tara on her feet in the bathtub, Chance poured fresh water from a bucket over her head to rinse the muddy swamp water off her body. Grabbing a towel, he patted her dry and then snagged her by the waist hiking her over the rim of the tub. He planted her butt down on the counter near the sink. Opening the medicine cabinet, he took out a white unmarked jar. After re-washing her ankle with fresh warm soapy water, he dried off the crimson gash with a clean towel and grabbed the jar off the counter.

"What's that?"

"Salve. It's a homemade concoction Grams made to help fight infection."

She reached out and snatched the jar away from him. "I can do it myself."

"Wait, Tara."

She ignored him and opened the jar taking in a good whiff of its contents.

"Whew! Geez, Louise! What the *hell* is this stuff made of? It stinks to high heaven!"

He laughed. "I told you, it's homemade, and no, you don't want to know what's in it."

"I am not putting that stuff on my leg. Un, un. No, siree."

"Tara. If you don't put it on..."

"What are you going to do, big boy? Beat me up?"

The thought of what he *wanted* to do to her had him staring at her... *hard.*

She stared right back.

For no fathomable reason, every ounce of control Chance had been fighting to maintain since he'd met this fiery woman shattered. Stepping up between her legs, he placed his hands on her knees and oh so slowly slid them up her soft thighs. Tucking his fingers under her legs, he pulled her to the edge of the counter close to his body, the center of her heat mere inches away from his own rock hard body. His hands once again glided up her thighs to the edge of her sinfully short shorts. Angling his head, he crushed her lips to his in an all-consuming powerful kiss. She moaned as he swept her lips with his tongue begging them to part. She complied allowing his tongue to enter the sweet hollow of her mouth.

Her taste was intoxicating. She hooked her fingers in his hair and gave a gentle tug which in turn caused a low rumbling groan in his throat. It matched hers as she tried to wriggle her body closer to his. His hands roamed over her tee shirt toward her breasts. His thumbs brushed the fringe of the firm mounds. He could feel her body shiver in anticipation.

He rubbed the calloused pads of his thumbs over the hardening tips of her breasts creating a friction which had her eyes closing as her head fell back. He whispered her name, his voice filled with unbridled passion.

"Tara. *Mon chat marron*. I want you. I need you."

Chance could see in her eyes that she needed him, too. His muscles tensed when he heard a strange sound.

"What?" She had picked up on the tenseness in his body.

"A boat motor's coming up the canal."

Tara's body tensed against his as he pulled away from her.

"You stay right where you are. Do not move a muscle until I tell you to." He gave her a warning look.

"But..."

"No buts, Tara. Stay. Right here. On this counter."

He leaned in and gave her another hard, quick kiss. Growling roughly, exasperated at the interruption, he cursed, "Dammit! If it's Remi, I'm gonna neuter him." Tara giggled. Chance placed a kiss to her lips to silence her. "Shh. Not a word." He moved away toward the bedroom to retrieve his gun.

*****

When Chance stepped out onto the porch, he caught sight of someone he didn't have a desire to see -- not now or ever again.

"Chance, darlin'. I didn't realize you'd be here. I've really missed you."

As he hit the path leading to the wharf, Lacy Lewis, his ex-girlfriend, jumped at him when he got within reach. She hugged him hard and long... a little too long for his satisfaction.

"What the hell are you doing here, Lacy?" He pried her arms off his neck.

"We wanted a little private time. This is Kenny, my boyfriend. Kenny, this is Chance, my ex-boyfriend."

Chance nodded to the man wishing he could tell him to be wary of this woman.

"And just how did you expect to get into the camp, Lacy? Breaking and entering?"

She dangled a key between her thumb and forefinger swinging it back and forth in front of his face. He made a swipe to snatch it from her hand, but she pulled it back out of reach making him grab air only.

"Hand it over, Lacy. You don't belong here anymore."

After taking in a deep breath, she gave in and handed over the key.

*****

Tara was peeking through the curtains at the scene unfolding near the wharf. She couldn't make out every word being said but she definitely caught wind of the blonde woman's name -- Lacy. Maybe now she'd find out what this woman was to Chance. Realizing she was feeling a huge tinge of jealousy at the sight of the woman's hands on his body, she made a bee line for the front door.

Walking down the worn path to the wharf, she heard the guy who'd accompanied the woman let out a low whistle. She noticed the tensing in Chance's shoulders. He was definitely pissed.

As she drew closer, she let her voice ring out. "Hey, sweetie. Who are our guests?"

With his back to her, Tara heard Chance murmur, "Freakin' woman *never* listens. Honey, didn't I ask you to stay inside?" His voice held a note of sarcasm. "Y'all need to leave, Lacy. *Now,*" he told her, his tone low and menacing. When Tara reached him, she wrapped a possessive arm around his waist.

"Well, well." Lacy's voice was filled with jealousy. "New bimbo?"

Tara moved away from Chance and stood toe-to-toe with the woman. He tried to grab her by the arm and pull her back but she shrugged him off. Eyeing Lacy from head to toe, she replied in kind. "Well, well. Old ho?"

Lacy moved even closer to Tara in an aggressive stance. Timmy, who'd followed her outside, stood at their feet and began hissing and spitting at Lacy. When the blonde noticed the cat, she backed away.

"Keep the mangy looking *thing* away from me or I'll kick it. I'm allergic to cats!"

Tara put on her best sarcastic smile. "You kick my cat, *bitch,* and I'll kick your ass."

Kenny pulled on Lacy's arm taking her further away from Tara. "Let's go, sweetheart."

Chance pulled on Tara's arm at the same time. "Back off, Tara," he warned. Kenny backed Lacy up onto the wharf toward their boat. Buddy, who'd been napping at the end of the wharf, ran toward the pair barking up a storm. He leaped into the air and caught Kenny at the back of his knees sending the man headfirst into the muddy water.

"Kenny!" Lacy shouted as her man flailed his arms trying to stand upright. Tara's laughter peeled through the warm summer air as Lacy leaned down trying to reach him.

"Grab hold of my hand, baby. I'll pull you up." Kenny extended his arm toward her outstretched one. As soon as he made contact, he pulled. She fell in the water head first right next to him. When she came up spitting and spewing, she pushed down on his shoulders sinking him under the water.

"You stupid idiot! Look what you've done! I'm all wet!"

Tara laughed so hard she had to grab her side to hold in the stitch tightening a muscle there. Chance groaned and then called off Buddy. He lumbered down the wharf and pulled out both water soaked idiots. Once they were back up on solid ground, he headed back toward the camp.

"Goodbye, you two. Have a nice life." He spun Tara by the shoulders when he reached her and they headed back toward the camp before she could cause any more trouble.

Chapter Thirty-Three

The fresh fish Chance fried for lunch was exquisite, but with her appetite diminished, Tara just shoved her food around the plate. Thoughts of Lacy and what she meant to the big Cajun man kept creeping into her brain making it hard to concentrate on anything else. She hadn't even realized she was frowning until he spoke.

"You mad at your food or somethin'?" he asked in between bites. She lifted her eyes toward him and dropped her fork down on her plate, mad because he'd caught her moping.

"Why won't you tell me about Lacy? Who is she, Chance? Or better yet, what is she to you?" She realized her tone was snippy, but he'd ignored her when she'd asked after the couple had left in the morning.

The corner of his mouth lifted in a sexy grin. "What, *chère*? You jealous?"

She picked up her fork and viciously stabbed a piece of lettuce. "No. Just curious is all."

He looked like he wished she'd said yes. "Lacy's my ex," he announced, his tone flat.

Her eyes widened in disbelief. "Your *ex-wife*?"

"No, *chat marron*. My ex-girlfriend. I never married."

She let out a huge sigh of relief. "So when did your relationship with her end?" She was compelled to find out about the woman.

"A long time ago. I want nothin' more to do with her."

"What happened between the two of you?" She knew she'd taken her questioning a little too far. He dropped his own fork and pushed himself away from the table, his chair falling backward as he stood. Glaring down at the fallen chair, he picked it up and righted it in place with some force. Without another word, he stalked out the room.

A little while later, Tara walked into the living room. Chance stood in front of the fireplace, his back to her, his muscles flexing with tension. She hadn't intended to make him angry. She was jealous at the sight of the other woman's hands on him.

She had to confront the truth. Feelings were rising within her for the handsome Cajun, but she just wasn't sure of his feelings about her. At first she thought he was holding back because of his commitment to his work, but they were safe and sound here in the swamps.

Maybe the kisses they'd shared were nothing more than moments of lust. One way or another, she had to know.

Stopping a step behind him, Tara lifted her hand to place it on his back, but he spun around and faced her, his sudden movement halting her momentum.

"Chance. I'm sorry. I didn't mean to pry into your past. It was rude of me. I just didn't know why I felt I had to push you. If you don't want to talk about Lacy, then fine, we won't talk about Lacy. I promise I'll never mention her again. In fact, I promise not to ask you anything whatsoever about your past again. Because if you really wanted me to know, you would have told me already, right? Anyway, I am sorry."

"Just shut the hell up and kiss me, woman." He pulled her toward him and locked his arms around her. The kiss he delivered was another scorcher. Every kiss he delivered filled her with heat.

Wrapping her arms around his big neck, she stood on the tips of her toes to get closer. In turn, he tightened his grip around her pulling her body flush to his. She let out a low, sexy moan when his hands started roaming down her backside landing on her butt. He reacted to the sound of her voice. The movement of his hands became more aggressive. She felt a blush rise to her cheeks when he made contact with the skin of her thighs. His touch was as smooth as silk against her skin.

His tongue sought hers. When she allowed access and their tongues met, zings of desire zapped the nerve endings all over her body. Her stomach muscles spasmed with delight. His velvet tongue performed an ancient ritual with hers driving her wild. From the sounds emanating deep in his throat, she knew he felt it too. Taking matters into her own hands, she placed them against his chest and shoved until his back was up against the wall near the fireplace. She leaned in and kissed him hard.

He groaned loudly with her show of aggression and pulled her legs up wrapping them around his waist. In one swift movement, he reversed their positions placing her back up against the wall. Their hands roamed and their kisses grew hotter. In another swift movement, he lifted his mouth off hers and shoved away from her making her off balance as she nearly hit the floor.

"What the hell is your problem now, Frenchie?" She was shouting at him trying to regain her balance, stunned and pissed to no end at his sudden rejection. She was getting damned frustrated with his hot and cold reactions.

*****

Standing a foot away from Tara so they had no contact, Chance took in a big gulp of air and closed his eyes as he tried to regain his pitifully meager self-control. When he opened them again and looked down at her, he couldn't mask the desire he knew was swimming in his eyes.

"Tara, *mon chère*." His voice was husky. "No matter how bad I want you, and trust me, I want you so bad I can imagine the taste of your sweetness on my tongue, I can't do this to you. You deserve the right to choose what you want on your own."

Furrowing her brows, she took a defensive stand. "Well what do you think I'm doing? You think you're forcing me? I *am* making my own choice. I'm an adult, you know. I can and do make my own choices. Grant it, I've made some pretty rotten ones in the past, but certainly I'm capable of having a fling and being able to walk away from it. You never give me any credit for anything. I can hold my own in a relationship without getting all possessive if that's what's stopping you. I'm not some pansy-assed virgin who would expect commitment. I'm a little smarter than that. And furthermore, I'm getting sick and tired of you coming on to me and not delivering the goods. If you want me, then take me!"

Her hands went straight to her hips in typical Tara's-pissed-at-something fashion and the sweet pink lower lip jutted out in full pout mode once again. Chance's honorable but meager self-control crumbled like a week old cookie.

He pulled her by the arm back into his personal space with an *oomph* slipping past her lips as she slammed into his body. Lifting her by the waist, he forced her legs to wrap around his torso to maintain her balance. He kissed her senseless while his hands roamed her back from top to bottom.

When they finally came up for air, he only had enough breath to utter one word. "Damn."

She leaned her head back to give him better access as his lips blazed a trail down her neck. When he reached her collar bone, he planted an open mouth kiss there and sucked on her sweet tasting skin. She all but growled making him do the same.

"So what the hell's been stopping you, Frenchie? Afraid you won't measure up?" She sure did like to taunt him.

He lifted his head and gazed into her emerald eyes. He saw so much desire in them, he was engulfed in it.

He lost the battle over his self-control. "Screw regulations." He headed toward her bedroom, the woman clinging to him like a fly stuck in honey.

"About damn time," she whispered in his ear. With her moist tongue, she licked his earlobe from top to bottom grabbing the lobe between her teeth just as he kicked open the bedroom door.

Like a man possessed, he growled as he dumped her on the bed making her bounce. Kicking off his shoes, he placed the gun tucked in his belt on the night stand and peeled the tight tee shirt over his head throwing it on the floor.

Tara whimpered when Chance's packs flexed in an age old male ritualistic display of strength and power.

Without hesitating, he unsnapped his jeans and yanked down the zipper. Hooking his thumbs in the belt loops, he shoved both pants and boxers down in one quick movement kicking them off. Still standing at the side of the bed, his heavy erection pulsed away.

"Good Lord," Tara said, her gaze fixed on his body. "No problem measuring up after all."

He grinned and lowered himself over her. With his knees tucked on each side of her thighs and his elbows caging in her head, he kissed her tenderly. Even though he was keeping his full weight from crushing her, he was close enough to cause a light friction between his body and hers.

A hungry groan came from somewhere deep inside Chance's chest. He'd felt Tara's nipples harden as he'd grazed her body. Blazing a trail of warm kisses down her neck, he met up with the plump curve of her breast, his tongue licking the salty-sweetness from her skin. She sucked in some air forcing her breast to swell up even closer to his mouth.

"Too much clothes," he murmured against her skin as he gripped the bottom of her tee shirt and yanked it over her head in one hurried motion. With a flick, he opened the front clasp of her lacey black bra exposing her rounded breasts. He couldn't help but stare.

"*Joli,* absolutely beautiful." Leaning down, he placed the tip of his tongue on the outer edge of one dark pebbling nipple. Her body jerked reacting to his touch.

"I love it when you talk that French crap to me."

He looked up at her with a playful smile. "I thought you said you hated it?"

"Only when you use it to keep me in the dark."

Without giving her warning, he captured the hardened nipple in his mouth and pulled. Her response became even more intense as he laved the bud with his tongue and then scraped his teeth over it before once again soothing it with his tongue.

After laying a line of wet kisses down the length of her body, he hooked his fingers in the waistband of her shorts and skimmed them down her legs leaving her in nothing but a lacey black thong. He smiled. "Nice. Matching undies."

"Uh, Chance?"

"Hmm?" He placed more hot moist kisses on her belly.

"Could you..."

"Could I what?" He kissed the spot just above her panty line. Her hips rose off the bed.

"Could you do it like in the romance novels and rip my panties off?"

He knew she could feel his smile break out as he pressed his lips to her tummy.

"Quit making fun of me." She swatted him on the shoulder.

He sat up with a smile and gazed into her eyes. His smile faded as he lost himself in the emerald green depths of pleasure reflected in them. Hooking a finger into the stringy panty, he yanked it away from her body just as she requested. With a moan, she threw her head back as he gasped.

"My God, Tara. You're beautiful."

"You're not so bad yourself, Frenchie."

He smiled as he slid his hands under her body and lifted. While she wrapped her arms around his neck and legs around his waist, he nibbled on her ear lobe. Goose bumps were visible on her skin. His body stiffened.

Tara sighed and plunked her head against his chest. Her breaths were coming short and quick. "What now?"

"Boat motor. Get dressed." Brusquely, he threw her back on the bed and jumped up grabbing his jeans.

"There's more damn traffic here than there is on the Vegas strip," she grumbled.

After zipping up his pants, he pointed a finger in her direction.

"I know, I know," she said in a sing-song voice. "Stay put. Don't move until I tell you, and don't utter a sound. I'm beginning to know the drill, Mr. FBI."

"Great. Now if you'd just stick to it, I'd be a happy camper."

He grabbed the Glock and stalked out the room.

Chapter Thirty-Four

Chance shouted as he stalked to the dock. "Remi Dubois! You have a cell phone. Couldn't you use it to call and warn me you were coming? I'm a little busy here."

"Now what would you be so busy doin' out here in the swamps?" Remi smirked.

Chance just bet he knew what Remi was thinking as he raked his eyes over Chance's bare chest and unsnapped jeans. "Just you never mind. Did you bring the supplies and ice?"

"Sure 'nuff. Why don't you give me a hand unloading?"

Chance glanced back at the camp and then dragged his fingers through his hair. "Yeah, sure. But first, I have to let Tara know everything's all right. You get started and I'll be back in a minute."

When Chance ran back into the camp to announce Remi's arrival and grab a shirt, he found Tara sitting on the side of the bed still naked, a dreamy look on her face.

"What the hell are you waiting for, woman? Get dressed before Remi comes in here, sees you *chu nu,* and I have to end up kicking his ass."

Tara let out an exasperated sigh as she slapped her hands against the sides of her legs. "See me *what*? Now what the hell does that mean?"

"It means bare-assed which is why I'd have to kill him. Get a move on, woman!" He took both ends of his shirt he'd picked up off the floor and twisted it around forming a rope. He let go one end in Tara's direction and swung it her way. It barely hit her shoulder, but the swat was meant to playfully sting.

"Ooh! You are so going to get it, Anselmi." She smiled while rubbing the offended spot on her shoulder. Remi's loud, booming voice filled the air.

"Hey, Anselmi! If you're gonna stay in there and play, I'm comin' up to join in the fun!"

Chance put his hand at the nape of Tara's neck and pulled her forward planting a whopper of a kiss on her lips. "Get dressed now or suffer the consequences," he teased.

Brows rising, Tara hopped to her feet like a professional gymnast and was half-way dressed before Chance could close the door behind him.

Chance headed back down to the wharf to help Remi unload the boat grinning at the thought of the woman in the camp. He couldn't believe his good fortune of finding a woman who challenged him at every turn and who appeared to be as faithful and as loyal as they came.

When he and Remi finished their chores, they met up with Tara sitting in the swing on the front porch, both Timmy and Buddy huddled at her feet.

"Well, well, Mr. Dubois. What brings you to Camp Fluffy on this warm end-of-summer afternoon?" Tara greeted him as he grabbed her hand and kissed it.

"*Mademoiselle* Roberts. It is truly a pleasure to see you again. My, but the weather here seems to agree with you. Your hair has the appearance of having been tousled by a gentle southern breeze and your face is flushed to a rosy hue by a kiss from the warm summer sun. Anyway, I assume it's the weather which has been kissing you and has you looking like a well-loved woman in the afterglow of passion."

Chance smacked him on the shoulder. "Shut the hell up, Dubois."

Remi's laughter floated on the warm southern air while Tara tried smoothing down her wild hair, her face growing redder by the second.

"Are you able to stay for supper?" Chance asked.

"Depends on who's cooking. If it's you? *Hell* no. If this pretty little woman is going to show off her culinary skills? *Hell* yes. I wouldn't miss it." Tara giggled.

"You're cruisin' for a bruisin', Dr. K." Chance huffed.

"What did you just call him?"

"Dr. K."

"Don't you start, Anselmi," Remi warned around a frown.

"Wait, Dr. K?" A confused looking Tara asked.

"Ask him how he got his nickname." Chance folded his arms across his chest as Tara looked back and forth between him and Remi. Remi let out a disgusted sounding groan.

"Body bags," Chance announced.

"Oh, hell!" Tara squeaked. "You've found lots of bodies."

Chance started laughing. "Go ahead, Dr. K. Tell her how you came by the name."

Remi just rolled his eyes and kept his mouth shut.

"We call him that because he's always got a stack of body bags in his patrol boat like he's going to find a freakin' load of bodies on patrol. Truth is, he's only found one: a mummified body which floated from its burial site at Chenierre near Grand Isle after a hurricane."

"I still don't get it." Tara still looked somewhat perplexed.

"Don't you remember the doc a while back who allegedly assisted mercy suicides?"

A look of recognition crossed her face as she finally caught on to the significance of the nickname. Her laughter was boisterous and had Timmy meowing and Buddy howling.

Taking the ball cap off his head and flinging it to the ground, Remi's face grew taut. "That's it, Anselmi. I'm going to kick your ass now."

"You've got to catch me first, Dubois." Chance made a mad dash down the steps with his friend in close pursuit.

*****

All three sat in the kitchen having coffee. Remi and Tara got to know one another a whole lot better while Chance had the opportunity to catch up on some hometown news.

The camaraderie between the two men was making Tara a little melancholy. She missed her friends. "I wonder if Logan had any luck at the contest." Her thoughts spilled from her mouth. Both men stopped talking and stared at her vocal musing. She noticed their glares.

"What?"

"Logan? Who's Logan?" Remi asked with a raised brow.

Chance put a hand on his friend's forearm. "Trust me. You don't want to go there."

Tara swatted Chance on the shoulder. "Damn, but you can be rude, Anselmi. Logan is my neighbor and friend, Remi."

"Stop while you're ahead, Dubois."

Tara sent daggers at Chance with her eyes.

"Okay. He's your friend and neighbor. What kind of contest was he in?"

Chance held his hands up. "All right, but I warned you. Keep in mind he's an ex-Army Ranger, stands a head taller than me, and is twice as wide in the shoulders."

Tara swatted him again.

"Go ahead. Tell him," Chance urged, grinning.

Remi sipped his coffee looking up at Tara above the rim of his cup.

"On his time off, Logan runs the clubs in Vegas -- in drag."

Remi spit his coffee out and started choking. Standing beside him, Tara patted his back trying to help him breathe.

"I'm fine, sugar." He hoarsely regained his composure. "Now let me get this straight. This big assed macho man neighbor of yours cross-dresses?"

"It's not like you think." Tara was defensive. "He doesn't just cross-dress. He's bi-sexual, but sometimes he acts and looks like a true-to-life gay guy. He knows a lot of famous drag queens, you know."

Remi lost it. He carried his coffee cup to the sink, his shoulders shaking with laughter.

Tara tapped on his quivering shoulder. She pointed her finger to the kitchen door.

"Out! If you want me to play hostess and fix you dinner, then get the hell out of my kitchen. And that goes for you too, Anselmi."

Both men hightailed out the door like flames were licking at their heels.

*****

Ensconced on the couch in front of the fireplace, the conversation grew serious.

"So what's your plan for dealing with this ass who's after her?" Remi inquired.

"To start with, I'm going to plant and camouflage a few traps out in the woods bordering the camp. If the time comes when I think he might be close, I've got a cache of landmines I intend to bury on the surrounding grounds."

"I don't like the sound of this, Chance. You're one person trying to protect her from a psychotic maniac. From the sounds of this joker, he's intent on getting to her."

"He's not getting anywhere near her. I guarantee."

"But you can't watch all the angles where he could come at you all the time. You need another set of eyes. Why don't you let me take some leave and help you?"

Chance shook his head. "Can't. I need your eyes and ears out ahead of me. Have you heard any more?"

Remi nodded. "Yes. I called Quantico this afternoon and spoke with your boss, Lyons, like you told me to do. I told him you contacted me through Water Patrol and requested interagency assistance. He's aware now I know your location, but he didn't even try to extract the information. In fact, he said if you considered me trustworthy, then he was all for us working together and keeping her location a complete secret from everyone."

"Reggie's a good man even though I'll probably get a reprimand from him for the way I took off with her, but it was the only way I could protect her. We have a mole within the bureau who's feeding Cruz information."

"Well now that just sucks, but it makes a bit more sense to me now."

"What do you mean?"

"Lyons gave me information to replay to you. He said when Dean regained consciousness, he told him minutes before the shooting in Tennessee, he'd received a text message from an unidentifiable source. The message simply said find Junior and you'll find Cruz. Reggie said as of yet, they haven't been able to identify this Junior person."

"Derek told me while we were in Tennessee things were in the works which would flush out the mole, but I haven't talked to him since the attack there."

"Hey, you two! Dinner's served!"

Remi rubbed his hands together in anticipation. "If the little woman cooks half as good as she looks, we're in for a gourmet meal."

Chance punched him hard on his arm.

"Ow!" Remi rubbed the sore spot.

"Don't even think about it, Casanova. She's off limits."

"All right, all right. I get the message. I'm starving. Let's go eat."

*****

Three salad bowls sat on the counter with wine glasses on the table.

"There's lasagna on the stove. Help yourself. Would you please do the honors, Chance?" Tara handed him a bottle of wine Remi stashed in their supplies. Chance smiled down at her as he opened the wine.

"No wine for me," Remi remarked. "I'm on call. This looks so good." After everyone served themselves, they sat at the table to begin their meal. "What kind of lasagna is this, Tara?" Remi stuffed a big bite into his mouth.

"Vegetarian. I hope you like it."

Remi's jaw stopped moving. He visibly swallowed. "What? No meat? Where's the beef, woman? I'm a growing boy, you know."

"Oh, stop your blubbering." Chance rebuked. "You sound like a damn TV commercial. I think it tastes great."

"At this point, you'd think anything this little woman cooked was five stars."

The pager hooked to Remi's belt went off. He looked at the message and stood. "Sorry. Gotta run."

Leaning over Tara, he placed his hands on her shoulders. "I was just funnin' with you, sweetie. It's really good." He placed a kiss on top of her head.

"Dubois!" Chance scolded.

Remi raised his hands in surrender laughing. "All right. I'm gone." As he walked out, he shouted over his shoulder. "Y'all have sympathy and think about me tonight while y'all are goin' at it and I'm slavin' away without any." The front door slammed shut.

Tara and Chance just stared at one another. Remi's mere suggestion she and Chance might have sex sent tingles through her body. Her appetite for lasagna disappeared and was replaced with an entirely different craving, one for Cajun cuisine. Specifically, one tall, dark and handsome Cajun man.

Both standing at the same time, Chance backed up his chair. She did the same. Simultaneously, they stepped to the side of the table and stood toe-to-toe, her looking up at him, him looking down at her. The electricity crackled between them.

He made the first move and grabbed her around the waist lifting her off her feet. Her arms went around his neck for support. With her dangling like a necklace against him, he headed for her bedroom while he nibbled on her neck, his hands finding purchase on the soft curve of her butt. Just as he got to the bedroom door, the front door flew open.

"Hey! I forgot my cap on the... *oops*."

"Get the hell out before I kill you, Dubois!" Chance bellowed without so much as a glance Remi's way.

The front door slammed shut amid Remi's raucous laughter.

*****

"God, the man sure knows how to kill a mood, doesn't he?" Tara remarked as Chance lowered her from around his waist.

"Yeah. He sure does." Sighing, Chance watched Tara go to the kitchen table and start picking up the dirty dishes. "No, *chère*. You cooked, so I clean. Now go sit on the couch and read your book or something. I'll take care of this."

She smiled at him so sweetly, Chance wanted to throw her over his shoulder and lock them up in the bedroom for the next day or two... or ten. As he cleaned the kitchen, he thought about the beautiful woman who was just a few feet away. She was intelligent, sweet, and so incredibly strong. The need to protect her from everything which could hurt her, not just Alvin, was now embedded into his soul.

There was this deep desire to make love to her. The need at times drove him to the brink of near madness. He was glad there was no hot water heater here at the camp. With the number of cold showers he was taking, the propane tank would be empty by now.

Each and every fantasy his mind conjured up during those long, cold showers starred his green-eyed, auburn haired beauty. Now if he could just stop putting his foot in his mouth all the time, he might be able to see if this was real or just lust.

Drying his hands on the dish towel, he leaned against the counter and watched Tara as she read from her book. After a few minutes, he spotted something on the wall near the door which he'd forgotten about. He set out toward the living room in hopes the idea he just had would go over well.

*****

Tara looked up from her book as Chance's shadow crossed over it. He was headed toward the wall by the door. Something on a shelf on the wall garnered his attention. She was getting ready to ask him what was going on when music filled the room.

Before her brain could process what was happening, Chance was standing in front of her, a smile plastered on his face. He extended his hand toward her. "May I have this dance?"

Laughing, she placed her hand in his. He pulled her flush with his body, wrapped one arm around her waist, and placed one of her hands on his chest covering it with his own. They swayed to the rhythm of a lovely beat.

"What type of music is this? I've never heard it before." She looked up at her protector and realized she found him pretty, in a rough and tumble sort of way.

Chance ran his knuckle across her cheek. She could feel the heat of a blush rising there. "It's called Zydeco and it's pretty popular in this area. They play it at all of the local fairs."

She felt his lips press to her hair. With her head against his chest, Tara could hear his heart beat solid and strong. As he took a breath, she felt the air whoosh out of his lungs.

"This is nice. I feel so safe like this with you, like nothing and no one can hurt me."

Chance backed up a little and lifted her face with his knuckle under her chin. "As long as I draw breath, no one will ever hurt you again." His arm tightened around her as his chocolate colored eyes darkened. He leaned down and caressed her lips. Butterflies took flight in her stomach. The kiss started out soft and very tender. Before long, he was kissing her hungrily, his lips hard against hers and fueled by passion.

He moved his hand down to the bottom of her tee shirt and slipped his fingers beneath the material. His other hand was tangled in her hair, the hairband she used to put her hair in a ponytail suddenly loose. He angled her head slightly to deepen the kiss. At this point, she was a moaning mess. When they pulled apart, they were breathing heavily.

"If someone comes by this time, I'm gonna shoot and ask questions later," Chance voiced as he threw Tara over his shoulder.

Chance flung her to the bed like a sack of feed falling onto the bed of a pickup truck. She landed with a grunt and a bubble of laughter. "Damn, Frenchie. Could you be a little rougher? I didn't land quite hard enough."

He gave her a sheepish grin. "Sorry. You're so damned light I got carried away."

She chuckled and grinned back. "Are you always so rough or was that for my benefit?"

His brows shot up. "Are you askin' for rough or just inquiring?" Her laughter tinkled.

She leaned against an elbow, placed her head in her palm, and gave him a sassy grin. "Too bad we don't have the right kind of music. I'll just let my imagination run wild while you do a strip tease for me."

He responded by pulling his shirt over his head. With his chest bare, his biceps flexed effortlessly.

Her eyes widened as did her grin. He seductively unsnapped his jeans and started pulling down the zipper, his eyes never leaving her face. Her smile started to fade as he hooked his thumbs in his jeans and boxers and slid them down slow and easy. He kicked them off his feet. Every part of his body stilled... well, almost every part. His erection was throbbing like crazy.

Totally flummoxed, Tara sat up and stared. A matting of fine curly chest hair the color of sweet maple syrup fanned across his wide chest and narrowed down to a thin line disappearing beneath his belly button. She was able to find her voice.

"Good God. I think I've died and gone to heaven."

*****

Breathing heavy, Chance looked at Tara. "Oh, baby. You are so going to get it now." As he climbed onto the bed, Tara backed herself up to the headboard.

"You have too much clothes on, *chère*. Chance grabbed hold of her shorts and slid them and her underwear off while she pulled her shirt up over her head. She unhooked her bra and tossed it aside.

Chance ran a finger down her face to her neck, then all the way down to her breast circling an already hard nipple. "You are so beautiful, perfect." He leaned in and kissed her with all the lust and passion inside him. His hand roamed down between her legs. He stroked her and found her swollen and soaking wet. Tara moaned into his mouth as he explored.

She was squirming. "Chance... oh. Oh, God," was about all he could make out moving down her body, licking and kissing his way to where his fingers playfully teased her.

Chance spread her legs so he could lie in between them. He blew his warm breath across her overly sensitive flesh. Tara moaned louder grabbing his hair. Using his fingers, he opened her up to him, following with a sweep of his tongue. He sucked. She bucked and cried out. The sound of her voice had him getting hard again.

Adding his fingers back to her opening, Chance watched Tara's reactions as she moaned and thrashed about. She started tightening around his fingers, so he removed them and pushed himself up to kneel between her legs.

Panting and out of breath, she sat up. "If you hear another boat, I'll be the one to shoot."

With a wicked look, Chance pushed her back down to the bed and pushed into her. She screamed coming hard around him. He fisted the sheets holding back his own release as he pushed in and out.

Leaning down, he captured her open mouth with a kiss. She dug her nails into his back making him hiss in pleasure. He grabbed hold of her hips and rolled so he was under her.

"Ride me, *chère*. Ride me hard."

Tara started moving back and forth, up and down, hard and fast. Chanced helped guide her with a hand on her hip while the other fondled her bouncing breast.

God, he loved the view with her on top. Watching her lose herself in ecstasy which he helped create was the best damn feeling he'd ever had.

Feeling his own release coming hard, he used both his hands to bring her down on him faster and harder. Screams and moans were the only sounds in the room. Chance brought her down one last time and held her there as her walls fluttered all around him. With one final moan, Tara collapsed onto his chest. They both were breathing heavy.

"I think that was the best sex I've ever had," Tara commented as she rolled off Chance which caused him to groan as he slid out of her.

Tara snuggled up to his side as he wrapped an arm around her. "Same here, *chère*. You have ruined me for all other women now." He pressed a kiss to her lips. Snuggling even closer, Tara threw her leg over his hip.

"Sounds good to me."

*****

In a rundown motel on the outskirts of Quantico, his eyes are glued to the TV, but a movie or show isn't what's holding his attention. It's what's happening in the room next door. When the guy in the other room had departed, he seized the opportunity and broke into his room. Poking holes in the walls between the rooms and planting cameras and microphones so he could watch and listen to the goings and comings of said room, he set himself up for a show.

The room's inhabitant had to be the sickest piece of trash he'd ever seen. He discovered Alvin Cruz was a heartless psycho who killed without thought to human life, but it was the one helping Alvin who was the focus of his interest -- the one known as Junior. That trash was sitting number one on his list of people who'd destroyed his life.

Junior had once been a friend but he'd used the friendship to bury him, but Junior hadn't done a good enough job which was why he was able to seek revenge for the life Junior helped take from him.

Movement on the screen caught his eye. Ah. Speak of the devil and he shall appear. Alvin opened the door and let someone into the room. Making his way to the dresser where his equipment was set up, he picked up the headphones so he could listen in on the conversation.

"*...found her?*"

Junior took something out of his bag. "*Yeah, I found her.*" Alvin made a grab for what looked like a map but Junior held it out of reach.

"*Just give me her damn location and you can go about your life.*" Alvin looked pissed.

Junior just shook his head. "*Not yet. They are deep in the swamps in Louisiana. You would never find them by yourself. I have someone in the area I can get in touch with who will help you get there.*"

"*Well, call him! I need to go and claim what is mine.*"

He shook his head. No woman should be subjected to a psycho like Alvin, especially someone like Tara Roberts. She'd had enough headache to last a lifetime. He focused his attention back to the action taking place in the next room. He could see the map. It displayed the very bottom portion of Louisiana which also showed a lot of water. He grabbed his camera and took a picture of it so he could study it later on.

Junior hung up his cell. He turned toward Alvin who was pacing the length of the room like a caged animal. "*He will meet you at the local airport and...*"

"*Well then, get me to the airport,*" Alvin interrupted Junior, rushing to the other side of the room to get his bag. Junior crossed the room and took the bag from Alvin dropping it at their feet.

"*No.*"

"*No? What do you mean, no? Screw you, Junior. I'm going to get her with or without your help.*"

Alvin was losing it, and if Junior wasn't careful, Alvin just might take matters into his own hands at Junior's expense -- meaning his life. He hoped it didn't come to that. He stood a better chance at bringing Junior to justice.

Calmly, Junior pushed Alvin down into a nearby chair. "*No. I have another plan to try before you go running around the swamps like an idiot. You would get eaten by an alligator or a shark.*"

Alvin crossed his arms over his chest looking like a child who didn't get his way. "*Well. What's this great plan of yours?*"

"*This.*" Junior pulled out a cell phone. Alvin looked at Junior like he was the crazy one. Junior continued. "*This is a cloned copy of the FBI Director's phone. I can't call Anselmi, but I can text him and get him to come to us.*"

Alvin jumped up from the chair. "*I don't give a damn about him. I want Tara!*" He objected sounding just like a spoiled brat.

"*He will bring her to us, dipshit! He isn't going to leave her there unprotected.*" Junior's face was red, a sure sign he was losing his temper.

Alvin still looked unconvinced. "*What if he decides to leave her?*"

Junior shrugged. "*Then you get to go hunting.*"

Crap! This new development wasn't good. He couldn't contact any of the agents because the only one he trusted was laid up in the hospital thanks to both of the assholes on the screen. What could he do?

Chapter Thirty-Five

"Tara, sweetheart. Time to get up." With her head buried under the covers, Chance tried stirring her, but she wasn't budging. "Hey. You still alive down there?"

"No." She was mumbling into her pillow.

"Would you like some breakfast?"

She managed to groan.

"How 'bout a tall glass of OJ?"

She groaned again.

"Okay. Since you don't want anything, I'll just go fix myself a steaming cup of coffee." She rummaged around under the covers but her head never appeared, her butt popping up as she poked her hands out from under the covers, fingers stretching toward the headboard. After the night of marathon sex, Chance figured she needed all the help she could get with sore muscles, but the sight of her butt in the air made him go a little crazy. He couldn't help but slap her behind with a playful swat.

Her body jumped and her head finally emerged. She looked over her shoulder at him, smiling.

Laughing, she asked, "Any more where that one came from?"

He gave her his sexiest grin. "Oh, there's plenty more, but not now. Breakfast first. I need fuel if I'm expected to perform." He swatted her again before heading for the bathroom.

*****

They sat across from one another in companionable silence having breakfast. Since they'd entered the kitchen, conversation had been at a minimum, but only because they'd both been famished.

Chance's burner phone dinged to alert him to an incoming text. He looked at the phone and frowned. "Sorry. Have to take this. I'll be right back." He went out the front door.

Tara stared into her coffee cup wondering if the call was about Alvin. Her breaths started coming quicker as the old menacing face of fear reared its ugly self in her mind. The reality of her situation struck her straight between the eyes.

Last night she'd been able to forget her troubles and the fact she was on the run from a psychotic killer. Her Cajun man had given her a memorable night in his arms and he'd managed to slip her into fantasy if only for one night. The ringing of his phone was like a pin bursting the bubble of pleasure his lovemaking ensconced her in.

Walking back into the kitchen, Chance sat down without saying a word. He took one more bite of his breakfast but then pushed the plate away.

Tara eyed him warily realizing something changed. "Everything okay?" His hesitation in answering spoke volumes. Her stomach twisted in a knot.

"Everything's fine." He reached across the table and squeezed her hand. "So what would you like to do today? Want to go fishing again?"

She smiled but shook her head.

"How about a long walk through the woods? Maybe we could find some healthy pieces of driftwood we could use for playing fetch with Buddy."

A lightning strike lit up the kitchen and rolling thunder filled the air. Tara almost jumped out of her seat. Chance offered her his hand. "Come here," he commanded, his voice soft.

She stood and allowed him to pull her into his arms. He turned her around so her back faced him and he tucked her into his arms, wrapping her up like a blanket.

"*Chère*. What's the matter? Why are you so jumpy and upset?"

She inhaled a quick breath and rested her head against his chest. "What is wrong, and don't give me some bullshit about everything being fine." She could feel his muscles tighten, but he remained silent.

"Whatever." She tried turning around in his arms, but he kept her tightly cocooned in his grasp. She tilted her head until she could see his face and eyes. "What was the text about?" A flicker of anger lit his dark eyes, but it faded quickly. "Be straight with me, Chance. I'm a big girl. I can take a little bad news."

His eyes were swimming in guilt. He looked upward as he took in a deep breath of his own. Finally, he turned her so she was draped on his lap like a child. She clung to his neck with one arm while her other rested on his chest.

"The text was from my boss, Reggie. He's summoning me back to Quantico. I could tell him no, but it would just send them all hunting us. Besides, I would end up unemployed. I don't have a choice here, *chère*. I have to go."

Tara's eyes were flitting about seeking out something in his face he might be holding back but she could detect nothing unusual.

"Is he getting closer, Chance? Is that why they're calling you back? Because of Alvin?"

He placed his hands on each side of her face. "*Non, chère*. Listen to me. This is just a formality -- a meeting. Cruz has been laying low since Tennessee, and we've hidden ourselves well enough it'll take him a while to find us. Everything's all right. There's no need for you to worry."

She took in a shaky, ragged breath and settled her head against his chest. "When do we have to leave?" She felt him tense.

When she lifted her face to his, he placed a tender kiss on her lips. "*We* are not leaving, *chère*. I am. I've already talked to Remi and Poppee. They'll come out here and keep watch over you. I won't be gone long. There's no need for you to come with me and no need for you to worry about anything."

Another quick shot of lightning lit up the room as the thunder rumbled through the air.

"So when do you have to leave?" she asked, just as huge raindrops pinged on the metal roof playing a melodic tune.

Tara accepted the finality of the situation even though she wasn't keen on the idea.

"Tomorrow morning." Chance nuzzled the skin just behind her ear. "Which leaves us all day and all night. So what do you want to do?"

Tara could feel his arousal coming to life beneath her. She squirmed to help him along.

He growled in her ear. "I have a friend who once told me making love during a thunderstorm heightens the senses. He should know; he's got six children and claims they were all conceived during storms. I've never made love in the middle of a thunderstorm before. Have you?" He licked the rim of her ear and then blew a soft breath over it making her shiver.

She responded with a throaty moan as he lifted her and carried her to the bedroom.

"Hold up." He gently laid her on the bed and started to take off his shirt. He stopped with his shirt midway up.

"What?"

"My turn." She hopped off the bed and helped him finish pulling off the shirt. She unsnapped his jeans and pulled the zipper down real slow. When his hands went to the waistband, she slapped them off and replaced them with her own. Shoving them down past his hips, she let them drop to the floor.

"Commando. I like." She smiled waggling her brows. Leaning in, she blew a soft breath over him. He grunted in approval. Then she stood and turned him around so his back was facing the bed. She shoved at him and he toppled. He straightened propping himself up on a pillow, his hands behind his head. He must have realized her intent and set himself up to watch her strip for him. Slow and methodical like, she pulled her shirt over her head baring her untethered breasts.

His breath audibly hitched. "You are so beautiful, Tara. There are no other words worthy of describing how you look."

She gave him a sexy grin as she slipped her thumbs into the waistband of her shorts. They slithered down her body and dropped to the floor along with her panties.

"Damn." His deep brown eyes glittered with lust.

She eased herself onto the foot of the bed. Keeping her eyes trained on his, she started by rubbing her hands over the top of his feet. Slowly, she worked her way up his calves weaving her fingers through the hair there and then continued up his thighs forcing his legs to part. When she got to his hips, she skirted around them and dragged her hands over his flat abs. When she reached his upper chest, she flicked a nail over his nipple. His body jerked. He tried leaning forward to kiss her but she turned her head away.

"Not yet." She straddled his chest as her hands went up his neck, over his jawline and into his hair. She splayed her fingers and hooked them tightly giving his hair a gentle tug. His head fell back and his eyes closed. She licked a spot near his temple and started a downward track of moist, hot kisses. When she got back to his chest, she grabbed his nipple between her teeth and gently pulled. Again his body jerked.

"Tara." His voice was low and husky.

She ignored him and continued with her trek of kisses. When she got to his abs, she sat up and stared into his eyes mirrored with lust. She jumped off the bed and walked back to the foot of the bed. With a wicked little grin in place, she tugged on his feet letting him know she wanted him to lie flat. He did as she requested and slid his body prone. She bounced back on the bed but turned her back toward him as she straddled him. Her naked rear end became his full frontal view. He growled and reached for her ankles but she slapped his hands away.

"*Mon Dieu,* woman. You're killing me here." His hands came around capturing her breasts.

"Condom," she commanded.

He grabbed one from atop the nightstand and placed it in her open hand. She rolled her body back up. The foil pack ripped open. She was poised with the protection over the tip of his erection, her fingertips ready to roll it down, when his hands went around her waist and he flung her to the other side of the bed.

"What the hell?" she exclaimed.

"Un, un. Can't take it anymore. If you so much as lay one finger on me, I'll explode." He grabbed the condom out of her hand and settled it in place.

He maneuvered himself between her legs and hooked them in his arms, her butt lifting off the bed. They both groaned at the contact. His eyes closed and he stilled inside her trying to regain his self-control. With a deep breath, he set a rhythm of thrusts which made her chant his name.

"Oh, God, Chance. Please. More." She begged between breaths as he picked up the pace and pounded her with deep full thrusts.

"Come for me, *chère*. Let me watch pleasure and ecstasy fill your eyes."

Tara felt a new sensation fill her heart. She gave in to the overwhelming emotion and granted his request as his relentless rhythm sent her flying higher than she'd ever flown.

*****

Some hours later after they'd both dozed, Tara wiggled her body closer to his. Chance sighed and pulled her in even tighter. "How about a warm shower?"

"Exactly what I was thinking, except I'm not sure I can move."

He chuckled and placed a kiss on top of her head. "Come on. I'll make it easy on you."

He rolled out of bed, picked her up, and carried her into the bathroom. After setting her down, he shoved the shower curtain aside and turned on the water letting it warm up. He picked her up by the waist and deposited her under the water.

"Oh, my. This is heaven."

He stepped in beside her. Squirting shampoo into his hand, he began washing her hair, massaging her scalp with his fingertips. He placed her where the water would wash away the suds. He wiped the water off her face. Then he soaped the towel and began washing her body. When he reached the juncture between her thighs, he knelt and gently washed her. Once he'd reached her feet, he stood and turned her around repeating the process on her backside.

When he finished with her, she took another towel from the rack and did the same for him in return.

"*Mon Dieu*. The simplest touch of your skin makes me crazy." He clunked the back of his head against the wall of the shower.

She continued her ministrations until he couldn't take it anymore. He took the towel out of her hand and flung it to the floor. After putting on protection, he lifted her, and pinned her body against the shower wall.

"Come here, *chat marron*." He entered her with a savage need to be inside her warmth. She whimpered and he stilled.

"Oh, *chère*. I'm sorry if I hurt you," he whispered near her ear.

She shook her head. "Good. All good. Don't stop."

He picked back up where he'd left off making sure he supported her weight and didn't hurt her. His primal need took over. With a deep grunt, he sank into her.

"Together, *chère*," he murmured as they both tumbled over the edge into ecstasy.

*****

Back in bed now, Tara felt sated, her body lax and ensconced in

Chance's hold, her head in the crook of his arm.

"You know, Anselmi? For a senior citizen, you sure have a lot of stamina. Is this what you do with all the girls in your protective custody?"

His chest vibrated with laughter. He pushed her back enough so he could look at her eyes. "No. Why do you think Derek calls me rookie? This is my first case, remember? Which means you're my first and only woman under protective custody."

"Oh yeah. I forgot." She smiled sheepishly.

Chance looked deep in her eyes. "*Chat marron.* You're the first in a very long time, and no one else has ever done the things to me you do."

"Chance?" she whispered as she nudged closer to him, her head resting on his chest.

"Hmm?"

"When are you going to tell me what that stuff you keep calling me means?" She felt him vibrate again with inner laughter and she swatted him playfully on the chest.

"When are you gonna stop beating me up with those tiny fists?"

She tried to rare back, but he held her firmly in his grasp. She sighed and gave in enjoying the comfort of his arms.

"Get some sleep, *chère,* before I prove to you once and for all older men make better lovers." She giggled against his chest which brought a smile to his face. They both took deep breaths and, within a matter of minutes, were fast asleep.

Chapter Thirty-Six

Tara sat on the swing watching the morning sun rise over the glistening water as she sipped her coffee. Chance was packing and getting things together to leave.

She wasn't sure what they were doing, but after last night's marathon lovemaking, she really didn't care. Well, maybe lovemaking wasn't the right terminology. Sex didn't hold the right emotion. Tara didn't think she was in love with him, but she was on her way. She wasn't sure how Chance felt about her, but she knew he at least lusted after her. Plus, she wasn't sure what his hang-up was with his ex, Lacy. Whatever happened affected him, and would he want to see her again once Alvin was locked up behind bars?

She didn't think Chance would or could be involved with her so he was already breaking the rules. She was getting herself worked up about something which may not even be relative.

She lived clear across the country in Las Vegas, and he lived... hell. She had no idea where he actually lived.

This just wasn't like her. She never just had sex without being in a relationship. Thinking back, she didn't know much about Chance's every day life. She could just hear Logan in the back of her head. "*But how does he make you feel, sugar?*" Which was the reason she was not totally freaking out. When she awoke in Chance's arms, she realized the hollow feeling she carried in her chest since losing her family felt smaller. The ache had been like a constant reminder of her loss.

But this morning, it wasn't debilitating as it had been. She didn't feel like curling into a ball and closing herself off to the world and she didn't want to drag herself out of bed and be off to work when she didn't have the strength for it. She didn't feel quite so alone.

As she continued musing, she heard a distant meow. Scanning the horizon, she searched for Timmy who was nowhere in sight. The meowing continued and became more distressed. By the sound of his cries, she knew something was wrong.

"Timmy! Where are you?" she yelled out searching the grounds in front of the camp.

Hanging over the porch railing, she peered off into the swamps. To the right near the dense wooded area surrounding the property, she spotted him. With his paws bogged down in the muddy ground, he was struggling trying to free himself.

"Timmy? Sweetie, hold on! I'm coming to get you!" She made a beeline for the steps taking them two at a time. When she hit the bottom step, she took off at a fast clip.

Just before she reached him, her momentum slowed and her own feet bogged down in the muddy water logged wet marsh land. It sucked at her feet until she couldn't lift them. The spongy earth was clinging to her ankles like quick sand.

"Help! Chance! We're stuck!" she yelled at the top of her lungs. Knowing he was in the bedroom packing for his trip to Quantico, she feared he wouldn't hear her distress call.

"Hang in there, Timmy. Chance will come and get us out." The feline was still meowing and struggling to gain purchase in the mud.

"Chance Anselmi! Get your backwoods southern ass out here and help us!"

Buddy came bounding up to them, his bark signaling frantic as he barked first at Tara and Timmy and then turned to bark toward the camp trying to summon Chance.

"Tara! Where are you?"

She heard his muffled cry from the porch. She let out a breath of relief. "Over here near the trees! We're stuck in the mud!"

"Hang on! I'm comin' to get you."

Timmy's meow became more of a screech as his paws and huge body sunk even lower. "It's going to be all right, big boy. Our Cajun man is coming to our rescue."

*****

Chance trudged through the dense swampy land almost to the top of his white shrimper's boots. He stood next to Tara and peered down at her. In her struggles to lift her legs out of the quagmire, she'd spread streaks of mud across her face making her look like a painted Indian princess. Chance bellowed with laughter while Buddy continued barking up at his master.

"Are you just going to stand there like a dumb frog or are you going to get us out?" With her frustration mounting, she took a hand and swiped at the hair falling across her face. The action put more mud on the tip of her nose and across her forehead. His laughter became raucous.

"Chance Anselmi! I swear. If you don't quit laughing at me, one of these days when you least expect it, you'll wake up to find your most prized possession super glued to your leg!"

His laughter died a quick death. Knowing her temper, he didn't doubt she'd do it in a heartbeat. He extended his hand to her, but she refused to take it.

"Un, un. Him first." She pointed to Timmy who was looking at Chance like he was public enemy number one.

Chance eyed the huge cat. The last thing he needed this morning was a tussle with a cat who, as of yet, had not shown him one iota of friendliness. He turned back to Tara.

"But, Tara. Don't you..."

She held up her hand to stop him. "Him first, Frenchie."

Resigned to the fact he couldn't deny her anything no matter what, he took a few steps toward the feline. When he got within reaching distance, Timmy hissed and spat at him something awful. He backed up a step holding his hands in the air.

"How 'bout I pull you out first and you pull out the cat?"

"Super glue, Anselmi!"

That was enough incentive for him. He lunged at the massive cat with both hands. Groaning at the added weight of muck clinging to the already rotund animal, he gave a mighty pull and freed Timmy from the mud. He turned back to rescue his damsel in distress. With his hands around her waist, he gave a strong tug and plopped her out of the mud. One of her shoes flew off her foot and landed right next to Timmy. The other shoe stayed mired in the muck.

Chance kept his hands firmly on her waist until her feet hit the ground next to the muddied cat. With his sexiest grin, he looked down at her mud smeared face.

"I love the new look, *chère*. They say mud is good for the skin."

She took her mud encrusted hands and splayed them across his massive chest, bits of muck flying in every direction.

"Stop it, *chat marron*!" He protested between fits of laughter. He let her spread more swampy mud on him until she was looking happy.

She looked up into his eyes. A slow grin emerged making her look so endearing his laughter faded. He rubbed the slick mud clinging to his hands around the bare strip of skin between her shirt and shorts. He watched her eyes dilate with desire. Leaning down, he kissed her hungrily as she wound her arms around his neck. He couldn't seem to curb the lust which rose within him with each contact of their skin.

A loud meow bellowed in the air. They both looked down and saw Timmy wedged between them, his muddy head plopped down on Chance's white boots. Noticing her bare foot and one shoe, Chance gave her a puzzled look.

"Hey. Where are your Cajun Reeboks?"

"My what?"

"The boots I gave you our first day here. We call 'em Cajun Reeboks. Where are they?"

She gave him a look which said if he was making fun of her one more time, he was history.

"Just never mind. Let's get cleaned up. I have to leave soon." Without a second thought, he picked up the muddy cat with one hand and took Tara's hand in his other. He guided them toward the steps to the camp while Buddy followed close behind. Amazingly, Timmy licked his face and never complained.

*****

"Remi," Chance warned. "Hands off!"

"Come on now, t-boy. You know me better than that. I'm not a poacher."

"And you'd best keep it that way. Poppee. Keep an eye on things for me, please?"

"You know good and well I will, son," the old man replied.

"Especially him." Chance pointed toward Remi who grabbed his chest feigning injury by his friend's untrusting barbs.

"Man, you wound me, bro."

"Just do what I told you and keep your hands to yourself or I'll cut them off."

Trying to incite further jealousy in him, Tara encircled Remi's waist with her arm. She flashed Chance a brilliant smile. "Don't worry about us. We'll be just fine, won't we, Dr. K?"

Remi jumped back so fast he almost tumbled. Holding up hands in self-defense, his look said he thought she'd lost her mind. "Now, Tara. I like you, sugar. A lot. But don't you go givin' the big ape ideas. He's just mean enough, big enough, and bad enough to bash my skull in if he *thinks* I looked at you much less if I touched you. So you just keep your hands to yourself and you and me, we'll do just fine."

With a wide grin on his face, Chance grabbed Tara's hand and pulled her away from his friend. She landed with a thud against his chest as his mouth quickly devoured hers.

Poppee shielded his eyes with his hand. "Lord have mercy. I'm too young to see such things goin' on."

Still kissing, both Chance and Tara stifled chuckles. With some hesitation on both their parts, they came up for air as he whispered in her ear, "Still want to flirt with Remi?"

She grabbed his shirt and pulled him down for one more long leisurely kiss. She was gasping for air when they parted. "Remi who?"

Chance's smile was heavenly. "You stay safe, *chat marron*. I'll be back as soon as I can." Unwilling to let her go, he gave her one more quick kiss before getting in the boat and heading out.

*****

Dressed all in black, he sat in the airport lobby with his cell phone in hand pretending to check phone calls. His eyes, hooded by the bill of the ball cap on his head, never strayed from the man at the ticket counter.

Earlier in the morning, he'd watched Junior, a man he'd once called friend, empty his bank account of an exorbitant amount of money. Now he watched Junior pay for a one way ticket to Rio under an assumed name.

So Junior was going to skip the country which meant Cruz would soon go to Louisiana to find the girl. With cell still in hand, he clicked a few pictures and began adding to the final proof needed by the FBI to prove Junior was the mole.

He thought back to the days when everyone who surrounded him was trustworthy including this man. One way or another, every last one of them who worked to ruin his good name and take away his freedom and family would fall, and he would exact sweet revenge on his own terms.

He looked up and stared at Junior. Junior lifted his head and looked straight at him, apprehension apparent.

Their eyes momentarily met, but it didn't matter. There was no way he could be recognized. He disguised himself well. With a wide smile on his face, he stood, dropped his phone in his pocket, and walked away.

Chapter Thirty-Seven

About an hour after Chance left, Remi received a callout from Water Patrol requesting assistance on a search for a group of missing fishermen near Port Fourchon, a twenty minute boat ride from Camp Fluffy. Poppee assured him they would be safe and sound without him. Tara, doubting the frail old man could handle himself much less her, asked Remi if he thought it wise to leave her alone with Poppee.

"Tara, don't y'all worry yourself none. The old geezer may look frail, but he can handle whatever comes his way. Why, he can pick a fly off a wild boar's ass from twenty yards out and leave the fly's wings intact."

"Well, that really makes me feel safer." She was in disbelief.

"See you guys in a couple of hours." Remi hopped down the steps and ran to the boat. He jumped in and took off leaving Poppee and Tara on the porch all alone.

"T-sha. How's about you take this old coon-ass around for a walk? My old bones don't move so well no more and they need some exercise."

"Sure, Poppee. I'd love to walk with you."

They headed down the steps of the camp, Tara helping the old man maneuver with his walking cane. She wondered why he needed it.

"So what happened to make you have to use a cane, Poppee?"

He tapped his right leg with the cane before walking on. "This here leg. It got chomped on by an ornery cai'mon back in nineteen eighty somethin'. Mean old cuss, he was."

She stopped walking to look at him. "Wait. I think I remember what it means. Alligator, right?"

"You got it right."

"Oh, my. What happened?"

The old man smiled pleased with her attention. "Well, we was two dumb Cajuns dat had gone cai'mon huntin', me and old man Boudreaux from Vacherie. They had just opened up da gator season because them gators was takin' over this here marsh. We was in my pirogue, me and him, huntin' gator tracks."

"Gator tracks?"

"Yep. Gators leave telltale signs all along da banks when they sun themselves." The old man scanned the banks on both sides of the canal. Pointing to a muddy area ten yards down on the opposite side of the canal, he smiled. "See dat muddy spot on da bank across?"

Tara's gaze drifted to where he was pointing. "Over there?" She pointed in the same direction.

"Yep. See how da mud is slick in one spot and leads down into them waters?"

"Yes. What does it mean?"

"Dat means an old cai'mon was sunnin' himself up on da bank and slid his old body down into them waters. You can tell how big he is by da size of da mud slide."

Tara's eyes widened in wonder. "Wow. He must be humongous."

"Nah. It's just a baby."

"A *baby*? If that represents a baby, I don't want to see his mama or poppa."

The old man laughed. They continued walking while Poppee finished his story of how, when he and his friend Boudreaux, had gotten the alligator into the boat thinking the animal was dead, he'd let the gator go and the beast flailed around to take a bite out of his leg.

They wandered along the tree line on the eastern most edge of the property and were beneath the tall cypress trees. Almost finished his story, Poppee grabbed her by the arm.

"What is it, Poppee?" she asked, sensing something amiss.

He snapped his cane upright. The cane was collapsible and flexed. Coming from somewhere inside the cane, a flash of metal shaped like a saber appeared. Before she knew what was happening, the old man swished the sword-like object to the side of her head. Reflexively, she leaned back out of the way, her heart pounding.

"Sorry, t-sha. I would've killed dat snake sooner, but I just noticed it. Damn. And it's a copperhead, too," he matter-of-factly reported and glared down at the fallen poisonous snake now resting near Tara's feet.

Her stomach roiled at the sight of the decapitated snake, its body still wriggling. "Ew!" She groaned in disgust and stepped away from its writhing body. She realized how quickly the old man had reacted. Now she was genuinely impressed with his swift reflexes. He snared the dead snake's torso on the end of the sword and flung it deep into the trees.

"T-sha. You ever hear of dat famous pirate, Jean Lafitte?"

Tara looked perplexed at the sudden change of subject. "Sure. Didn't he roam somewhere here in the south?"

"Sure 'nuff he did. Supposedly he buried his riches right here in these swamps."

"Wow." Tara was amazed. "Have you ever found any of his treasures?"

"Sure did. Oh, nothin' worth much, mind you, but me an' old Boudreaux was out one day diggin' around and we come up with a fine lookin' bracelet. You know, legend says dat Lafitte buried his treasures all along these swamps 'neath da cypress trees. He marked each tree by tyin' a knot in da small tree trunks. See dat one?" He pointed his saber toward the cypress tree nearest the camp. "See how dat tree is deformed in the middle with a big knot in its trunk?"

Tara eyed the tree, her eyes widening. "Wow. You think this is one of the trees he buried stuff under?"

"Why of course. That's why da tree grows crooked. Listen, sweetie. While you here, you just feel free to get you a shovel out dat tool shed and dig until your little heart is content. Maybe you might get lucky and find somethin' real fine dat you can keep."

"Why thank you, Poppee. I might just do that."

Tara hooked her arm around his as he locked the cane back in place and they started walking again.

"Tell me something, Poppee."

"What's dat, sugar?"

"What does t-sha mean?"

He smiled down at her. "The't' means little or petite. 'Sha' means *chère* or *chèrie,* which means *cherished one*."

Little cherished one. She liked that.

"And what the heck is Chance saying when he says '*chat marron*'? I've noticed he only says it to me and he won't tell me what it means."

The old man rared back and laughed. "He never told you what dat means? I can't believe dat boy sometimes."

"No. He's never translated most of what he spouts in French. Don't get me wrong. It's a beautiful language and all, but it pisses me off every time he uses it and won't tell me what it means. Makes me think he doesn't want me to know."

"Well that's probably why he don't tell you, I imagine. Chance has pretty much been a loner all his life you know and has a mind of his own. He lost his parents when he was a young'un. Eight years old if I recollect right. It's when he came live with me and Grams. Didn't have many friends while he was growin' up. Had this big chip on his shoulder. Not havin' parents at dat age is hard for a boy. Me and Grams did our best for him, but nothin' replaces a parent's love."

Tara nodded recalling her own lost family. It had been hard on her too, but she'd been old enough to deal with her loss. For Chance, he'd been forced to grow up way too soon.

"Anyhow," Poppee continued. "At least he had Remi. I practically raised dat boy too. He spent most of his days with us. Remi's ma and pa were just plain old mean. They didn't treat none of their kids right. So Remi, he would trail after Chance like a lost little puppy. Man, da trouble them two got into. I could tell you stories but you wouldn't believe 'em."

It brought a smile to her lips. She'd love nothing better than to hear stories of Chance and Remi in their youth. "Would you tell me some stories about them, Poppee?" They walked into the shade underneath the camp.

She helped him sit in an old rocker and then she planted herself on a nearby log. The old man's eyes twinkled with love when he spoke of the two boys he'd taken under his wing and watched grow into fine strong men under his tutelage. After twenty minutes of storytelling, Poppee had Tara laughing at the stunts the two pulled off as youngsters. She gleaned a much better insight into Chance's personality as well as his heart, but the old man was smart. He'd distracted her from her original question.

"Hey. You never answered my question," she huffed.

"What question was dat?" He sounded so innocent.

"What does '*chat marron*' mean?"

He laughed before answering. "'*Chat*' means cat. '*Marron*' means wild. Together, they mean wildcat."

"Ooh, that man! You mean he's been calling me a wildcat all this time? Well you just wait until he gets home. I'll show him who's a wildcat. He's going to hear a word or two from me in straight up English. Why the brainless twit. Just who does he think he is calling me names like that? When he gets his ass back here, I'm going to give him a piece of my mind. Yes, sir, I am. He won't know what hit him up side his fat, brainless head when I'm finished with him."

Poppee was laughing so hard he had to grab his side. Tara stopped ranting and stared at him. "What?"

"Now I see why he gave you dat name, t-sha. You certainly are a little wildcat!" The old man laughed some more.

Tara couldn't help but smile. When his laughter died down, he turned and looked her straight in the eyes with a serious look on his face.

"Tara? You do know dat grandson of mine loves you, right?"

Tara was so taken aback by his matter-of-fact statement, she couldn't speak. She gulped in a big breath but couldn't muster a response.

"And now I see dat you love him too, *non*?"

The lump in her throat subsided enough so she was able to speak. "Poppee. I've known Chance a very short time. A person can't fall in love so quick. Can they?"

The crinkles around the man's eyes lifted as did his crooked smile. "I don't know why not. Me and Grams fell in love overnight and we were married forty-five years when I lost her to da cancer. Why can't you two fall in love in a matter of days?"

She mulled over his question. Could a person fall in love quick like? And how did he know Chance was in love with her, anyway?

"Just what makes you think he's in love with me?" she asked, dubious.

"Oh, sweetheart." The man sighed. "Anybody with a lick of sense can see da love in dat boy's eyes when he looks at you, and when you look at him, you have dat look too."

Could the old man be right? Could Chance be falling in love with her? "Poppee. Have you ever seen him in love before?" She thought about the woman who'd barged in on them, the one he refused to talk about.

"Humph. You must've met Lacy, huh."

She was surprised. "Yes, I did. She came here the other day."

"Chance didn't tell you nothin' 'bout dat girl, did he?"

"In case you haven't noticed yet Poppee, he doesn't open up much."

The old man chuckled. "I've noticed, sugar, but don't hold it against him. It's just his nature to hold everythin' inside his self. I suspect he didn't tell you about Lacy because he's embarrassed."

"Embarrassed? Why? We all have things in our past we're not proud of."

"Sure 'nuff, but you see, when Chance was a senior in high school, he started datin' Lacy. By da time he went in da Army, he got himself hooked up good with dat girl. Had even bought her a ring. He planned to marry her."

Tara frowned at *that* revelation.

"See, da boy thought he was in love, but me, I knew better. Dat woman was no good for him. I tried warnin' him, but you know young'uns; they don't listen worth a damn. Especially da hard headed ones like Chance. Anyhow, he found out just what I was tryin' to warn him about on his own."

"What happened?"

"He came home on leave for Christmas one year. Got here two days early only to find dat woman in his own bed with another man who happened to be one of his best friends.

Shocked, she had to ask. "*Remi*?"

The old man's brows shot up. "Oh, *hell* no. You think Remi would still be standin' right side up if dat was da case? *Non*, sha. One of his other friends."

"You had me going for a minute there, Poppee."

"Yeah, well. Chance walked in on them two in da middle of what they was doin', if you catch my drift. Dat boy went straight to his closet, grabbed his shotgun and pointed da barrel smack dab between dat fella's eyes."

"Don't tell me he shot his friend?" She was incredulous.

"Nah, but dat young man damn near messed on his self, let me tell you. He never showed his face in this town again. I heard tell he moved on over to Victoria, Texas, and has a passel of little ones with some woman he shacked up with."

"Humph. Interesting." So that was why he hadn't explained Lacy to her. The woman had wounded his manhood by screwing around with another man while he was away. In Tara's viewpoint, it was a dirty thing to do. One thing she firmly believed in was fidelity.

"What happened to Lacy?"

Grandpa smirked. "No one else was there to witness, mind you, but I here tell he pulled da sheet out from under her behind and dumped her butt on da floor naked as a jaybird. Then he told her to skedaddle and not to let da door hit her in da butt on her way out."

Tara couldn't help it. The old man's way of telling a story was just so hilarious, she couldn't help but laugh out loud. Poppee told her a few more stories about Chance and Remi's youthful escapades and then they walked up the steps of the camp and settled in for the night.

Chapter Thirty-Eight

Reggie Lyons was ensconced behind his desk mulling over evidence from the Roberts case. Some things were not adding up. He'd once considered each member of SIU7 trustworthy and loyal, but all evidence was pointing to someone within the group having turned traitor. Someone was passing information to a known murderer and there had to be a reason.

He was determined to flush out the mole and find out what his or her motivation was. He also intended to see the traitorous agent behind bars. A light rap came from his door.

"Enter."

Chance Anselmi poked his head in. Reggie was taken aback by the presence of the agent who was supposed to be deeply ensconced in a secret location hiding the Roberts girl. He hadn't expected to hear from much less see the agent in question. He stood up so fast his chair banged against the wall of cabinets at his back.

"What the hell are you doing here, Anselmi?"

A look of confusion crossed Chance's face. "You're the one who called me and told me to come back because I had no choice, but Tara is not with me. I didn't bring her with me like you asked."

Reggie bent forward and planted his palms on the top of his desk. "What do you mean, like I told you? I never called you."

He watched Chance's eyes widen. The agent turned to go for the door. Now on the other side of the desk, Reggie grabbed his shoulders and spun him around. "You are not going anywhere, so sit your ass down and tell me just how it is I called you and told you to come back here."

Reggie leaned back against the front of his desk. He hoped like hell he wasn't putting his trust and Miss Roberts's life in the hands of the mole. Derek spoke highly of this guy saying he felt him to be on the up and up. Reggie respected Derek's judgment which was the only reason he didn't have Anselmi in handcuffs right now for disobeying orders.

"You sent me a text." Chance pulled his cell phone out of his pocket, looked something up and shoved the phone in Reggie's direction.

Reggie grabbed the phone out of his hands and examined the text. It had been sent from his number, but he himself had not sent out the text. He pulled out his own cell phone and checked it to make sure. There was no corresponding message on his phone.

Chance stood and began pacing. "I need to call my friend, Remi. He's watching Tara and needs to be on high alert." Chance ran his hands through his hair. "What a dumb-ass move, Anselmi! You left her alone!" He gripped his hair with both hands now. He continued his ranting and then came to an abrupt stop. "I have to go. I have to get back to Tara before Alvin does."

Reggie put himself between the door and Chance. "Wait a minute, Chance. We need to find out what's going on before you go running off again."

Chance looked like he was about to rip Reggie's head off when there was a knock at the door. Neither of them moved or responded to the intrusive knock.

A small female voice sounded from the other side of the door. "Sir? It's Izzy, sir. I have the info you wanted."

Chance's shoulders dropped. "Is the info about whoever is the mole?"

Reggie nodded. Chance returned and dropped in the chair he'd vacated earlier. "I'm not leaving until I hear this information."

"Sir? If right now is a bad time, I could come..."

Before the tech could finish her sentence, Reggie opened the door.

Izzy entered the room looking from Reggie to Chance and back to Reggie again. "Oh. I can come back, sir."

"No, Izzy. Come in and have a seat."

*****

As soon as the door opened and the woman started walking their way, Chance remembered her from the session in the bullpen when they received word of having a new case. He was once again struck by her distinctive appearance. She was five-four in height if she was lucky with straight-as-nails glossy brown hair cut short in the back, bright red highlights tapered in front down to her chin, and what was a feather light dusting of blue on the tips framing her face. Her big brown eyes were partially hidden behind a pair of black nerdy looking glasses. A butterfly pendant hung around her neck and was nestled in her well-endowed bosom while butterfly earrings dangled from her ears and a similar butterfly pin adorned her shiny hair. All in all, she was kooky looking but cute. She handed Reggie a folder.

"Thanks, Izzy. Chance? Have you met Izzy yet?"

"No. We went on assignment before we could make acquaintances."

"Special Agent Chance Anselmi? Meet our Technical Analyst and all around brainiac, Isabelle Roth. Izzy? Meet Chance."

He stood and shook the young woman's hand. "Please to meet you, ma'am." He gave her his most pleasant Cajun accent. Her eyes widened as she perused his massive build.

"Pleasure to meet you too, Agent Anselmi. My, but they must grow them big wherever you're from."

Don't know, ma'am, but I do know a few fellow mud runners from back home who are bigger and badder than me."

"Impossible. There can't be anyone bigger than you. Where's home?"

"Southern Louisiana, ma'am."

"Interesting. Are you full blooded Cajun? Because their culture has always peaked my curiosity. I've done cultural studies on several different ethnicities, but haven't had time to research Cajuns. I only know they're of French, Acadian, and Canadian descent. Oh, and call me Izzy. I'm sure we will be working closely together in the future."

Chance instantly liked the woman. She had a friendly demeanor and yet exuded a superior intellectual aura. "Yes, Izzy. We are of Acadian and Canadian descent and have a rich French heritage also. Some of my ancestors made their way from France to Louisiana via Canada."

"Uh, if you two want to have a historical discussion, please do it on your own time. I hate history."

"Oh, right, sorry, sir." Izzy stammered. "I get carried away sometimes. I've got the search going into the..."

She stopped dry and looked toward Chance, her eyebrows drawing together. Then she looked back at her boss with confusion written all over her face.

"Oh. It's all right, Izzy. Anselmi's been cleared."

Her facial features relaxed. "Oh. Okay. As I was saying, I've got a search going into the financial backgrounds of the agents in question. We should receive results within, oh," she checked her watch, "five minutes and forty-three seconds," she said matter-of-factly. "Exactly."

Reggie grinned. "Thanks. Let me know when you get the info. I have another problem I need your special touch on, Izzy."

"Oh? What have you got for me?"

"It seems somehow someone sent Chance a text and it was made to look like I was the one who sent it, but I didn't," Reggie explained to Izzy the situation which brought Chance back to Quantico and the reason Reggie's stomach was twisted in knots at the moment.

Izzy took both Chance's and Reggie's phones. "I'll look into this right away." She turned and headed out the door.

"Nice girl."

"Not only nice, her IQ is off the charts. She's got more info in one brain cell than the rest of us have in all our brains combined. Okay, on to business. There are some things we need to discuss. First and foremost, is the Roberts girl still safe?"

Chance nodded as he sat across from the Deputy Director. Even though he was currently working directly for Derek in the field, Reggie was top dog while Derek held command as lead field agent with Travis second in command. Closing the file folder open on his desk, Reggie looked up at him.

"I should have your badge for the stunt you pulled running with the Roberts girl, but I can't. Your task force commander heaped so much praise on you for how you handled the situation, he's tied up my hands. Besides, I wanted to commend you myself on your quick reaction at both safe houses. You used sound judgment in protecting our vic. Derek briefed me on both incidents. As I've said, he also thought highly of your quick responses."

"Thank you, sir. And how is Derek?"

"Spoke with him this morning. He's complaining like an old woman about being cooped up in a hospital bed, but all in all, he's recovering well. Dean will take a bit longer to heal but he's coming along fine too. He'll probably squawk just like Derek when he's a little better."

Chance grinned. "Good. Sounds like both of them."

"We've got a rat in our organization, Anselmi." Reggie's voice was filled with disgust.

"I suspected as much, Director. Someone's feeding information to Cruz about the safe house whereabouts. SIU7's members were the only ones who knew both locations. One of us had to leak the info."

"I agree and so does Derek. He told me he let you in on the fake safe house trap we set up on the west coast as a decoy. The site was hit by Cruz the second day you guys spent in Tennessee as you already know."

The wheels in Chance's brain started turning. "And how did he learn the location of the fake safe house if you were the only one who knew?" He was getting tenser by the minute.

Lyons held up his hand to halt his momentum. "Hang on, there. I'm getting to it." Chance took a deep breath calming his nerves as Reggie explained.

"The three of you in Tennessee were left in the dark about the decoy. The rest of the team members were told Roberts was being held at the west coast location. We even had a double posing for Roberts. Once the west coast location got it, it cleared the three of you in Tennessee. The others remain suspect. One of them passed the information to Cruz."

Chance could feel his blood beginning to boil. One of his fellow agents was selling them down the river and he wanted to know who and why. Whether he'd befriended him or her yet didn't matter. He'd find out who the asshole was and show him what happened to someone who turned traitor against a brother or sister.

"So what do you think is the motivation behind the mole?" Chance wanted to get back to the matter at hand.

"Don't think we'll know for sure until after we flush him or her out. Most of the pieces to this puzzle are in place now, but we still need one or two more to complete it. I was hoping you might have noticed something unusual, a conversation maybe, which might give us a clue."

"No, sir. I haven't, but I've been tied up with the Roberts case. I haven't had much contact with other agents except for Dean and

Navarro."

"It's a shame about Navarro. Although he wasn't with us very long, it's always upsetting to lose a fellow member of the bureau."

"I fully agree, sir. He was a nice guy, although a bit quirky."

"Yes, he was." Another couple of minutes passed in general conversation when Reggie's phone buzzed. He glanced at the ID. "It's Izzy." He placed the phone on speaker. "You're on speaker, Izzy. Got something?"

"Reggie! You two have got to see this. Come quick!" Her voice was animated.

"Be there in a second. Come on, Anselmi. Her office is just down the hall."

As both agents entered the tech's office, Chance took in the massive bank of computer monitors covering an entire wall. They were set in a semi-circle, various shapes and colors, three monitors high in height and ten monitors in width. They all had the same image plastered across the screens.

"Reggie, you've got to read this. I received this email two minutes and thirty-four seconds ago. There was no subject line and no sender ID."

"Yes!" Reggie pumped his fist in the air. "We've got him!"

Chance read the email and was stunned. It detailed a large deposit at a local bank the same day Cruz escaped from the psych hospital and a huge withdrawal made a couple of hours back from the same bank. Today's transaction consisted of withdrawal and closure of an account which was wiped clean of one point five million dollars.

The account holder's name was none other than Joe Scott.

Chapter Thirty-Nine

"Okay. So Scott cleaned out his bank account this morning. It doesn't prove he's our mole." Chance played devil's advocate.

"True, but keep reading," Izzy advised as she twirled a pen over her fingers with some kind of fuzzy thing on the end of it.

Another transaction flashed on the screen. It detailed the transfer of one and a half million dollars to an offshore bank account in Rio de Janeiro under the name Malcolm Bennett.

"Who's this Bennett guy?" Chance asked not following.

"Which is the beauty of it all," Izzy answered. "The name is fictitious. There is no Malcolm Bennett. I know it still doesn't prove Scott's the one feeding Cruz information, but when you couple those with these, I think you'll be convinced."

She clicked away on the keyboard in front of her. Half of the monitors changed from one email to another. There again was no subject line and nothing identifying the sender. The rest of the monitors now displayed photographs, one popping up over the other.

The pictures were of Joe Scott meeting with Alvin Cruz in what looked like a café. The date and time at the bottom of the screen were crystal clear. Scott met up with the psycho only hours after Cruz's escape from the psych hospital. Chance didn't know how or even why they had pictures of the meeting nor did he care.

"And wait! There's more!" Izzy was excited. She fiddled with the keyboard a couple of seconds and turned to face both Reggie and Chance. "A courier delivered this to us this morning in an unmarked brown envelope with my name on the front. Forensics is checking out the envelope as we speak. Anyway, listen to this."

She dramatically pressed a pink fingernail on a key. A voice Chance didn't recognize floated in the air. From what was being said, it was Alvin Cruz's father, John Cruz. The second voice was much more familiar to him -- Joe Scott, his task force team member, and Cruz was calling Scott *Junior.*

Chance focused on the second email displayed on the second set of monitors. Despite lack of identity as to its sender, the body of the email was loud and clear. Joe Scott, Jr. purchased a one-way ticket for Rio de Janeiro and his flight was due to leave in an hour.

Reggie picked up the phone on Izzy's desk and dialed. "This is Lyons. Get me the location of Special Agent Joe Scott, ASAP. A gag order is in effect." He clunked the receiver back down.

"He's on the run! He'll get away with it if we don't stop him. We have no jurisdiction in Rio," Izzy pleaded.

Chance turned toward the door. "Oh *hell* no, he won't!" His hands fisted in anger.

"Wait, Anselmi! Let me gather a task force," Lyons yelled.

But nothing was going to stop Chance. He pulled the door open with a jerk and glanced back at the Deputy Director.

"Send them to meet me if you want, but I'm not letting this asshole get away." He slammed the door shut and never looked back.

*****

Chance flipped his FBI badge over his jacket pocket out in plain sight. He'd called the airport on route and found out Scott's plane was due to take off in fifteen minutes. He just hoped he wasn't too late to nail the turncoat.

Flying through the terminal as fast as he could, he made it to Gate C where the flight to Rio was currently boarding. The walkie on his side went off.

"Agent Anselmi. Agent Bordeaux here. SIU7 has arrived and is converging on Gate C."

He grabbed the walkie, keying the mic. "Roger. I'm there now. Any word on Scott?"

"Negative. He hasn't been spotted."

"Send agents out on the tarmac to stop that bird if it tries to take off."

"They're already in place. Task force entering the terminal now."

There was a crowd of people at the doorway entering the plane. Scott was nowhere in sight. He cursed, realizing the rogue agent already boarded. He scanned the terminal and saw a clerk at the check-in counter. Rushing over, he held out his ID so she could see it. "Special Agent Chance Anselmi, FBI. I need you to stop boarding the plane immediately. It needs to be searched."

The young girl at the counter appeared dumbfounded. She must have been new at the job because she obviously didn't know what to do.

"Now!" Chance shouted.

She flinched and grabbed the phone as he headed for the doorway leading to the plane. Shoving people left and right out of his way, he gained entrance through the plane's open portal. He announced himself to the flight attendant at the door and flashed his badge.

"I need to search this plane. Keep anyone else from boarding until I give the go ahead."

"Yes, sir," the attendant replied.

He pulled his service revolver from its holster and kept both hands on it tucking it down low as he checked first class, his eyes searching the faces of every passenger there.

No Scott.

He drew the curtain separating First Class from Coach back slow and steady until he could peer in at the already seated passengers. Three rows down the left isle, he spotted the agent. Even though Chance had only seen Scott a few times, he recognized him from a picture which hung on Reggie's office wall, a picture of his task force team.

Joe was sitting alone in an aisle seat, his head bent distracted with something on his lap. Chance took a deep breath and swished the curtain out of his way.

With his feet firmly planted, he lifted the revolver and aimed it at Scott's chest. A woman seated in the first row let out a vicious scream when she saw his gun. Joe lifted his head and stared straight into Chance's eyes.

"FBI! Everybody down!" Chance yelled.

When his view cleared, he saw the blood drain from Scott's face but noted the man's quick recovery from his surprise at being caught.

"Chance Anselmi. Fancy meeting you here. Didn't think I'd ever get to see you again."

Joe shifted a hand toward the inside of his jacket. Chance knew he had a revolver stashed in a shoulder holster. "Freeze, Scott. You're under arrest."

Joe's hands stopped moving. "What's the problem, Anselmi? You've lost your mind over the woman or something aiming a gun at me? I'm your team member, for God's sakes. Whatever your problem is, I'm sure we can hash it out."

The bastard thought he could talk his way out of his predicament. Chance had another thought coming for him.

A wicked smile full of menace crossed Joe's face. "Come on, man. Don't you want another opportunity to screw the little bitch one more time in your little backwoods hideaway?"

"Shut the hell up, *Junior.* You're under arrest, remember? You do have the right to remain silent. I suggest you exercise your right before I put a damn bullet through your thick skull." The walkie at Chance's side went off.

"SIU7 in place at Gate C. Any sign of Scott?"

Joe seized the distraction from the radio transmission to reach for his gun. He stood and aimed it directly at Chance's heart. Before either had a chance to squeeze the trigger, a pop of gunfire exploded in the air.

Scott flinched, a look of total surprise covering his face. He crumpled to the ground, his gun clanging against one of the nearby seats before landing in the middle of the aisle.

With a now unobstructed view to the back of the plane, Chance saw Derek at the end of the aisle, one arm extended with his smoking weapon drawn, his other arm in a sling.

In a rush, Chance picked up Scott's weapon while keeping his eyes trained on the agent's slack body. Derek walked forward until he stood directly over Scott, his gun still aimed at the agent's head. Holstering his weapon, Derek bent over Scott's body and placed his fingers over the carotid artery in his neck.

"Is he dead?"

"He'd better not be. I aimed to wing him, not kill him." A moment passed and Derek smiled. "Nope. The traitor's still kicking."

Extracting his walkie from his belt, Chance informed the task force the subject was apprehended. Within moments, the inside of the plane was flooded with fellow agents who proceeded to empty the plane and secure the scene.

Chance shook his head in dismay as he holstered his weapon. "Damn, Derek. I thought your ass was still in the hospital."

"Lyons called me as soon as you lit out of Izzy's office for the airport. He knew better than to leave me out of this bust. You should've heard the nurses yelling at me on my way out the hospital. Such dirty words coming from such dainty mouths."

Chance chuckled. "I should've known they wouldn't be able to keep you down."

"You better believe it."

"Had you figured out it was him?"

"Yes. Travis showed me an anonymous text he received just before everything went from sugar to shit in Tennessee. It said if we figured out who Junior was we'd have our mole, but I needed proof before I could act. Thanks to Izzy, Lyons, and whoever sent Izzy the tape recording, we've got what we need."

The plane was becoming a bustle of agents and medical personnel. Derek and Chance moved out into the terminal waiting area so they could speak freely.

"So, tell me, rookie. How are you and Tara getting along these days?" The senior agent had a look of amusement on his face. Before Chance could answer, Derek's cell phone rang.

"Ross here. Okay." Derek handed the phone to Chance. "Izzy wants to talk to you."

Chance put the phone to his ear. "Hello, Izzy."

"Oh my God, Chance! I just figured out how Reggie's phone sent you the text, but it really didn't send it."

Very confused, Chance's brows furrowed. "What are you saying, Izzy?"

"What I'm saying is Reggie's phone was cloned! Someone made a copy of Reggie's phone number and all."

Chance felt the blood drain from his face. He felt a little dizzy.

"Chance. Are you okay?" Derek sounded concerned.

"Izzy. I need you to write this number down. A guy named Remi Dubois will answer. Tell him who you are and let him know what's happening."

Derek and Izzy were both squawking at him wanting to know what changed.

"Joe Scott is the one who sent me the text. He also referred to our 'backwoods hideaway', which means he knows where I'm hiding Tara. And it all means Cruz knows her location." He glanced Derek's way and saw the moment the truth hit him. He continued talking to Izzy. "Izzy. Tell Remi I'm on my way."

"Okay, Chance," Izzy's voice wavered. "Please be careful."

Chance couldn't help but grin. The technical analyst had a soft side. "I'll do my best, ma'am." He ended the call and handed the phone back to Derek.

Shaking his head, Derek shoved the phone back into Chance's hand. "Take it. You don't have yours and you'll need one. Now go. Be careful. I'll fill everyone else in."

Retrieving a notebook and pen from his pocket, Chance wrote down numbers and handed the paper to Derek. "These are the coordinates to the location of my camp where we will be."

Derek and Chance shook hands. "Wish I could go with you." Derek looked like he regretted sending Chance off alone.

"Yeah, me too. I'll call you as soon as I get there." Chance turned to leave, but turned back toward Derek. "Oh, and if Dubois tries to give Izzy a hard time, tell her to tell him I said if he still wants one of those brunette Georgia peaches, he'd better do as she says or I'll kick his ass from here to kingdom come and beyond, and tell him he'll never set his eyes on another fine Georgia peach again for the rest of his pitiful life."

*****

Remi just finished writing up his report about the missing fishermen. They were some guys who'd been drinking too much and had fallen asleep. They would be okay after their sunburns go away.

He shook his head in disbelief. *When will people ever learn? Drinking while boating is never a good idea.* When his cell phone rang, he figured it was Chance checking in. He pushed the button and answered the call.

"Hey, brother. What's happening?" There was a hesitation on the caller's part before he heard an answer.

"Um, hi. This is Izabelle Roth. I'm a technical analyst for the FBI. Is this Remi Dubois?"

Now Remi was on high alert. Dammit! Had something happened to Chance? "Yeah. This is Remi. What's going on? Where's Chance?"

"Agent Anselmi asked me to call you. He's fine and on his way back to wherever you are."

Okay. Something was just not right. Chance wouldn't have someone else call for him; he would simply call himself. What if this woman was the mole Chance referred to? Or she could be someone helping the mole.

"Look, baby doll. I don't know what's going on out there, but Chance would not ask someone else to call me; he would call himself, and he definitely would not have some computer geek do it." Remi grabbed his department issued phone and dialed Chance's personal cell number. Just as soon as he heard a phone in the background start ringing, the computer geek started speaking.

"Look, Mr. Big, Bad Cajun Dude. I don't have time to deal with you... uh, are you trying to call Chance's cell phone?"

Caught red-handed. So the geek wasn't just computer smart, she had common sense.

"And before you ask, the reason I have Agent Anselmi's phone is because the text he received calling him back to Quantico was a fake sent from a cloned phone. I have been analyzing it for the past thirty-six point four minutes."

For half a second, her precise time frame messed with Remi's brain. Then it hit him. Chance lured back on false pretenses wasn't a good sign.

"Anyhow, Chance asked me to contact you and let you know he is now on his way back to your location. He also wanted you to know Alvin Cruz might be on his way to your location as well."

Definitely not good.

"Oh. And he also said if you gave me any trouble, I was to tell you he would not get you the Georgia peach you wanted and he would, and I quote, 'kick your ass from here to kingdom come and beyond.'"

And double damn. The message could only be from his best friend who was the one person on earth aware of his obsession with fine southern women.

"Okay. So what do you need from me, sugar?"

"Now that is more like it."

Remi could almost hear a purr in the cute sounding analyst's voice, and from the sensual sound of the sexy little purr, Remi thought maybe a sweet Georgia peach might not be what he wanted anymore.

Chapter Forty

"What the hell are you doin', woman?" Chance stared at Tara who was hunched over where she stood under the old cypress tree shading the right side of Camp Fluffy. She was dressed in a pair of *Party Hard* shorts and a tank top, hands encased in gardener's gloves and a small shovel stuck in the ground at her feet. Buddy was right next to her, his paws digging away in the same hole she had been digging.

She pivoted and stared at him. Traces of dirt smeared her cheeks. Her expression turned from one of frustration to one of pure joy when she realized he was home.

"Chance!" She ripped off her gloves running to him at full speed. He caught her mid-air, her arms going around his neck and her legs wrapping around his waist. He couldn't help but smile as he inhaled her sweet scent which was now mixed with a little clean sweat and freshly turned earth.

"What are you up to, *chat marron*?" he questioned her again as he set her down on her feet. Poppee was sitting in the old rocking chair in the shade under the camp. Remi was next to him on a log, a pair of binoculars hanging from his neck.

Tara glanced at the old man and smiled. "Poppee and I took a walk yesterday. He told me the legend of Jean Lafitte and where the pirate marked his buried treasure by tying knots in small trees like that one. I thought I could dig up some of it."

Her look was so youthful and innocent, it made Chance angrier. "And you believe everything the old codger says? Tara, he's full of it. Haven't you caught on to him yet? He'll fill your head so full of bogus stories you won't know what hit you." Her face crumpled with his words.

Poppee grabbed his cane and stood mumbling as he walked out from under the camp. "Guess my welcome is over. I'll just get my stuff and ease on outta here."

Chance glared at Remi still sitting on the log. "And you! Why didn't you stop her? You know the old man is full of it."

Remi shrugged his shoulders and grinned. "Hey! Me? I was just sittin' here peaceful like watchin' a fine lookin' woman dig a hole." He lifted the binoculars toward Chance. "Wanna take a look?"

Chance eyed the binoculars in Remi's hand. His eyes followed a straight line from the binoculars to where Tara was digging under the cypress tree. His gaze then returned to Tara. Taking in her skimpy wardrobe, he shot a wicked look back at his friend.

"You son of a bitch! I told you to keep your hands off *my* woman. That meant your eyes too. I swear, I'm gonna twist your balls in a knot and cut you up into tiny little pieces! I've been warnin' you, and now you're gonna pay the price!"

He let go of Tara and took off in a dead run toward his friend, but Remi was just too quick. Throwing the binoculars on the ground, Remi shot up off the log in one fluid motion and broke into an all-out sprint toward his boat docked at the wharf, Chance in pursuit stringing French cuss words his way. Remi shouted out to the old man who was already in the boat.

"Hey, Poppee! Start up the engine quick! He's madder than the wild gator that bit you and he's fixin' to take a chomp out of *my* leg!"

Remi took two steps on the wharf and leaped into the boat like a cat on a hot tin roof. Taking over the wheel, he urged the boat out of the slip. When he was safely away from the wharf, he turned back to see Chance at the far end of the wharf, red faced with a murderous look. He was shaking his fists at them.

Remi smiled. "Call me if you need backup, *mon ami*! Bye y'all. Be in touch soon. And Tara, honey? Thanks for the memories, sha!"

Chance took a deep breath trying to curb his jealousy and headed back toward Tara who was rooted in the same spot he'd left her. His mood still black, he glanced down at her with furrowed brows.

A huge dopey smile broke out on her face. "I'm your woman?" She sounded... *hopeful*?

"Damn straight." Brusquely, he pulled her into his arms and kissed her senseless.

*****

Chance stared down at the woman draped over his chest, exhausted and sated from another round of lovemaking. Time was ticking. He knew Cruz was closing in on them. His sixth sense was tingling and there were things to do to get ready for the showdown. Rubbing his hand on her bare back, he managed to elicit a moan as she slid higher up his chest and kissed the tip of his chin.

"*Chèrie*. It's time to get up. I've got things I have to take care of."

"Do we have to?" she grumbled.

He chuckled. "Well, I don't want to either, but I have no choice."

Tara pulled herself into a sitting position. "What's going on, Chance? What happened in Quantico?"

He didn't want to frighten her any more than she already was, so he hadn't yet told her about Scott, but time was up. He needed to prepare her for whatever they were about to encounter.

"The reason Alvin was able to find us in Ohio and Tennessee is because one of the agents on the task force was feeding him information about our locations." Tara's body stiffened. "Now wait a minute. Don't jump to conclusions. We found out it was Joe Scott. Instead of him keeping tabs on Cruz's whereabouts, he's been feeding Cruz information on ours. Scott's in the hospital now with a bullet in his shoulder. He'll be locked up for a long time."

"Does Scott know where we are now?"

Hesitantly, he answered. "Yes."

She covered her mouth with her hand and gasped. "So, if he knows where we are, then Alvin..." Her voice trailed off.

He pulled her into his arms and held her tight, her body trembling beneath his grip.

"Can't we leave now and find another hiding place?"

"*Non, chère*. It's too late to run. Cruz has the jump on us. Scott gave him a head start. If we try to outrun him now, he'll just end up finding us someplace else where he might have the advantage. At least here I know every spot he could hide. The advantage is ours. Which is why I have to get things done before night falls."

"What kind of things?"

He didn't want to tell her, but the more he thought about it, the more he realized she had to know so she wouldn't stumble across traps unknowingly. "I've set traps along the tree line. Now I have to bury a few landmines in the yard around the camp."

"Like what you see in the movies?"

"Yes. The ones when you step on it, it triggers the firing mechanism. Once you lift your foot and take the pressure off the firing pin, it explodes. What I need you to do is keep Buddy and Timmy inside as much as possible. If they need out, put them on a short leash and don't venture away from the path leading to the wharf. I won't set out any in the area since we can see through the window and can hear a motor running. Better yet, don't let them out until I come back. We can take them out together."

"When do you think he'll come?"

"Soon. Maybe even tonight, which is why I need to get goin'."

Tara moved off the bed to get dressed while he did the same. "Stay inside until I come back." He took her in his arms and kissed her. "Don't worry, *chèrie*. He won't get near you."

Chance knew full well his statement was a promise he might not be able to keep.

*****

Just before daybreak on day five at Camp Fluffy, the day after Chance's return, he peered over Tara's shoulder at the clock on the night stand. Five-thirty a.m. He saw Buddy sprawled lazily on his back across the foot of the bed, paws straight up in the air. Timmy was there too with his paws and head draped over Buddy's stomach. The cat was snoring like a buzz saw.

Having been unable to sleep for the last hour or so, his internal radar was humming telling him Alvin was close -- real close. He would have to check the perimeter soon just to make sure everything was all right. Cruz was not going to get close enough to smell her much less touch her.

He couldn't bring himself to leave her side. As he watched Tara sleeping peacefully sated from a full night of lovemaking, he thought about all she did to him. Somehow she managed to turn him inside out. He didn't think he'd ever feel this way about anyone.

He loved her sassiness and her whit, her laugh and the way her nose crinkled when she ran across something she thought was unpleasant. He loved the tenacity, fortitude, and brave attitude she always exhibited through an air of confidence and ferocity while she was fragile and vulnerable inside. He even found himself growing fond of her damn cat. In fact, there wasn't a thing he didn't love about her. His heart thumped hard in his chest.

He loved her.

He looked down again at her sleeping form, her back pressing against the entire length of his body. His arm draped across her waist, he palmed her breast and then moved his thumb in slow, soft circles around her nipple. He felt it pebble and tighten. The one little touch sent him to attention. He wanted her again. He always wanted her.

Nudging her hair away from her ear with his chin, he placed a gentle kiss on her lobe. "Mmm, *chat marron*. You drive me crazy," he whispered as he stroked her breast with his hand. She squirmed moving tighter against him as she purred with a low groan. He so loved her purr.

"What time is it?" Her voice was throaty, sexy.

"Just before dawn. Go back to sleep."

She rubbed her butt against him making him groan. "Can't. There's a piece of steel poking me in the back."

He laughed. "You put it there, woman, now deal with it." He gently squeezed her nipple once more.

Buddy let out a low feral growl breaking the intimate spell. Chance's head whipped up and his eyes scanned the room. Buddy's growling continued.

"Something's wrong." He felt Tara's body stiffen.

"What is it?"

Buddy barked roughly and jumped off the bed. They heard him rumbling through the living room, barking and growling at the front door. Chance jumped out of bed and started pulling on his jeans.

"Chance?"

He saw the damn fear fill her eyes once more as she realized Buddy's bark was a warning. Opening the drawer on the night stand, he retrieved his Glock plus an extra clip of ammo along with the gun she'd used for target practice. He jammed the Glock in the back of his jeans and took the safety off the other gun pointing the butt end of it in her direction.

"Take this. If anyone other than me comes in here, aim and shoot till you're out of ammo."

"Chance, you're scaring me." Her voice wavering, she grabbed the gun with one hand and tried to hold up the sheet over her body with the other.

"Get dressed and stay put." He leaned over the bed and grabbed her head with both hands, then planted a firm possessive kiss on her lips. When he lifted his head and looked into her terrified eyes, his heartbeat took off like a bottle rocket. He was not losing this woman.

His woman.

He glanced down at the gun in her hand. "Use it."

The front door of the camp was still locked. Buddy was practically dancing in front of it whimpering and wanting out.

Pulling the Glock out and extending his hands ready to shoot, Chance unlocked the door and opened it slow. Buddy shot out like his paws were on fire.

As Chance cautiously walked out onto the porch, he peered through the early morning mist for Buddy or for an intruder. He could see paw prints in the morning dew, but there was also a set of men's shoeprints. Chance had just started following the prints when a howling bark from Buddy split the air followed by an agonizing yelp... then silence.

Cursing and hoping Alvin had not hurt, or worse, killed Buddy, Chance ventured slowly, his eyes peeled searching for anything unusual. Scanning the area near the wharf where Buddy's prints lead, he saw the basset hound lying in a crumpled heap at the wharf's edge.

His throat clogged. "Buddy," he whispered dejected. As he approached the fallen animal, he stooped down to check him out keeping his eyes ever vigilant of his surroundings. A quick glance down at the dog confirmed his worst fear. Buddy was bleeding across the neck and wasn't breathing.

His beloved friend was dead, but the loyal animal hadn't gone down without a fight. Chance noted shards of human flesh in the dog's teeth. Buddy was able to take a chunk out of his attacker.

Livid over the loss of his companion, he stood and surveyed the property. No sign of anyone. The hairs at his nape stood on end; he could almost smell him. He began his hunt.

Cutting through the thick cypress trees circling the camp, Chance found the evidence he'd been searching for. Boot imprints which weren't his littered the ground just inside the tree line at the back of the camp -- Alvin's. Somehow the idiot had missed the traps.

Huddled down close to the ground, Chance surveyed the back of the camp. He could see parts of two sides of the building plus the entire underneath area. A blurry movement caught his eye on the left. A cloaked figure was moving toward the front of the camp darting in and out of the pylons. The figure stopped and hunkered down. Chance seized the opportunity and advanced toward him.

*****

Alvin listened for sounds of movement in the camp above his head, but there were none. He wondered if the two were sleeping all snug as bugs on a rug. The son of a bitch FBI agent better not have ruined her. She was *his* woman. He'd cut the bastard if he'd messed her up. Tara Roberts was his and his alone.

It had been hell getting to this God forsaken land. A non-stop flight turned into two layovers due to mechanical failure of one of the planes. *Mechanical failure? Who the hell wants to hear their plane has mechanical failure?* He had trouble getting a rental car, and then he'd had to scrounge up a whiskey addicted scum of a man who had a boat which could take him out here to this rodent, bug, and alligator infested creepy-as-hell swamp. Of course the scumbag didn't have to worry about his addiction anymore. In fact, he wouldn't have any more worries, period.

On top of all that, the damn dog grabbed hold of his leg and wouldn't let go. He had no choice but to cut the dog's throat. Too bad he'd had to kill the animal; he liked dogs.

Yeah, it had been a rough ride getting here, but she was worth it. *After all, she's the love of my life.* He was just about to make a move toward the front steps of the camp when someone jumped him from behind.

*****

Chance lunged for Cruz and caught him around the shoulders. They both fell to the ground grunting. "There you are, you sicko." Chance turned Alvin to face him and straddled over him. He slugged the psycho square in the jaw with his fist. "You will not touch her, do you hear me?" He pummeled his opponent again and again until Alvin's body slumped. *Dammit. I hope he's just unconscious and not dead.* Chance straightened up gulping air like he'd run ten miles.

He patted his hip where he normally kept his handcuffs. *Dammit, forgot the damn things.* His thoughts were cut off when he was pushed in the chest so hard it knocked him off his feet. The impact as he met the ground made his gun skid under a pile of wood.

"You'd better not have ruined her. She's mine!" Alvin bellowed as Chance stood facing him. They resumed fighting, arms and fists flying. In a quick move, Chance grappled with him until they both hit the ground rolling away from the camp out into the open.

"She'll never be yours, you psycho asshole."

He got the upper hand when they'd both managed to stand upright once more. "This one's for Buddy." Chance cold-cocked Cruz with a stiff upper cut to the jaw. Alvin's head flew backward but he was able to withstand the punch and threw one of his own, catching Chance square on the tip of his chin.

Stunned, Chance reset himself and started throwing body punches trying to cut off the other man's breath. He maneuvered until he was able to grab Alvin around his neck from the back. A loud click rent the air.

Both men froze in place.

Chance glanced down at their feet and saw one of the pegs in the ground where he'd marked a landmine.

"Oh, damn."

*****

Tara was hunkered in the middle of the bed with the gun in her hand. Her whole body was trembling, fear fueling her motion.

Where the hell is he? Doesn't he realize by now how terrified I am of Alvin? How dare he just dump a gun in my hand and take off leaving me alone. There's no way I can face my tormentor without him.

Maybe she'd stop shaking if she could take her mind off what was happening outside. She thought about waking up this morning in Chance's arms. He'd spooned her close to his body and draped his big arm over her resting his hand on her breast. She'd been roused by the feel of his fingertips as he made her nipple grow hard to his touch, and she'd fully awakened at the feel of his rock hard erection rubbing up against her butt. There was no longer any doubt in her mind. She had some serious feelings for the man, and he was out there somewhere trying to rid her of the maniac who had occupied every waking and sleeping moment of her life for what felt like forever.

She wished Remi would have come by and stayed with them. Two would have been much better than one. She knew Chance was capable of handling the situation alone. He was an ex-Army Ranger and FBI to boot. He'd had lots and lots of training, but Alvin was a certified lunatic and Chance was not invincible. Now that she'd admitted to herself she had deep feelings for Chance, she wanted the opportunity to explore those feelings.

She kept her eyes and ears vigilant for any sight or sound, but none were forthcoming. In fact, other than her own heart hammering in her ears, there was no sound at all... not even Buddy. Her heart gave a twist at the thought something might have happened to the beloved pet. Chance loved the dog. In fact, so did she.

A loud *boom* echoed through the air shaking the building. Tara let out a scream. *Oh my God. What the hell was that?* Timmy leaped off the bed as the loud noise struck. With the gun still in her hand, she followed Timmy's lead and jumped off the bed too.

"Timmy, where are you?" she whispered as she entered the living room. Keeping her voice low, she continued calling for her precious cat, but he wouldn't come to her.

"Damn stubborn animal." She heard another noise coming from outside. Frightened, she fell to the floor scooting back on her butt until she hit the cabinets. Footsteps now echoed off the front porch steps.

She raised the gun with trembling hands and aimed at the front door. It flew open and hit the wall with a bang. Her heart thudded in her chest.

Alvin Cruz now stood menacingly in the open doorway.

Chapter Forty-One

"Ah. There's... my baby. You've been... hiding... from me." Alvin gulped in air between words. "Junior finally... got something... right."

Tara's heart was beating a quick time tempo as she viewed her nightmare in the flesh. He was beaten and battered, cuts and scrapes over his arms and a bloody gash running down his left leg. A huge red whelp was blossoming above his already swollen right eye. His clothes were tattered and disheveled, his blond hair stringy. From his bedraggled appearance, he and Chance must have struggled, which meant Chance had found him, which also meant the loud booming noise had come at Chance's expense, not Alvin's.

Her wildly beating heart stopped. *Oh God. Oh God. Oh God. Had Chance triggered one of the mines?*

Quickly, she rationalized what his absence meant. Her heart tried to deny the fact something bad happened to him. She thought he was invincible.

"Chance. No," she whispered out loud while she shook her head in denial and her heart began to split in two. He would never leave her all alone to deal with this maniac, not unless he'd succumbed to a mine. Surely he couldn't have survived that kind of blast.

She could feel the rapid return of the dreaded emptiness he had managed to fill in her heart. Tears began trickling down her face. She cringed from the thought of seeing his body broken and defeated.

"What's the matter, baby? Aren't you glad to see me? Here I've been roaming all over the country trying to find you so we could be together again and you call out for the FBI asshole? What, you don't want me anymore? I've done everything for you, dammit. Yeah, I saw you dressed up in the skimpy outfit yesterday. I've been watching the two of you... you and the dumbass you've been with here. But it's okay. He won't be bothering us anymore, just like Mommy and Daddy stopped bothering us, remember?"

Fear clogged her throat at the mention of her parents and his confirmation Chance had indeed lost the fight of his life. She became aware of his movement, which he was inching his way toward her as he tried distracting her with his ramblings.

She unfolded her legs and scrambled around the kitchen table back away from him, the gun still clutched in her hand. She was hoping she could make her way to the living room. That way, she would be able to keep some of the furniture and obstacles between them, but she cleared the table when Alvin was trying to catch her. It caused her to fall to the floor, but she somehow managed to stand upright once more.

He lunged for her ankle, but she was able to scoot out of reach. She turned to run but he caught her, toppling her over. The gun flew out of her hand and skidded across the floor out of sight. He was on top of her pinning her body to the floor. He wrapped both hands around her throat. With his back facing the bookcase, he stood and lifted her off the ground.

Tara could hardly breathe let alone scream as Alvin kept a tight grip on her throat. She couldn't get any leverage as the tips of her toes scraped the floor. Alvin continued his earlier tirade.

"You know I killed them all for you -- for us, so we could be together. They didn't want me to join your little family. They were all trying to keep us apart, just like the bastard out there. Even he can't stop us now."

Tara grew weaker as she gasped for what little air she could manage, tears streaming down her face. She looked past Alvin and saw Timmy perched on top of the bookcase ready to pounce, baring teeth. Her eyes drifted back toward Alvin.

"Do you have anything to say about your recent slutty behavior? No?" He loosened his grip just a hair so she could speak. She sucked in a huge gulp of air as she tried to catch her breath. Her throat was scratchy and raw when she tried to speak.

"It wasn't my family who didn't want you. It was me. I don't want you. Never did and never will, you sick bastard!" She turned just enough to spit in his face.

"Why you damn little bitch!" He let her go and backhanded her across the jaw, the blow so powerful she fell back on the floor. "If I can't have you, no one will!" He pulled out a knife from behind his back.

Tara's heart tripped as she recognized it as the knife Chance had used when he'd cleaned their catch of fish. As Alvin lifted the weapon in the air, Timmy let out a feral shriek and pounced on Alvin's back digging in with his claws between the maniac's shoulder blades. The knife fell to the floor with a clang but remained out of Tara's reach.

Struggling to wrestle the heavy tabby off his back, Cruz flailed his arms in the air. While he was preoccupied with Timmy, Tara scurried across the floor to the fireplace. She grabbed a poker iron and gripped it firmly in her hands. Finally able to reach the cat, Alvin hurled the still hissing feline to the floor.

Anger flooded Tara's brain when she heard Timmy's screeching cry. His treatment of Timmy pissed her off even more and sent her into a rage.

She charged at Alvin with the poker iron. When she got close enough to strike, he turned in time to grab the poker twisting it out of her hands. He shoved her away throwing her into the bookcase where she landed with a thud. Her body stunned, she slid to the floor as books fell all around her.

"You stupid bitch. All you have to do to stop this is to accept fate and say you're mine."

"Never!" she screamed at him. "Never!" She threw book after book at him trying to upset his grip. He dodged them all and came after her with the poker raised high over his head.

The front door swung open banging against the wall. A disheveled and bloody Chance charged into the room and hurtled his massive body at Cruz.

Tara's heart raced at the sight of him. Bloody and banged up, he was alive.

Just as Chance shoved Cruz away from her, the madman shifted his stance and caught Chance solid on his shoulder with the poker iron. Chance buckled from the blow, but recovered quick. Lunging at Alvin once more, he was able to force the poker iron from Alvin's grip where it flew out of reach. They both fell to the floor rolling back and forth as they fought for dominance.

A flurry of blows ensued as their bodies shifted across the floor. Chance was beginning to get the upper hand when Alvin turned around just as Chance was about to grab hold of him. Alvin was no longer empty handed -- the poker iron was now firmly in his grasp.

Alvin tried to stab Chance with the iron, but Chance dodged the steel rod in time. Alvin hit him across the chest with it. The hit was so hard, Tara could tell it cut off Chance's breath. That gave Alvin the break to take aim again. Just as he was ready to drive the pointed end of the poker into Chance, a furious Timmy landed on his back once more.

Tara appeared to have been forgotten in the fight. She was looking for a weapon to help Chance. Spying a metal baseball bat in the umbrella stand next to the door, she raced over and grabbed it.

Struggling to free himself of the cat, Cruz held the iron with one hand and reached around his back with the other. His arm holding the poker iron dropped down to his side but he still held it in a death grip.

When he was able to free himself of the angry cat, he looked up. Tara faced him, a metal baseball bat in her grasp ready to strike.

Placing the tip of the cold steel poker on the spot near Chance's heart, Cruz poked him with it. A droplet of blood oozed down.

"Drop the bat or he gets gored."

Without a second thought, Tara let the bat fall to the floor. Her stalker grinned just before he brought the poker iron down on Chance's head.

Tara let out a bloodcurdling scream as she watched Chance slump to the ground with a thud. A large gash was visible on his head and blood was beginning to pool beneath it.

"Don't worry. He's not dead. I didn't kill him just yet because I want him to watch. I want him to know you belong to me and no other."

Tara fell to her knees in agony. Cruz dropped the poker iron and faced her, his intent obvious. She fell back on her haunches and started a backwards crawl until she butted up against the couch. Something poked her hand from beneath it. She reached a hand there and realized she'd found the misplaced gun.

Bracing herself against the couch, she jumped into a shooting position with gun in hand. With the sight directly aimed at Alvin's heart, she lowered the weapon about an inch and placed her finger gently on the trigger.

Cruz stopped in his tracks, his eyes glued to the gun. A slow grin emerged on his battered face. "Know what, baby? I'll bet you're going to be the best piece of ass I've ever had."

Tara cocked the trigger in response.

"You're not going to pull the trigger. You don't like guns. Have you tried shooting that thing? No? I'll bet you suck at it. Besides, I think you don't have the guts to pull the trigger."

Tara looked straight into her nemesis's crystal blue psychotic eyes.

"Think again, *asshole*!"

Without flinching, she pulled the trigger slow and easy. Once. Twice. Three times. Mouth agape in surprise, Alvin's wicked blue eyes were wide open. With blood blooming from three bullet holes in his chest, Alvin slumped to the floor.

Tara fell to the floor and crawled on hands and knees to Chance. Timmy was already at his head licking him in the face trying to rouse him. As she got to him and tried rolling him over, he groaned, his teeth clenched and a grimace on his face.

"Oh, God. Chance. Tell me you're all right. Talk to me, Chance, please. Tell me you're all right!" Tears streamed down her cheeks.

Chance's eyes opened slowly and Tara's breath came out in a whoosh of relief.

"Alvin?" He was weak as his eyes closed once more.

"Dead. I shot him," she replied without an ounce of remorse in her voice.

Chance's left eye re-opened. "In the head or the foot?"

Reflexively, she bopped him on the shoulder.

"Ow! *Maudit*!" he cursed, a little chuckle coming from him.

"Sorry! I didn't mean to..."

"It's okay, *chat marron*. You didn't hurt me any worse than I already am. Get my cell phone out of my pocket and call Reggie."

She did as he instructed giving Reggie all the gruesome details of their encounter. When she hung up, she sat and placed Chance's head in her lap. Stroking his hair back, her hand started visibly shaking.

The nightmare was over. Her stalker was dead. Tears flowed down her face like a torrent of rain. Chance's eyes flew open. "*Chèrie. Mon Dieu.* Good Lord, please don't cry. It's over. You're safe now." He placed his hand over hers.

"I almost lost you too," she blurted in a voice overflowing with emotion.

He shook his head. "No. Don't be sad at what might've been. Now is the time for you to start a new life free from him and free from fear."

With a weak smile, she bent down and gave him a gentle kiss. Timmy meowed, and then hissed right by Chance's ear.

"Go find your own girl, you big fur ball," he chided.

*****

A few minutes later, the front door to the camp swung on its hinges with so much force, it banged against the wall. Remi stood in the doorway, his left hand holding a pistol, his right hand beneath it steadying his aim. His eyes were sharp as he hunted for the source of the gunfire. He swung his arms first to the left and saw Alvin's body slumped on the floor in a pool of blood looking deader than a doornail. He then swung to his right and saw Chance and Tara both sitting on the floor, Chance's head in Tara's lap. When he realized they were both alive, he expelled his worried breath and lowered the gun.

"Y'all just had to do this all by yourselves, didn't you? Y'all couldn't call me first and at least invite me to watch the show?" He marched to where Alvin's body lay on the floor. Placing two fingers to Alvin's carotid artery, he pressed down and found no pulse, not that he expected to from the way Alvin was shot -- three bullet wounds straight to the chest.

"Be damn glad you weren't here," Chance remarked. "The pretty little woman as you so fondly call her was hell on wheels."

"Well somebody had to shoot him. You tried blowing him up and instead almost got yourself blown up. So, naturally I stepped in," she gloated, her mood seemed good considering what had just transpired.

"From the looks of him, you could qualify as an expert in field training," Remi teased.

"Hold up. Wait a minute. Where'd she get him?" Chance voiced sounding confused.

Remi faced Chance and tapped his own chest right over his heart.

"No way. She hit a damn rabbit five yards in front of her target when she was practicing."

Tara gasped, obviously insulted.

"She closed her eyes for Chri'sakes!"

Tara stood letting Chance's head drop to the floor with a thud. "Ouch! That hurt!" He rubbed his head where it had met with the hard floor. He grabbed Tara by the ankle and ran his hand over it.

Tara looked down at Chance, his head still oozing blood from his wound. Thankfully, Alvin hadn't hit him so hard as to knock him out.

"I'm only picking with you, Tara. You did great," Chance complimented her.

Remi watched as Tara dropped down on the floor and leaned over. Grabbing Chance by the ears, she kissed him silly.

"I'm with Poppee. I'm too damn young to watch such goings on," Remi retorted as he strode toward the couch where they were now sitting.

He surveyed Chance's wounds, what little he could see of them Tara's body wasn't covering. There were several cuts and scraped on his arms and neck as well as the head wound, an ugly welt across his chest where he'd been hit by something and a pretty deep gash on the side of his head. But considering he'd damn near been blown up by a landmine, Remi thought he was in remarkably good shape. Alvin definitely got the raw end of the deal in their fight.

When Tara came up for air, she looked straight at Remi. "Don't you have a body to add to your long list of pick-ups, Dr. K?"

Chance's laughter rang through the air.

Damn, Remi felt his cheeks flush.

Chapter Forty-Two

A matronly nurse taped down fresh sterile gauze bandages with a vengeance over the gaping wound on Chance's head using a mile of silk tape. There wasn't a stitch of bandaging which could escape the confines of the tape.

"There. Better." She blew an exasperated breath causing her salt and pepper bangs to flare. "Maybe now you'll keep your hands off this one and I won't have to come back a *fourth* time to re-bandage your wound. Do you understand what I'm trying to tell you, Mr. Anselmi?" She gave him a stern look and a cocked brow.

"Hey. I can't help it. The paper tape was eating my skin. If you understood me the first time, you would've switched to silk tape on re-bandaging number one."

Remi listened to the argument as he tried unsuccessfully to remain still in his chair. Chance's anger was uncharacteristic and it was making him uncomfortable. In the last two hours, this had been the third time the same nurse came in to re-dress the wound on his head. She also came in twice during the same time frame to change his IV site which kept infiltrating because the big dummy wouldn't keep still.

Ever since Chance's boss, Derek, had barged into the room and whisked Tara away for debriefing, Remi watched his buddy's disposition turn from sunny, happy, and lighthearted to grumpy, grouchy, and plain old mean.

In all the years Remi had known him, which was for most of their lives, he'd never seen Chance fly off the handle like he'd been doing this morning. Well, except for the time six years back when Chance came home early for Christmas and caught his fiancée in bed with one of his buddies. Livid with anger, he'd flown into a murderous rage. When Remi got there and realized what happened, he'd been afraid Chance had killed them both, but somehow, the big man had managed to subdue his anger. He'd scared the piss out of both of them when he drew his shotgun out of the closet and aimed it between their eyes. Instead of firing, he'd walked out without so much as a backward glance at his unfaithful woman and the low-life he had once called friend. His unshakable military bred self-control remained steadfast and strong then and ever since, never wavering... unlike now.

Remi pondered the situation. Chance's mood had been fine before Derek showed up and pulled Tara away, which meant Tara must mean something more to Chance than just a casual affair, something deep, and something profound... and *that* thought made Remi smile.

"What the hell you smiling for, Dubois? Enjoying my misery?"

"Oh hell yeah, I'm enjoying it... every damn minute of it."

Chance was growling his disapproval when the door to the room opened and Tara bounded in. Remi looked on as sheer relief washed over Chance's face the minute his eyes lit on the woman. Yep. The big Cajun man finally met his match. He'd been out-fished -- caught hook, line, and sinker, by a wiry little California bred woman... and Remi loved it.

*****

Tara slid her fingers in between Chance's long and warm ones. As always, the skin-to-skin contact sent butterflies flitting about in her stomach. She stared at Chance. His eyes were luminous with his adoration for her.

She just couldn't believe it was all over. With Alvin dead and no longer a threat, she was free from the fear which gripped her for what felt like forever. She took in a huge gulp of air, her lungs filling rapidly. She exhaled as if she'd been holding her breath for all those years which, pretty much, she had been. She frowned when she realized in actuality, she didn't know what it was like to not feel fear.

Chance squeezed her hand. "What's wrong, sweetheart? You look like something's bothering you."

She did a mental headshake to clear her mind. "I'm fine. I was just thinking. With Alvin dead, I don't have to be afraid anymore. Maybe now I can breathe again."

Chance squeezed her hand again. "That's right, *chère*. Now you can lead the life you want free from fear, and you'll be able to enjoy yourself again. I'm very happy for you."

Tara gave him a fragile smile. "I know, but it almost feels like I'm hovering in a state of limbo. What's worrying me is I don't think I know how to be free."

"Well, now you'll have the time to figure it all out. You can do whatever your heart desires, *chat marron*."

She'd almost forgotten. She pulled her hand free of his and swatted him on his shoulder.

"Ow! What the hell was that for?" He sounded vexed.

"You've been calling me a wildcat! Poppee told me what that shot thing meant. I can't believe you think I'm such a hell raiser -- a damn wildcat!"

Chance laughed. "You *are* a wildcat -- a bold, brazen, hellacious wildcat of a woman."

He grabbed the front of her tee shirt and pulled her down. His hand slid behind her neck as his mouth nipped at her ear. "And I love it about you, my *chat marron*."

He kissed her like a starving man massaging her lips with his own, nibbling them and forcing hers apart as he explored the inner depths of her mouth. His tongue parried with hers. Her nipples were swelling and pebbling, becoming rigid nubs. She moved her body so she was draped against his unwounded side. He repositioned himself in the bed allowing her access to the full length of him. She slid her body over his, their kiss deepening as their other body parts came into full contact.

*****

"Ahem." Remi cleared his throat to get their attention. Chance and Tara pulled apart to look at him, neither of them looking the least bit guilty about ignoring him. He laughed.

"Since you two don't seem to need my help with anything, I think I'll just mosey on out and see if I can find the gorgeous bombshell of a brunette who came in here and re-bandaged your head, Anselmi. You know the one I'm talkin' about, the one who was rubbing up against you, the one stacked like a brick house?"

"*What*?" Tara gasped.

Remi couldn't help but laugh at Tara's reaction. He held up his hands in self-defense as Chance grabbed a half-empty bottle of water off the night stand and threw it at him. He missed which made Remi laugh even harder.

"Dubois! When I get out of this damn bed, I'm gonna skin you alive for tryin' to cause trouble. Get your skinny ass out of here before I get up and hurt you."

Remi headed for the door at a quick pace laughing like a fool.

Chapter Forty-Three

Travis groaned. Every muscle he owned was racked in spasms. His leg itched to high heaven. The gauze patch on his side covering a gaping wound the doctors had left open to drain was aggravating the crap out of him, and the silk tape they'd secured over each and every little patch of gauze covering his entire body was eating up his skin. All in all, he was freaking miserable. The door to his hospital room creaked opened.

"Up for some company?" Derek peaked through the door grinning like crazy.

"Only if you've got a hot blonde hanging on your arm. Other than that? No."

Derek walked in the room followed by Chance, Tara, and some fellow Travis didn't recognize. Tara went straight to the side of his bed and draped herself across his body giving him a big hug. He grunted from the pain as she pressed down on his injured side.

"Oh, sorry. I didn't mean to hurt you. I'm just so glad you're alive."

"Thanks, but if you want me to stay that way, ease up on the hugs, okay?"

An elderly, somewhat rotund nurse entered the room and eyed the visitors one by one. "I thought I told you no visitors, Mr. Dean?"

"I didn't invite this bunch. They busted down my door and invited themselves."

The nurse opened her mouth ready to shoo them out the room, but Derek flashed his badge at her and gave her a you-better-not look. She shut her mouth, grabbed a glass of water off the tray next to the bed, handed Travis a cup with his meds in it, and gave him an evil eye until he swallowed the pills. She put the cup back on the tray and left without another word.

"Great way to clear a room, Ross."

Derek smiled. "I have a way with women."

Travis started laughing but it quickly turned into a groan. "No jokes, dammit. It hurts."

"All right. We'll behave. So how's it been going?" Derek asked.

"What are you? Blind? I've been freaking shot to hell and you want to know how it's been going? Want to trade places?"

Before Derek could answer, another nurse entered the room. This one, on a one to ten scale, was a nine and a half. She walked up to the bed, placed a stethoscope against Travis's chest, and gazed into his eyes the entire time she listened to his heartbeat. The monitor above his head picked up a quicker pace, his heart rate accelerating.

She smiled at him, placed her palm against his cheek, and turned to walk away. When she spotted the unknown guy standing by the door, she halted. Eyeing him from head to toe and back, she gave him a radiant smile.

Eyeing her in like fashion, the guy returned the smile. "*Mon Dieu. Manifique.*" He watched her leave the room.

"Who the hell are you?" Travis asked.

Chance made the formal introduction. "Travis Dean? Remi Dubois. Remi's with Water Patrol back home. He helped us hide Tara."

Remi walked over to the bed and shook Travis's hand. "Good to see you're alive. I'm not sure why, but Tara seems to think you're some kind of hero or something."

"Right, some hero. I was the first one shot to hell and back. I missed the whole shooting match."

"Travis. I don't care what you say. You're a hero in my book and I'm the only one here who counts," Tara informed him.

"Thanks, Tara. So, Remi. I see you have an eye for beauty." He waggled his brows.

Chance jumped in. "Travis. Don't you get him started. This man is a womanizing..."

"Anselmi! I have a tongue. Let me speak for myself," Remi retorted.

"Oh, yeah. You have a tongue all right, and I know what you like to do with it too. So keep it in your mouth."

Tara laughed. "Boys, boys. We're here to make Travis feel better, not to fight."

The door swung open again and a nurse's aide walked in. Dressed all in blue, she stood close to six feet tall, was slender with an hour glass figure and a head full of long brunette curls cascading down her back. She grabbed Travis's medical chart hooked at the foot of the bed and walked over to him. Placing her fingers against his wrist, she turned her other arm up to look at her watch. Her eyes flittered upwards to meet his. She gave him a wink, wrote something down on the chart, put it back on its hook, and walked out.

"She winked at you," Remi announced.

"Humph. It would've been more than a wink if I would have been alone."

Derek broke into their conversation. "Okay. Enough female ogling. We've got a meeting to go to. Just wanted to stop in and see how you were doing, Travis."

Chance hadn't been able to get a word in edgewise so he seized the opportunity to speak. "Travis. We all wanted you to know how much we appreciate everything you did on this assignment. I especially wanted to tell you how sorry we are you were shot and I wanted to thank you for watching over Tara."

"You're all part of the team now, Anselmi. We're family, and protecting family around here is a given." The injured man turned his head to stare at Tara. "You're worth it you know." A single tear fell from her eye. She blew him a kiss.

Yet another pretty nurse entered the room. This one stopped in front of Remi, mouth agape. He placed his finger under her chin and lifted it shutting her mouth.

"You are one gorgeous specimen of womanhood," he told her, smiling.

She took a couple of steps backwards and ran into Travis's bed giving him a jolt.

"Ow! Don't do that!"

The nurse turned around stunned by his reaction. She was so flustered, she forgot why she had come into the room and left fanning her face with her hand.

Remi moved to the side of Travis's bed. "Are there more like her around here?"

Travis nodded. "Lots. They'll be changing shifts in a few minutes. It gets even better on the evening shift. Stick around if you'd like."

Remi pulled up the chair next to the bed and plopped down in it. "Don't mind if I do. I'll catch you guys later. Give me a call when y'all are ready to leave."

They all laughed and headed for the door. Chance grabbed Remi's arm and pulled him out the chair forcing him to follow as everyone bid Travis goodbye.

Chapter Forty-Four

Chance and the entire task force minus Travis waited in the conference room at FBI headquarters for the Deputy Director to show. He'd called for a debriefing and had also requested Tara's presence. She and Izzy were having a woman-to-woman conversation in a corner which Chance wanted no part of. He was talking to Derek about Travis's condition. The door to the conference room opened and Reggie entered.

"Everyone, please be seated. I've gathered you here today to congratulate this task force on a job well done. The apprehension of the assailant, Alvin Cruz, was handled with true professionalism. You all epitomize the FBI motto of 'Fidelity, Bravery and Integrity.'

"We lost a valuable team member in Agent Navarro. He will be missed by one and all. A memorial service will be held next week and I'm sure you will all want to attend.

"We also lost another member of our team, Agent Joe Scott. He will *not* be missed. For those of you who have not yet been debriefed, Joe Scott had ulterior motives for passing information to Alvin Cruz concerning Ms. Roberts's whereabouts.

"While attending college, Scott raped a young co-ed and threatened her life if she revealed what he'd done. John Cruz, Alvin's father, attended the same college and had befriended Scott. The elder Cruz was witness to the crime and was sworn to secrecy.

"Over the years, Cruz kept Joe's secret but held it over his head using it to extract certain favors from the agent. When Alvin escaped the psychiatric institution, Alvin enlisted Scott's aide in his search for Ms. Roberts. The elder Cruz confessed to authorities Scott's extorted thousands of dollars from him to finance the aiding and abetting of his son's flight across the country. In addition to the funds Scott extorted from the Cruz family, he also had a million and a half in funds stashed sway obtained from an unknown source. More than likely, he was into other illegal dealings which we have yet to uncover.

"As for Scott's condition, he's currently recovering from his wounds and will be sent to a maximum security facility upon his full recovery to await trial. Charges pending against him are extortion, aiding and abetting a known criminal, and attempted murder of a federal agent just to name a few."

"Excuse me, Director?" Lucien Bordeaux interrupted. "Have we been able to identify the sender of the emails which exposed Scott?"

"If I may, sir?" Izzy requested. Reggie nodded his approval. "The emails were encrypted. Each one was sent from a different computer with a different IP address. All three of the accounts have since been closed and are untraceable. Whoever sent them has superior knowledge of cyberspace and computers. I tried to track them back to their sources but was unable to do so."

"Well if *you* couldn't track the guy, Izzy, then we don't stand a chance of finding him either," Lucien commented with a smile. Izzy blushed.

Reggie also grinned. "We intend to continue searching for this mystery person. Had it not been for him or her, we might not have intercepted Scott before he fled the country. Now, if all will excuse me for a moment?" He stood and left the room. When he returned seconds later, Chance's best friend accompanied him.

"Ladies and gentlemen, this is Officer Remi Dubois who is employed by the Lafourche Parish Sheriff's Office, Water Patrol Division, in south Louisiana. In cooperation with the FBI, Officer Dubois went above and beyond the call of duty to assist in the sequestering of Ms. Roberts after the hit on the Tennessee safe house. Since Scott was always aware of her whereabouts, we would not have been able to adequately protect her were it not for Officer Dubois's assistance.

"I've brought him here today not only to commend him on his actions and allow you all to meet him, but also to see if we could talk him into becoming a permanent member of the FBI. We're in bad need of reliable and trustworthy agents these days and Officer Dubois has demonstrated he possesses the qualities needed to become a special agent. So, what do you have to say, Officer Dubois? Would you consider a transfer to our organization?"

*****

Remi paled. Chance, who was grinning from ear to ear, nodded his approval and mouthed "say yes" to him. The praise being bestowed upon him was unwarranted and unnecessary as far as he was concerned. He'd done it for his friend. Hell, from what he'd been told, the only reason Cruz found Tara in the first place was because they'd followed him to Camp Fluffy.

The offer of a position with the FBI was something he hadn't anticipated. Even though secretly he'd longed for just such an opportunity, it was impossible for him to accept.

"I truly appreciate the offer, sir. Really, I do, but I'm afraid I have to decline. It's just not a viable option for me at this time." He watched Chance's face drop into a frown.

"I understand." Reggie's voice held a note of disappointment. "But if you change your mind in the future, please don't hesitate to contact me or one of these agents. I'd be more than happy to sponsor your entrance into the Academy."

"Thank you, sir."

"Now. Ms. Roberts." Reggie turned to face Tara. "Cruz's parents have been slapped with an injunction prohibiting either of them from any contact whatsoever with you directly or indirectly... that is, once they're out of jail which won't be for a long time. They each should receive ten years minimum in federal prison for fraud and tax evasion in regards to their car dealership not to mention further charges pending against John Cruz for his involvement with Scott. With the entire Cruz family out of the picture, you can resume your life without fear of retribution or retaliation."

*****

Tara swallowed the lump forming in her throat. It had taken five long horrific years to free her from the constant grip of fear, but finally she felt the weight of it lift from her shoulders. "I can't thank you all enough. Without the efforts of this team, I may not be alive today, and if I gave any of you a hard time, I am truly sorry."

Looking directly at Chance, she smiled. He returned her smile with one of his own. "You've all been wonderful. Thank you."

"We were only doing our jobs, Ms. Roberts. No need for thanks. Is there anything else the FBI can do for you before we consider this case closed?" Reggie inquired.

She shook her head and gave him a wistful look. She missed her boss and her friends while on the run, but in truth, she would miss the new friends she'd made through this ordeal, not to mention her Cajun man. She was reluctant to return to her former life because, when she did, she would be leaving her heart down in the swamp lands of Louisiana.

"No, sir. I think you've all done more than necessary."

"Will you be returning to your jobs in Vegas?"

She put on a sad little grin. "Actually, I think I might go back to school and get a degree so I can find a better job." She was looking at Chance.

He shook his head. "You hold down two jobs which are both decent and respectable. Go to college if you want to, Tara, but don't do it because you feel you have to."

Reggie stood and gave Tara a big smile. "There is one more thing I have for you before you go, Ms. Roberts."

He walked back to the door, leaned out, and summoned someone in the hallway to enter. He was followed back by Bob, Tiffany, and Logan.

"Oh my God! Guys!" She bolted from her chair and ran into Logan's arms. He caught her midair as she wrapped herself around her friend.

"Hey, cookie. It's great to see you," he whispered in her ear, his voice wavering with emotion. When he let her down, she ran to both

Tiffany and Bob and hugged them in turn.

"What are you guys doing here?" She was breathless.

"We've come to take you home, cookie. This nice FBI man called us and offered to let us come here and get you."

"Actually, he called me," Bob corrected. "These two refused to stay back and wait so they got on the plane with me."

"Well, if no one else has anything further, this meeting is officially adjourned," Reggie announced.

Everyone rose and started milling about having private conversations. Chance walked up to Remi and shook his hand.

"Why the hell won't you accept Reggie's offer, Remi? You know this is a once in a lifetime thing here. It's something you've mentioned quite often, and I'd sure love to have you as a team member someday. What's stopping you?"

Tara watched silently as Remi put his head down and averted his eyes. She couldn't think of a reason why he wouldn't want to join the FBI with Chance. When he lifted his head and looked at his best friend, Tara thought his look was one of pure guilt and sadness. "I can't, Chance. Not right now."

"Why not?"

"Just forget it, all right?"

Chance nodded, but Tara knew he'd pursue the subject later on with Remi. "Come on then. I'll introduce you to my fellow agents.

"Ladies and gentlemen, I'd like you to meet my good friend, Remi Dubois."

One by one, Chance introduced him to his team members. He shook each agent's hand murmuring greetings to each one with a smile. When they got to Izzy, Remi's smiled faded.

"This is Izzy Roth, our Technical Analyst. She's a crackerjack with computers. Oh, right. You guys already met through a telephone conversation, right?"

The kooky little woman stared open mouthed at the tall Cajun man. Her eyes were wide with wonder. She extended her hand toward Remi who looked down from her face to her hand and back up again, his eyes sparkling. Hesitantly, he reached out. When their hands touched, they both jumped back at the same time. After regaining some composure, Izzy spoke.

"Mr. Dubois. It's a pleasure to meet you in person."

Remi just continued to stare unable to utter a word. His brows furrowed. He leaned in a little closer to Izzy. "You wouldn't by any chance be from Georgia, would you?"

Izzy's face lit up. "Atlanta!" She announced this proudly as Remi's eyebrows shot up. He stood stone faced for what felt like forever.

Chance nudged him on the shoulder. "Uh, Remi?" He prodded his friend. Remi shook his head, cleared his throat, and spoke once more.

"Ms. Roth, ma'am. The pleasure is all mine." He gave her a tight smile then spun around when Tara placed her hand on his back. "Tara, sugar. What is it you need?"

Reaching up to hug him around the neck, she planted a big kiss on his cheek. "Thanks so much for everything, Dr. K."

"He's a doctor too?" Izzy chimed in sounding amazed.

Tara started laughing. "Far from it, but it's a long story. Remi. Let me introduce you to my friends."

He smiled and nodded as she glanced at Chance. "Coming with us, Frenchie?" She couldn't stop the hope dripping from her words. He nodded and followed them.

"Ooh, la, la! Frenchie!" Derek teased.

Walking beside Tara, Chance turned his head toward his partner sporting a grin and flipped his middle finger up near his face. Derek's laughter peeled.

Chapter Forty-Five

"Tara, it's time we head out if we're going to make our flight." Bob was back in his familiar fatherly persona.

Tara took in a deep breath. "Can I have a minute?"

Bob smiled down at her. "Sure, honey. We'll be waiting outside."

They closed the door to the conference room on their way out. Everyone else had left earlier for the hospital to go visit Travis. Remi, Chance, and Tara remained.

Walking up to Remi, she tilted her head back giving the tall Cajun man a wistful smile. "I sure am going to miss you, Dr. K. Come and visit me sometime?"

He grabbed her hand, bent her fingers and gave them a gentle kiss. "You bet. And Tara? You are one class act, *mon ami*. I'll miss you too." They hugged one last time.

Remi looked at Chance. "I'll be waiting down the hall." He eyed Tara with a smile. "No hurry. Take your time." He turned and left the room.

Chance took in a deep breath and looked down into her eyes. They shimmered; she was holding back tears. "Tara." He pulled her into his arms and hugged her with all his might resting his chin atop her head. He felt her draw in a deep, ragged breath against his chest. His voice came out in a whisper. "*Mon chèrie*. No matter what you do with the rest of your life, please be happy."

She pulled away from him and gazed longingly into his eyes. The tears fell like rain down her cheeks.

"Tara, I..." he tried to voice what was hammering to be let loose in his heart, but the words wouldn't come. He couldn't bring himself to take away her opportunity to have a normal life, one in which she could make her own choices and feel no pain or fear.

Chance watched her throat bob as she tried to speak. "Chance, I can't put into words what I... I need you to know..." She was having trouble getting words past her lips.

She pulled him down and gave him one last soul filled kiss. "Thank you," she whispered, and then walked away.

When the door slammed shut and she was no longer in sight, Chance's eyes misted. The door swung open again. Remi marched right up to him and shoved a hand against his chest catching him off guard and almost toppling him over.

"What the hell did you say to her? Why are you letting her walk out that door?"

"You don't understand, Remi. She deserves a life of her own now. She should have the chance to make her own choices, no matter how I feel about her."

"You stupid *coullion* -- you idiot! She's already made her own choice. She's taken her chance. That *chance* is you. You're just too damn stubborn headed and ignorant to see it."

Chance looked disbelievingly at his friend. "What are you saying?"

Remi rolled his eyes. "I knew there was nothin' in that damn coonass head of yours, but I didn't think it made you stupid. You're in love with the fine little woman, and even though I can't understand why, because you sure don't deserve it, she's in love with you too." He sighed. "Chance. If you let her leave now without telling her, you'll regret it for the rest of your life. Once in a lifetime thing, remember?"

After smiling at his buddy and slugging him on the shoulder, Chance took off in a flat out run toward the door.

*****

Logan held the car door open so Tara could get in. Just as he was about to close it, someone yelled from behind.

"Wait up!" Chance slowed his pace as he approached the vehicle. Tara got out of the car looking befuddled.

"What's wrong?"

"Tara, I..." he hesitated as he realized her friends were intently awaiting his words too. "Come here." He grabbed her arm dragging her away from the car across the parking lot to the side of the building.

With his hands on her shoulders, he spoke the words his heart wanted him to say.

"Tara. I love you."

Tears flowed from her eyes as she grabbed her chest. "I love you too, but I just don't know if it would work, Chance."

His heart stopped beating as he bolted upright, all muscles stiffening.

"I mean, do you think you could put up with my relentless ramblings, my faults, and all my little quirks?"

He nodded vigorously.

"Do you think you could handle it if I decide to stay with *Party Hard*?"

"Whatever you want to do, wherever you want to do it, is fine by me."

She inhaled a deep breath. "Would you be willing to take me to Vegas every once in a while to visit my friends if I choose to stay with you?"

He drew her even closer. "Every damned day if that's what you want."

She slowly nodded and sniffled giving him a lopsided grin. "Are you promising to love me forever?"

"And beyond," he replied.

"And you'll love Timmy too?"

He pretended to think the last question over. She furrowed her brows.

"Can I get back to you on that one?"

She hit him in the chest as he corralled her in his arms laughing. "Whoa, *chat marron.* I was just kidding. Timmy's your family. He's part of you, and I love every single part of you, so the answer is yes." He pulled her closer and kissed her senseless.

"Go, cookie, go!" Logan shouted.

They both started laughing. "I love you too, Frenchie." He picked her up and swung her.

"Go back with your friends and enjoy their company for a change. Take as much time as you need. I'll be waiting for you when you're ready to come home."

"You'll let me go back?"

"Tara. I told you. Make your life your own. Whenever you're ready to move on, I'll be right here waiting with open arms. Plus, I'm on medical leave until I'm one hundred percent, so I can meet you there in a day or two. I love you, *chèrie.*"

"Damn, Frenchie. You're actually good for a lot of things after all."

They both laughed.

Epilogue

The crimson colored evening sun was slowly sinking causing ribbons of shadows to dance around the sleepy swamp land surrounding Camp Fluffy. Crickets chirped and bullfrogs croaked out a harmony worthy of a symphony. Chance sat on the front porch swing, his new bride tucked in tight between his legs, her back to his chest and his massive arms encircling the woman he'd come to love more than life itself.

"Happy, *chère*?" he whispered in her ear.

"Mmm, very." She gazed up into his eyes as she rubbed her hand across his forearm.

They'd decided to spend a week of solitude at the camp before heading out on their honeymoon. They both needed a few days to come down from the adrenaline rush of a full blown Cajun wedding complete with rebel rousers and a fiddle playing band.

"Thanks for seeing Bob, Tiff, and Logan made it here for the wedding which was a wonderful surprise."

"Glad it made you happy, sweetheart. They're important people in your life. They needed to share some happy time with you."

"And they did. I liked to pee my panties laughing when I saw Logan hit the floor doing the alligator dance with Remi."

Chance laughed. "It was a sight all right. Never thought I'd see an ex-Army Ranger with muscles like his make moves like that."

Tara giggled. "Yes. It's one for the record books. Have you heard from Derek? I wish he could have been here."

"Me too. He called me last night to congratulate us. He's out on some new case. I'm a little worried about him. He didn't sound too happy."

"I wonder why? And what about Travis?"

"Time is Travis's best friend right now. He'll need lots more of it before he's recovered, but from what I understand, he's on his way. He's been flirting with a new bunch of nurses on a regular basis when he goes to physical therapy. He and Remi hit it off so well, they call each other all the time to talk about women."

Tara laughed. "Sounds like them."

The faint purr of a boat motor drifted in the air. Tara felt Chance's muscles tense as the sound grew nearer. Even though the threat from Alvin no longer existed, he was still very protective of his woman. He always would be.

As the boat rounded the bend in the canal, they caught sight of the reflective "Water Patrol" emblem on the side.

"Come on." Tara jumped out the swing and tugged on his arm trying to get him to follow. Physically, of course, she couldn't budge him, but he played along and allowed her to drag him down to the wharf.

"*Bon soir, mez ami*! Good evening, my friends," Remi shouted out his greeting and waived just as his boat drifted into the slip next to the wharf. Chance grabbed the anchor rope Remi tossed his way and secured it to the pylon.

"Remi Dubois. What the hell brings you to Camp Fluffy this evening?" Chance extended his hand toward his friend.

"Wait up a minute." Remi bent down and picked up what looked like some sort of cage covered with a drop cloth. He handed the cage to Tara then grabbed Chance's hand pulling himself up onto the wharf next to his friends.

"I'm just playin' delivery boy tonight is all. You two doin' okay out here all by yourselves?" He winked.

Chance looked at Tara with adoring eyes and grabbed her by the waist pulling her in tight by his side. "We're doin' much better than you are for sure. Remi. When are you gonna stop sowin' your wild oats and settle down with a good woman? Gotta tell ya, bro. So far for me, it's pure heaven."

Remi placed his knuckle under Tara's chin lifting it and stared into her eyes. "I'll stop sowing right now if you give me this one here," he said with a playful smile.

Chance put his hand on Remi's chest and shoved almost knocking him off the wharf.

"No way. Keep your grimy paws off her. She's officially mine."

Tara and Remi both burst out laughing at Chance's instant possessiveness.

"So, Dr. K, why don't you stay for dinner?" Tara asked her new friend.

Remi grinned hearing Tara use his nickname. "Sorry, darlin'. I know when a threesome is good and now isn't one of those times. I promised you I'd make this delivery and here it is."

She gave him a big smile and moved into his personal space, then hugged him. She pecked a kiss on his cheek. "*Merci, mon bon ami.* Thank you, my good friend."

Remi chuckled, his eyes twinkling as he looked at his best friend over his wife's head. "Well I'll be damned. I do believe we're gonna make an honest-to-God transplanted Cajun out of this woman yet."

Chance couldn't help but laugh. Remi turned around and hopped back into the boat. He leaned down and started up the motor. As the boat began its backward drift, he waved.

Tara and Chance rejoined with arms around each other and waved back. The boat slowly disappeared down the canal and out of sight.

Chance turned to face his wife. "All right, woman. What have you and wonder boy been conspiring about?" His gaze went down to the cage at her feet.

"I wanted to get you something special as a wedding present."

"*Chèrie*. I have everything a man could want. I have you."

She blushed still when he spoke sweet love words to her. "Yeah, but I'm not a present you can unwrap."

"Wanna bet?" He waggled his brows making her laugh.

"Behave. That comes later. Anyway, I couldn't come up with anything decent on my own so I picked Poppee's brain the other day and he gave me an idea."

"Oh, Lord. If Poppee had his hands in this, it can't be good."

She leaned down and removed the cover from the cage. Curled upon itself and sleeping soundly was a puppy, a miniature version of Chance's beloved Buddy.

He gasped and bent down opening the door to the pet carrier. The puppy stirred a bit but didn't awaken. Reaching in, he stroked his finger over the soft fur on top the puppy's little head. A shimmer of light glinted off something around the puppy's neck. Lifting the dog tag affixed to a beige collar, he read the inscription out loud. "Buddy II." He looked up at his wife with misty eyes.

She spoke, her voice quivering. "Poppee told me when he kept Buddy for you while you finished up your training at Quantico a while back, Buddy decided to make a midnight run one night next door to visit the neighbor's basset hound."

Chance looked down again at Buddy II who was now licking his finger. He started to chuckle. "Why you old dog, Buddy. I never knew you still had it in you," He mused. He bolted straight up, a look of panic crossing his face.

"What?" She was worried as usual by his sudden tenseness.

"Timmy. How do you think he'll react to Buddy II?"

"I don't know. He's been moping ever since we lost Buddy. I think he misses him. Why don't we go find out?"

She picked up the carrier and headed for the porch where Timmy was curled up beneath the swing. She reached in and extracted the sleepy-eyed puppy. Timmy lifted his head and watched as she placed the furry pup next to him. They sniffed each other for a moment. Timmy stood and pranced all around Buddy II like he was assessing a possible new threat to his domain.

The puppy kept his eyes trained on the cat but didn't budge. Timmy looked up at Tara, then at Chance. He meowed once and plopped his big body down next to the puppy. Buddy II sank down on his belly. Timmy put his head on the puppy's back.

"Awe," Tara purred.

"Welcome to our family, Buddy II." Chance encircled his wife's waist with his arms and planted a kiss atop her head. He leaned down and whispered in her ear.

"*Je t'aime avec tout mon coeur, mon petit chat marron.*"

She glanced up at him waiting for a full translation.

"I love you with all of my heart, my little wildcat."

She gave him a radiant smile. After losing everyone she'd once loved, Tara finally had the beginnings of a new family she could love forever.

The End

Look for *SIU7 Book Two: Cold Obsession*
Coming April 2017

About Genevieve Williams

With a panoramic view of Bayou Lafourche in Louisiana as a backdrop, Genevieve pens stories with quintessential southern flair. Many of the scenes and four legged friends featured in those tales are based on real places and real furry friends. A knowledge of most things military also manages to worm its way into these yarns of suspense and romance.

Her first published work, *Wild Obsession,* captured first place in the Sixth Annual Dixie Kane Contest for SOLA, the South Louisiana Chapter of the Romance Writers Association. An active member of the Romance Writers Association, she loves making the conference circuit rounds meeting other authors and avid book readers.

Travelling, watching movies, and, above all else, reading are a few of her favorite activities not to mention loving up on several of those fantastic furry friends.

62345465R00140

Made in the USA
Lexington, KY
04 April 2017